THE DEVIL TAKES YOU HOME

Gabino Iglesias is a writer, journalist, professor, and literary critic living in Austin, Texas. He is also the author of the critically acclaimed and award-winning novels *Zero Saints* and *Coyote Songs*. Iglesias's nonfiction has appeared in the *New York Times,* the *Los Angeles Times, Electric Literature,* and *LitReactor,* and his reviews appear regularly in media outlets such as NPR, *Publishers Weekly,* the *San Francisco Chronicle,* the *Boston Globe, Criminal Element, Mystery Tribune, Vol. 1 Brooklyn,* and the *Los Angeles Review of Books.* Iglesias has been a juror for the Shirley Jackson Awards and the *Millions* Tournament of Books, and is a member of the Horror Writers Association, the Mystery Writers of America, and the National Book Critics Circle.

Praise for **The Devil Takes You Home**:

'Some of the finest, most terrifying and heartbreaking writing you will read this year. *The Devil Takes You Home* is not to be missed.'
– S.A. Cosby, *New York Times*-bestselling author of *Razorblade Tears* and *Blacktop Wasteland*

'*The Devil Takes You Home* is an unforgettable neo-noir nightmare written with a poet's heart.'
– Steve Cavanagh, bestselling author of the Eddie Flynn series

'Complete horror sung by an angel. I was transfixed. This is superb writing.'
– Harriet Tyce, author of *Blood Orange* and *It Ends at Midnight*

'Gives the genre a welcome shot in the arm'
– *Guardian*, the Best crime and thriller books of 2022

'[A] haunting noir thriller . . . a borderlands odyssey that blends noir and magical realism'
– *New York Times*

'Masterful. [A] brawny, serpentine and remarkably poignant novel.'
– *BookPage*

'A meditation on grief and rage.'
– *Vanity Fair*

'Here there be bloodshed, oh yes, sudden lyrical frenzies peppers over the main course of calamity. Every time you think the book got quiet, it screams again.'
– Josh Malerman, *New York Times*-bestselling author of *Bird Box* and *Daphne*

'With a noir voice reminiscent of Jim Thompson, this book charges into rage and despair, sparing no one, least of all the reader. Strap yourself in.'
— Chris Offutt, author of *The Killing Hills* and *Country Dark*

'Some nightmares you wake from just leave you in an even worse nightmare. And then Gabino Iglesias holds his hand out from that darkness, takes you home.'
— Stephen Graham Jones, author of *The Only Good Indians*

'*The Devil Takes You Home* is carried by a voice and rhythm, shaving sharp and wholly indelible. Iglesias never fails to keep a masterful foot on the pedal, feathering off the gas at times only to inevitably press it to the floor and pin us to our seats.'
— David Joy, author of *When These Mountains Burn*

'Pure noir, overflowing with the rage and sorrow of our times, *The Devil Takes You Home* is brutal, hallucinatory, and somehow, beautiful. This novel confirms what some of us already knew: Gabino Iglesias is a fierce, vital voice.'
— Paul Tremblay, bestselling author of *Survivor Song*

'The line between noir and horror not only gets blurred in Iglesias's *The Devil Takes You Home*; it gets obliterated. His barrio noir is a new kind of fiction, profoundly moving, despairing and scary all at once.'
— Brian Evenson, author of *Last Days*

'An excellent crime novel driven by righteous grief, fierce narration, and raw violence. Iglesias takes us on a vivid exploration of pain and rage, along the Southwest border where the horrors of reality and the supernatural intertwine.'
— John Woods, author of *Lady Chevy*

'A dark and disturbing tunnel into another world, Iglesias deftly walks the line between beautiful and haunting. A tense and unapologetic story, I devoured this in a weekend, my eyes widening with every unflinching word.'
— Sam Holland, author of *The Echo Man*

'*The Devil Takes You Home* is an almighty powder keg of a novel that explodes across the page, filling the reader with shock, awe, terror and pity. A hypnotic marriage between jet-black narco noir and magic realism, it's a high-octane road trip you'll never forget.'
— Tim Baker, author of *City Without Stars* and *Fever City*

GABINO IGLESIAS

THE DEVIL TAKES YOU HOME

WILDFIRE

The right of Gabino Iglesiasto be identified as the Author of
the Work has been asserted by him in accordance with the
Copyright, Designs and Patents Act 1988.

First published in 2022 by Mulholland Books, Little, Brown and Company

First published in Great Britain in hardback in 2022 by
WILDFIRE
an imprint of HEADLINE PUBLISHING GROUP

First published in paperback in 2023 by
WILDFIRE
an imprint of HEADLINE PUBLISHING GROUP

1

Cataloguing in Publication Data is available from the British Library

ISBN 978 1 4722 9107 3

Offset in 11.12/13.67 pt Perpetua Std by Jouve (UK), Milton Keynes

Printed and bound in Great Britain by Clays Ltd, Elcograf S.p.A.

Headline's policy is to use papers that are natural, renewable and recyclable products
and made from wood grown in well-managed forests and other controlled sources.
The logging and manufacturing processes are expected to conform to the
environmental regulations of the country of origin.

HEADLINE PUBLISHING GROUP
an Hachette UK Company
Carmelite House
50 Victoria Embankment
London
EC4Y 0DZ

www.headline.co.uk
www.hachette.co.uk

A mi familia
And to the city of Austin, for trying to kill me

CHAPTER 1

L eukemia. That's what the doctor said. She was young, white, and pretty. Her brown hair hung like a curtain over her left eye. She talked to us softly, using the tone most people use to explain things to a child, especially when they think the kid is an idiot. Her mouth opened just enough to let the words flow out. She said our four-year-old daughter had cancer in her blood cells. Our Anita, who waited in the other room, playing with Legos and still wrapped in innocence. Acute lymphoblastic leukemia. Those strange words were said in a voice that was both impossibly sharp and velvety. Her soft delivery didn't help. You can wrap a shotgun in flowers, but that doesn't make the blast less lethal.

The young, white, pretty doctor told us it was too early to tell for sure, but there was a good chance that Anita was going to be okay. *Okay,* that's the word she used. Sometimes four letters mean the world. She immediately added that she couldn't make any promises. People fear being someone else's hope. I understood her, but I wanted her to be our hope.

The doctor gave us a moment to process what she'd said. Silence is never as cold and sterile as it is in hospitals. My wife, Melisa, and I breathed in that silence and waited. We didn't look at each other, but I could feel the panic setting in, circulating through my wife like she was radioactive. I wanted to hold Melisa, to comfort her and say it'd be okay, but I was scared of making any sudden movement. I gently cupped my hand over hers, but she pulled away, quick and violent like an invisible shanking, so instead I stared at the doctor's white coat. Embroidered in blue right above the pocket, it read: *Dr. Flynn.*

The doctor inhaled. From the other room, the sound of Anita giggling reached our ears. It felt like God had punched me in the heart, and Melisa choked back something. A sad woman is a blade hanging over the world, threatening to fall at any moment.

Dr. Flynn inhaled again and then explained to us that acute lymphoblastic leukemia is a type of cancer that affects bone marrow and white blood cells. It's a relatively unexceptional error in the body, the most common childhood cancer. A glitch in the bone marrow, she said. Then she looked at us and said bone marrow is the spongy tissue inside our bones where blood cells are made. You know, because she probably thought we were stupid. When you have an accent, people often think you possess the intellect of a fence post.

Dr. Flynn wanted us to know many children make relatively quick recoveries from leukemia if they are diagnosed early and start treatment immediately. But she reiterated that they couldn't make any promises because cancer is always a tricky thing, "a slippery opponent," she said in an attempt at levity that must have gotten a strained smile from some bewildered parent once upon a time and the good doctor had kept it in her repertoire ever since.

When your child is healthy, you think of sick children and feel like crying, like helping. When your child is sick, you don't give a shit about other children.

Dr. Flynn tilted her head, shifted the curtain over her eye an inch to the side with her fingers, and placed a manicured hand on Melisa's shaking shoulder. Dr. Flynn's rehearsed sympathy looked as legitimate as her perfect nails. I knew we were just another case on her stack and she was throwing us a sliver of hope so we could hold on to it, hold on to anything at all. Still, we believed her. We needed to believe her. I looked at her snowy coat and thought about an angel. She would deliver us a miracle. There was no other option. Not believing her meant something so horrible my brain refused to acknowledge it.

When the doctor walked away, my wife started saying "Mi hija." *My daughter.* She sat down. She cried. She repeated "Mi hija" again and again. She said it until it became the heartbeat of our nightmare.

Mi hija. Mi hija.

I said nothing, fear something I couldn't or wouldn't speak to. All I could think of was getting into the other room and scooping Anita up into my arms and holding her there forever. Melisa's big brown eyes were wild. She gulped air and looked around, surely trying to calm down so we could go see our daughter without alarming her. Funny how parents can take a bullet and smile if they think it'll keep their kids from worrying or crying.

Anita was only four years old and had always been healthy up to that point. She'd never had anything worse than a cold, a few ear infections, and the random teething fever or stomach bug. Chemotherapy would work wonders on her. It had to. Medical research had made tremendous advances in the field. We lived in the future. It would all be okay. All we had to do was stay strong. Our little angel would go into remission in no time. God was good. He wouldn't let a baby suffer. No one deserves miracles more than unlucky angels. It would all be fine. God and chemotherapy, a winning duo, right? We convinced ourselves of this. Our baby was too full of life, too strong-willed, to lose that battle. Our baby was too loved to die.

Finally, Melisa let out a shuddering breath and looked at me. Something cold had crept into her eyes. She twisted her mouth into something akin to a smile as her eyebrows fought to bring her whole face down.

"Let's go get our baby," she said.

Melisa walked into the room and scooped our daughter up. She buried her head in her neck and tickled her with kisses to hide her red eyes and nose. I hugged them both and felt fear stab my heart.

I couldn't breathe right for two days. I felt like an alpinist who runs out of bottled oxygen near the summit of Everest. But then I saw Anita's smile, and hope blossomed in my chest. It was a warm, comforting feeling that allowed me to start breathing normally again.

Then came the nasty surprises.

CHAPTER 2

Turns out we hadn't caught the monster as early as they thought. It also turns out little brown girls with acute lymphoblastic leukemia tend to have a lower cure rate than children of other races. Oh, and the incidence of leukemia is higher among Hispanics. Even awful diseases are fucking racist. And you know the worst part? The wonderful doctors at the hospital couldn't tell us why. Yeah, the difference between a curandero spitting rum in your face and a doctor looking at you with no answers is a white coat and the smell of disinfectant that surrounds the latter.

The poison in Anita's veins wasn't happy with invading her blood; it also wanted to know what she was thinking, to ride the contents of her dreams, so it attacked her cerebrospinal fluid. Le invadió los pensamientos. Se metió en sus sueños and it slowly killed ours.

The strangest thing about it, the thing that made me so mad I forgot to be sad for a while, was that I've had a gift my whole life. When bad things are about to happen, I get this cold feeling in my gut. I hear things. A word. A whisper. A waking dream. Something that keeps buzzing around me until I pay attention. Whenever that happens, I've kept alert, stayed sharp. Been that way since I was a kid.

My junkie mother always said I had angels floating above me. I'd been born inside the amniotic sac, and she claimed that gave me the ability to see both sides of the veil. On dark, quiet afternoons when my mother only left the beige to go to the bathroom, she would look at me and declare she could hear the angels talking, showering the top of my head with secrets of things to come. She told me I had to learn to listen to them. "Escucha a los angelitos, mijo," she'd say. Then she'd grab her stuff from the small box next to the sofa, cook herself a fix, and plunge a syringe full of warm visions into her destroyed veins. I guess she wanted the angels to talk to her too. She wasn't entirely right about the voices, but she wasn't entirely wrong either. No one talked to me, but I knew things, heard things. Sometimes it was even in the absence of sound. For example, I woke up to an eerie silence one morning and knew that the lack of a second breath in our trailer meant Mom was gone. I didn't even have to get up and check. Tears were streaming down my face before my feet touched the floor. I also thought about my friend Hector while doing homework one day and then the world stopped humming for a few seconds. I knew he was gone. The next day at school, they told us his dad had been driving while intoxicated. The man had wrapped his car around a pole, killing himself, his wife, Hector, and his baby sister, Martita.

The point is that my little angel had always been okay and I had never gotten the sense that something awful was about to happen. No dreams, no worries, no words in the wind, no whispers in the middle of the night, no fear, ni una corazonada. Whoever or whatever took care of letting me know about bad things coming had decided to keep quiet about the most important thing in my life. This time, sadly, los cabrones ángeles decidieron quedarse callados. When it came to Anita, nothing had looked out of place. Melisa hadn't even thought to mention that the pediatrician had noticed some unusual swelling at

Anita's yearly checkup and ordered some additional bloodwork "just to be safe." Melisa probably didn't want me asking if our crappy insurance would cover that expense.

Within weeks of the diagnosis, our Anita went from a ball of unstoppable energy to a thin bird with broken wings. I'd hold her tiny body against mine and feel everything inside me break at once. An invisible monster was devouring her, feasting on her innocence, and there was nothing I could do about it.

So we prayed. Melisa and I prayed with clasped hands and gritted teeth. We prayed with a rosary clutched so tightly in our hands that our palms would sport tiny half-moons for hours. We prayed with spittle flying out of our mouths and tears in our eyes. We prayed and made deals, made promises, made threats. We prayed with every ounce of energy in our bodies. We asked La Virgencita to save our baby. We asked God to intercede. We asked the angels to lend a hand. We asked the saints to help us win this battle. They all stayed quiet, and death lived in that silence.

When Melisa started lighting strange candles, tying blessed ribbons to Anita's hospital bed, and using holy water to make crosses on our baby's forehead, I didn't ask questions or try to stop her. She was sad and desperate. She was willing to try anything to bring the holy into that hospital room. She had carried our child for nine months, and I knew losing her was like someone pulling out her heart and lungs. On good days, I understood her and prayed with her. On bad days, I stayed in the cafeteria, sipping atrocious coffee, thinking about punching doctors for not doing their job, and having a hard time process-ing just how pathetic Melisa had become, begging for a miracle that was obviously not coming our way.

You don't know horror until you've spent a few hours inside a hospital looking at the fitful sleep of a loved one who is being taken from you. You don't know desperation until the uselessness of praying hits you. I stopped eating and sleeping. I became a fuzzy copy of the man I used to be, an unshaved mess full of anger and pain and tears. Me llené de odio y desesperación.

A few weeks into our new reality, a human resources specialist from my office called. It was someone I'd never met. She said she was sorry to hear about Anita's health and then said she regretted to inform me they had to let me go because I'd used up all my sick days, personal days, PTO, and then shattered every absenteeism record in the company. I hung up. Your daughter has cancer, but you're not being productive, motherfucker, so we're firing you. Welcome to the American Dream.

The medical bills had already started showing up. "Every time we breathe in that hospital, someone writes us a bill for it and now we don't even have insurance," said Melisa. Her voice was full of quiet anger. She'd lost weight, and her cheekbones looked like weapons constantly threatening the world.

"We'll get the money somehow."

"You always say the same thing. We'll get the money somehow. We'll make it work. We'll be okay. I'm tired, Mario. Estoy tan cansada. Every day Anita spends in there, every new treatment and test she gets, adds to the pile of bills. What we have is not enough now and won't be enough anytime soon. It's never enough! We've been doing our best for so long and we're still more or less where we started. And now our baby—"

Her voice broke like a glass thrown against the floor, fast and sharp. I got up from the sofa and held her. It was the only thing I could do. Her body trembled in my arms. Anita's sickness was a new reality we woke up to every day, but this scene wasn't. Holding her felt old already, like something I'd done too much and was ready to never do again. Talking about money was worse. The discussion felt like a nightmare we'd carried from a time before we met each other, and then we'd created a larger

10

one by putting our problems together. Every time the car broke down. Every time we needed dental work. Every time bills piled up and we felt like we were losing control, we'd end up like this. I wished I'd held her for different reasons.

Melisa looked up at me. Her brown eyes shiny, her face red and still beautiful.

"What are we going to do?"

"We'll think of—"

She pushed me away. Hard. I wasn't expecting that.

"Don't say it. Don't fucking say it. God always takes from those who have nothing to give, and I'm tired of it."

The next day, God kept punching. We spoke to Dr. Flynn first. She said she was surprised at the inefficacy of the treatment. She had one of her colleagues, a chubby man with big ears and yellowing teeth, talk to us.

"This is a fascinating case," he said. "The survival rate is about 98 percent, and the small percentage of deaths we see can be mostly attributed to late diagnoses. In Anita's case, we're not within the optimal window of time in terms of detection, but we're also not too far from it. The aggressiveness of her leukemia is bizarre. She is truly a fascinating case."

Something stirred in me while he spoke. The doctor droned on and on, talking about Anita the way someone would talk about a lizard with three heads. Then he pulled out some papers. As he fingered through the pages, I had the sudden urge to grab them out of his meaty hands and shove them down his throat. Anything to make him stop talking. Melisa squeezed my arm. She always knew when I was tuning out. Squeezing my arm was her way of telling me to pay attention.

"There is an experimental treatment I'd like to run by you. We've seen great results with monoclonal antibodies in children that don't take to chemo the way we'd hoped. I won't chew your ear off, but Anita could be part of this clinical trial. We're talking about really potent man-made antibodies that can attach themselves to certain proteins found on cells. What the——"

"I'm sorry, Dr. Harrison, but who pays for these clinical trials?" Melisa interrupted.

"Insurance should pay for most of the costs. Once you meet your deductible that is, but that shouldn't be a problem for you." He chuckled again. "And of course you'd have to be in network and there are always the costs of extra meds——"

My hands were on Dr. Harrison before I even realized I had jumped out of my seat. "Fuck you, fuck the treatment, fuck the insurance, and fuck this damn hospital!" The papers he was holding flew up and then drifted down to the floor like wounded birds. No one spoke for a moment. Tennis shoes squeaked against the floor, and Melisa's hands were on my shoulders. She was saying something, but it was like this thing inside me had taken over.

I wanted to hurt the asshole who'd called my baby a "fascinating case," but Melisa pulled me away, apologizing, as Dr. Flynn looked on in horror, her one visible eye wide with fear.

"This isn't you, Mario," Melisa said as we made our way to the parking lot. "I need the sweet man I married with me right now, not . . . whoever this is."

I had nothing to say. We reached our car and climbed in.

Melisa turned to me, took a deep, shaky breath, and squeezed my hands harder.

"Agárrate de mi mano, que tengo miedo del futuro . . ."

Her soft voice filled the car. It was an old Ismael Serrano song. The darkness receded.

"Look at me, Mario." I did. "We'll get through this. It's what we do. We'll make it work. We'll get the money."

CHAPTER 3

I checked a few sites and sent out some résumés, but nothing happened. I'd gotten used to that. If your name has too many vowels, getting a job is ten times harder than if your name sounds like it belongs in the credits of a Hollywood movie.

When you're poor, getting money occupies your mind at all times anyway, but this was different. We needed a thousand dollars a month just to cover Anita's meds for the clinical trial, and that didn't include insurance costs or the back-and-forth visits between our home in Austin and Houston's med center. Finally, when it was clear even the McDonald's wasn't interested in an interview, I called Brian.

We'd worked together years ago at the insurance agency. Now Brian was a dope dealer and habitual meth smoker. Not exactly friends, we'd been two souls caught in the same soulless gig, and that made us gravitate to each other, to talk about movies and places we'd like to visit, celebrities we'd like to sleep with. When he got fired from the insurance place, allegedly for selling pirated movies out of the trunk of his car during his lunch hour, we kept in touch with occasional texts.

A year or so after he left, Brian had asked me to collect credit card info at the insurance company and give it to him.

He had someone interested in buying it. Third parties would use the info. "They won't be able to track it back to you," he had said. I processed credit card payments from all over Latin America, so it would have been easy and we needed the money then too. I collected the information in no time but backed out at the last minute. I was too afraid of getting caught and leaving Anita and Melisa to fend for themselves while I rotted away in prison. Brian understood and said he always had gigs waiting. "No biggie, man," he said. "You're a good dude. Call if the damn poverty noose gets too tight, yeah? I got you."

Melisa was at the hospital they'd moved us to in Houston when I finally took him up on that offer. By then she was staying most nights. At the start we alternated nights because only one parent could stay, but then getting a hotel stopped being an option because we were too broke. I often slept in the car. Every few days, one of us would drive home to do laundry and bring other things to the hospital. I was home on one of those trips when I decided to call Brian. The medical bills were too much, the insurance that we paid for out of pocket even crappier. Brian picked up on the second ring.

"How much do you need?"

"I need . . . as much as I can get."

"I can get you money. That part's easy. You willing to do anything?"

The question was unsettling, but Brian's tone remained up-beat. I said yes. And I meant it. Those fucking medical bills stood on top of all the others. Rent, electricity, car insurance, and phone bills didn't give a shit that our daughter was beating back death.

Brian came over a few hours later. He twitched like a broken toy as he pulled out a crumpled piece of paper. There was an address scribbled on it, somewhere on the outskirts of Waco, about halfway between Austin and Dallas. Then Brian handed me a torn photo of a large man wearing an ill-fitting blue suit in front of a beige door. The photo was damp. The man's red nose spoke of booze, bad nights, and high blood pressure.

Brian got up with a grunt and reached behind him. His hand came back holding a gun. "That's the dude," he said while inspecting something on the side of the weapon. His words seemed to ignore the fact that he was holding a gun.

"Here, you'll need this." Brian handed me the weapon while mumbling something about the safety and making sure it ended at the bottom of a lake and not in my car. I took the gun from him and looked at it. It looked just like the guns in movies but was heavier than I expected. There was writing on it: 9MM LUGER. SMITH & WESSON. My gun knowledge was limited, but I knew the thing could spit death and that was all that mattered. We've been strangling and beating each other with rocks and sticks since we stopped dragging our knuckles and swinging from branches. Guns are the natural next step. There is something unsettling about how we're given life and then spend a large part of it trying to engineer better ways of killing others. That said, the cool, hard metal made me feel good.

Brian plucked the gun out of my hand, turned it to the side, and pointed at the safety he'd been talking about. He showed me how to use it. "Two hands," he said. "Don't turn it sideways like the idiots in the movies, and for God's sake, don't forget the fucking safety."

His hands were shaky, but I got the gist. When his little class was over, Brian told me to drive to the address he'd given me. Once there, I'd see an abandoned VW van.

"Show up late," he said. "Go on a weekday. The guy leaves his office around seven or eight every night. He's one of those assholes who think they can become millionaires if they put in the hours. Anyway, he always stops for a drink or three and a little ass. Fat man loves the sauce and he likes them young, but he's usually home before midnight. Tries to look normal and shit, you know? Show up before he does and park a few blocks away. Dress like someone out for a walk. You know, like you're trying to lose a couple pounds or whatever. If no one sees you, hide behind the van outside his house. Wait until the asshole walks up to the door and then shoot him in the back of the head. Then get your ass outta there as quickly as possible."

The ease with which those words left his mouth shocked me. He was talking about murder. He didn't mention the sound of the gunshot. He didn't talk about nosey neighbors. He wasn't worried about cops immediately pulling up to the property, lights on and guns out. He talked about killing a man with the tone others use to tell you how they prepare their favorite sandwich.

"So just . . . shoot him?"

"Yeah," he said. "Show up. Boom. Get back. Collect six stacks. Easy gig. Oh, and make sure you get rid of the gun. It can be the one thing you forget about and then it comes back to bite you in the ass."

He replied with something akin to a smile on his face. I'd get six grand for the job, which was way more than I made in a month at the insurance place. More important, it'd cover Anita's meds. Then Brian looked at me and, placing his right hand on my shoulder, said, "This is a bad guy. You're doing the world a favor, man. I fucking swear. You don't even want to know what this motherfucker does when he thinks no one's looking. Just trust me, man. This guy is scum, okay? You're doing the world a favor."

He was overselling it. I knew Brian was using me and pocketing more than he was giving me. I didn't care. I needed the money. It was all about Anita. Six stacks wouldn't be enough to get us out of the hole. It wouldn't even make a dent in the stack of angry letters and final notices. But if it came down to Anita or this motherfucker, I knew it had to be done. I told myself that if God was busy making little angels sick instead of protecting them, there was nothing wrong with me picking up the slack and putting an end to those who actually deserved it. However, none of that worked too well. Killing is killing. I felt like I was trapped inside a skin that didn't belong to me. I didn't even know if this guy was as bad as Brian was saying or if he was feeding me a line to get me to do the job. Maybe the guy just owed the wrong person some money. Maybe he had crossed someone who didn't have the guts to take him out. The possibilities were endless, and they would all stop mattering the second I pulled that fucking trigger. Bullets don't believe in remakes or second chances. The thought traveled from my brain to my heart and wrapped itself around it like a creeping vine covered in thorns.

After Brian left, I turned on the computer. The idea of pulling the trigger in a neighborhood didn't sit well with me. Was there a way to make a homemade silencer? I'd seen them in movies and they always sounded like someone spitting instead of a gunshot.

If a gun embodies everything that's wrong with humanity, the internet is a festering mirror that shows us what happens when humanity has been completely lost.

I quickly learned a few things. It's legal to make your own silencer, though those in the know liked to call them suppressors. I read hundreds of comments about using a car oil filter or potatoes or a pillow. I doubted any of it would really work, and all the websites telling you how to build a suppressor belonged to the kind of white supremacist who likes to use the word *patriot* instead of *racist*. Buying a suppressor was an option, but that took time and left a trail. Since I had no interest in learning how to use my suppressor to survive once the minorities take over the country, I decided to log off and just hope that shooting the man and running would work.

I showered, dressed like someone going for a walk, and left the house.

Melisa called as I was getting dressed. She sounded awake, almost happy, and wanted to know if I'd thrown some chicken breasts in the slow cooker so I could bring her some when I drove back to Houston in two days. I knew I could take care of this guy and fix her up a meal that wasn't from a hospital cafeteria before she even had a chance to miss me.

Finding the address was easy thanks to my phone's GPS. The robotic voice mispronounced streets, making me think of an android that was also an angel of death.

A few hours later, I stood behind a rusty VW van with little curtains that had flowers on them. My heart slapped against my chest. There was no one around. I stood behind the van and pretended to look at my phone for a minute. The street was lined with quiet driveways and trees. A few lampposts vomited yellowish light onto cracked sidewalks and tufts of grass. Four houses down, a few toys were lying on the grass. Their loud colors were strident notes in an otherwise mellow suburban symphony. They stabbed my heart with memories I fought to keep locked away.

Sure that no one was looking, I hid between the van and a wooden fence. Vines poured over from the neighboring yard and made for a nice shield. Suddenly the gun weighed too much. It was pulling me down, making me want to melt into the ground and vanish.

Thirty minutes passed. The street was silent. Hiding like this reminded me of playing hide-and-seek with Anita. Children never really hide. They think they can't be seen if they hide their faces or head. We laugh at that. We find it cute. It's not. All grown-ups do the same shit. We're in plain sight, but we hide because we're using a mask, hiding our real faces from the world. Anytime we'd play, I didn't even have to look for Anita's tiny feet poking out from behind the sofa or an arm holding on to the side of a dresser. Every single time we played, her giggling gave her away. Where could she be hiding? I'd ask, sending her into fits of laughter. Before I knew it, I had tears running down my cheeks. She wasn't playing games now. There were so many cool places to hide in that hospital, but we'd never played hide-and-seek there. The gun stopped feeling so heavy. I was there for her, and I would do the thing for the money. I'd kill a thousand men to get my little angel out of that fucking place.

Another half hour went by. The darkness around me stuck to my skin with the insistence of a child asking an uncomfortable question.

Finally, a car pulled up and the chubby, balding man from the picture slammed the door and made his way up the cracked pathway to the house, breathing like a wounded hog the whole time. I moved to the front of the van, between the grill and the garage door, and focused on my target, letting everything else fade away. Even from a few feet I could see that his pupils were dilated, probably from whatever cocktail of drugs and alcohol he'd partaken of that night, but they looked like two black holes sitting on his ugly face. The man fiddled with his keys as he stumbled up the steps. His stump-like fingers were like useless insects that didn't know which way to go. It reminded me of that bastard doctor who called Anita a fascinating case.

Suddenly, I wanted to tear those keys out of the man's hands and use the serrated edges to run through his shadowy eye sockets. I wanted to kill him, to inflict as much pain on him as possible, and I couldn't explain why. He was a bad man, but I didn't know how bad. I didn't know if he deserved to die, but that wasn't as much of a deterrent as I knew it should have been. Maybe the man had stolen from rich assholes just like him. Maybe he liked blow on the weekends and had snorted more than he could pay for. I didn't know his crimes, but the desire to punish him was there, as strong as anything I'd ever felt. The feeling scared me, but I kind of liked it too.

I stepped from behind the van as the man finally jammed the key into the door and turned the knob. I took four quick steps forward, placed the gun against the back of his head, and pulled the trigger.

The night exploded in my ears.

The man's head jerked forward violently as gore splattered against the door. He pitched forward and crumpled at an impossible angle, his face — or what was left of it — leaving a wild smear of gore on the door. In the dark, I couldn't see much of what the bullet had done to the back of his head, but I could tell my work here was done. He wasn't getting up. I didn't feel bad about it. I felt good. It freaked me out a little and I couldn't breathe, but it also felt like energy was coursing through my veins. The body on the floor with its brain leaking out, that was a bad man. He deserved it. He was as guilty of Anita's illness as everybody else.

Those reasons sounded great to me, but they didn't explain, or excuse, the sense of joy that was blossoming in my chest and threatening to pull my mouth up into a smile.

Something snatched the edge of my vision and I looked down. Pools of red liquid still covered the man's face, but there was something rippling under the skin. It looked like a ball of the wriggling maggots burrowing in and contorting the flat features of his face. The worms slid down the rolls on his neck, and a thick squelching sound followed.

It was like something was feasting on the man's flesh, but from inside his skin. Whatever it was, I wasn't about to stay to find out. As I ran, the blast from the gun was a ghost clacking its teeth at my heels. Only when I got to my own car and tried to pull my keys from my pocket did I realize the gun was still in my hand. Shit. I opened the door, threw it on the passenger seat, and turned on the ignition. I sped all the way to the end of the street.

I was about to blow through the intersection when a woman on foot crossed the street in front of me. She was wearing a dirty white dress, and long hair covered her face. She turned to me and I saw a gaunt face and black holes where her eyes should've been. La Huesuda. Death was coming for me.

It looked like she was about to speak, but I didn't need any messages from the other side when they'd fucking abandoned me when I needed them the most.

I blinked and saw her eyes. The holes had been a trick of the light, shadows playing with my fear as she, a slim woman — probably a homeless person — walked under a street-light. My heart didn't slow down, but my fear receded a bit. However, I remained alert, my eyes open and scanning the road and sidewalks ahead. A message could be coming.

I'd had these sorts of waking dreams all my life. For the longest time, I thought everyone had them. What people meant when they said they were daydreaming. My second girlfriend, a young Puerto Rican named Katia who had just moved to Houston and hated everyone in our school, told me that wasn't the case. It came up in a conversation we had where she told me she knew where people had died in car accidents because she could see the bodies even though they were no longer there. She had to go to school every day and see the headless body of a child near the entrance. I asked her if the dead bodies were ever part of her waking dreams. She had no idea what I was talking about.

Remembering Katia made me think about Melisa and Anita.

These dreams or visions usually arrived when something bad was about to go down, and something awful had already happened. I didn't have time to worry about visions or anything else right now, not if I was going to get back to the hospital before my girls missed me. I drove on.

Normal people can't imagine committing a crime, much less killing a person. People who are dead inside are different. Una vez miras a los ojos vacíos de La Huesuda, todo cambia. La muerte recluta soldados sin anunciarse porque su poder es innegable. Besides the money, what Brian gave me that night was a way to make the world pay for hurting mi angelito. I blamed everyone, and now I was getting some revenge. Yeah, any revenge would do. Violence was soothing, a strange balm that made me feel better. The threat of death ruined my life, and in death I hoped to find something like it again.

I was driving into Austin when my phone rang. It was Melisa. All I heard was screaming and crying. I understood her clearly.

I dropped the phone. I stopped the car and instinctively looked back. The car seat stared at me, its emptiness an attack, and my world went in and out of focus. My lungs refused to expand. Something that sounded like the end of the universe erupted from my throat. In front of me, the dashboard became a wet, shivering mess.

CHAPTER 4

O ne day Anita was there and the next she was gone.
Gone.

Gone even after all our prayers. Gone without mercy. Gone while I was putting a bullet in the head of a man whose evil had wormed its way out after I shot him.

Gone was the only word I could use. All other words sliced my soul with their implied finality. *Gone* works because it's just an absence and at its core there's the possibility of return behind it.

In the days after Anita's death, Melisa and I hugged each other and left trails of snot-filled tears on each other's shoulders, but guilt and anger were the cancers growing inside us. We hated the doctors and the nurses; we hated the guy who gave us coffee at the hospital's cafeteria because he dared to smile; we hated ourselves. La muerte de Anita mató a Dios en mis ojos. Anita's death killed my family.

The gigantic sudden nonexistence of a beautiful soul that was supposed to always be there was the universe, y era un universo eternamente negro, triste, y frío. Melisa y yo morimos en vida, and that's the worst kind of death. It shattered our will to live while stealing from us the strength it'd take to kill ourselves.

We didn't have anyone to blame, so we blamed everybody, anybody, el maldito universo, el cielo, la tierra, y el mismísimo infierno. We blamed her toys and pollution. We blamed our cell phones and her tablet and the fucking microwave. We blamed God and the food we gave her and the clothes she wore. We blamed the doctors and the machines they used to see inside her and the chemotherapy and the chemicals they pumped into her frail body. We blamed her lazy, alcoholic guardian angel for falling asleep at the wheel and causing a horrendous, irreversible accident. Most important, we blamed each other, and that filled us with a kind of loathing that was as strong as the love we had for our dead daughter. We blamed ourselves, and the pain and guilt that seeped from that wound kept us in bed for hours, staring at the ceiling as the shadows crept up and then started sliding down the walls in the changing light.

Ningún matrimonio sobrevive eso. No one should witness the death of an angel.

Five weeks after throwing white flowers on Anita's tiny casket and ruining my only suit because my legs couldn't hold me up as they lowered her remains into the dark ground, I put my hands on Melisa.

We were in the kitchen. She was grabbing a glass of water beside me and I was doing the dishes. She said there was a leak under the sink. The garbage disposal was acting up again. Dirty water was dripping on everything we kept under there. She said the smell of rotting food and dirty water was getting on her nerves, making her think of dead things. I told her I'd contact the property manager.

"You won't," she said. "You always say you're going to do things but then you forget about them a minute later. You've always lived inside your head. Pinche despistado. You're fucking useless. I'll do it tomorrow."

The resignation in her voice stung. She didn't scream. She didn't move her hands aggressively like she did when we had an argument. She didn't spit the words out like she would when I had messed up big-time, raw hatred clanging against her small white teeth. The words came from a frozen wasteland where the only vestiges of love were buried fossils under fifteen feet of permafrost. I heard them and saw the monsters hiding behind them. I looked into her eyes and saw two small pools of emptiness where the light used to hit her pupils. Melisa was broken, a walking hole of anger, just like me. Her bitterness cracked against my back like a whip and tore my flesh open. Se me clavaron sus palabras como un millón de diminutos cuchillos.

Her darkness, her heaviness, was so close that I couldn't breathe.

"Fucking useless." The words hung in the air for a second. She had to walk behind me to return to the living room, so she came closer. Then she stopped. I could feel her body behind me, her warmth too close to my skin.

"Fucking useless." She was too close. Her words were too sharp, her tone a knife in my back.

Anger erupted in my chest. I wanted her away from me, so I shrugged my shoulder and turned around to let her know she was in my personal space. But she was too close. And she was too short. My elbow smashed against her nose. Her arms flew up. The glass she was holding went flying as she staggered backward. The glass hit the floor and exploded. Melisa moved two steps back and her feet hit something. She was about to grab her face, but her arms jumped again, one up in the air and one behind her. Melisa's lower back hit our cheap dining table with enough momentum to send her through it. The sound of the glass breaking was the sound of a thousand nightmares.

Sitting on the floor, her nose a bloody mess and shattered glass around her body, Melisa looked up at me. Her mouth trembled and her hands shook, but the anger in her eyes carried a weight that crushed me. In a single look, every ounce of hatred, every argument, and every accusation landed on me. The worried apology that had been climbing up my throat froze and died, became a lump instead of words.

I elbowed my wife and the mother of my dead daughter in the face.

I had tried to shove the love of my life away the way you shove a man who tries to steal from you.

I had wanted her away from me because my pain was her fault and her words stung. I wasn't fucking useless. None of this was my fault. Her defective genes had killed my daughter. Two dozen articles saying the exact cause of most cases of childhood leukemia is not known came to me, but at that moment, I knew better. I could see beyond the veil, right? It was her fault. Her lack of attention made us realize our baby was sick too fucking late. Melisa believed in God, but maybe not enough, and her lack of faith had denied us a miracle. Having a baby had been her idea, and everything that followed was her fault.

Melisa stood up, her body swaying, and held her left hand against her bleeding nose. She wobbled upright like a broken machine and looked at the blood in her hand. Then she looked at me again. There was too much red in the whites of her eyes, too many tiny capillaries mapping out months of despair.

Women are pillars. The only thing that changes is what or whom they hold up. Take a woman out and you're left with just the spaces between the other elements and a lot of debris. When Melisa brought up her other hand and saw the blood flowing from the damage the table had done, her legs gave out from under her and she slowly returned to the floor, scooting away from the glassy mess. I felt her tiny body drag the world down with it. She settled into a sitting position on the cold tile, her arms curled around her in a protective shield even though I knew I could pull them out of their sockets without much effort if I wanted to. The anger in me was a coil of power ready to explode.

A part of me told me to go to her immediately, to kneel down and pick Melisa up and beg for forgiveness, to explain that it had all been an accident, to somehow turn back time and undo the damage. Another part, however, a part that felt stronger and more immediate, wanted to leave her there, to push this human that had the same strong ties to our dead angel out of my life and let her bleed alone. I couldn't deal with Melisa, or myself, so instead I left my wife on the floor and locked myself in the bathroom.

I took a hot shower that lasted so long my hands became creased, pale alien spiders at the end of my arms. The water stung my face and eventually became cold. I didn't care. Reality was on the other side of a door I refused to open. After shutting off the water, I threw my towel on the floor and lay down on the bathroom tiles.

At some point Melisa got up. Her faint steps were an angry tattoo on the floor, announcing the possibility of an explosion. None came. I eventually slunk out of the bathroom. I pictured Melisa coming at me, teeth bared and fingernails ready to collect strips of my skin as payment for what I'd done. I saw her walk into the room with a large chunk of glass from the table in her hand.

But Melisa had locked herself in Anita's room. There were drops of blood leading to her door, a smear near the doorknob. I went up to the door and heard her sniffling on the other side. She stayed in there for hours. I eventually passed out on the sofa, an old movie about a spaceship that comes back from hell playing on the TV.

The next day I woke up and Melisa was gone. I found a note next to the remains of the kitchen table. She was moving back in with her parents, who lived in Orlando. "Don't come looking for me," read the last line of the note. "The thing that held us together is now food for the worms."

CHAPTER 5

Ten days after elbowing Melisa in the face and sending her crashing through our table I received divorce papers in the mail. I signed them and placed them in the mail the next day. I had enough money to survive a couple weeks, but that was it. And the bills kept coming. The thought of having to interact with other people at a job made my skin crawl.

I wandered around the house aimlessly for hours every day. There was this constant buzz in the air, like static on a neighbor's television. The sound would stay there for days, both driving me insane and blending into the background like the refrigerator's hum. I'd go into Anita's room to get away from it. I'd sit on the side of the bed where I could still smell her tear-free shampoo if I leaned my head into the pillow.

Sometimes I'd cry myself to sleep on the floor of her room. Other times I'd stay awake for days, the insomnia making me feel nauseous. On nights and days when I did sleep, dreams of Anita rushed in. I held her again. I tickled her again. Jugamos con sus muñecas otra vez. Her voice and laughter and energy invaded everything. Every time she came to me in dreams, I would wake up crying and kept crying until I passed out from exhaustion.

*   *   *

One day, about a week after Melisa left, I heard the patter of small feet outside her room. I held my breath as I walked to the hallway to take a look. It was empty. The rooms were empty. There were no tiny feet in the house. The sound was all in my head.

I stood there, listening, hoping. Nothing. After a while, my mind drifted and I decided I needed some fresh air. I couldn't even remember the last time I'd gone outside, but as I stepped off my porch I was taken aback by how dilapidated all the houses were around me. I'd never lived in a fancy neighborhood and this one was no better, but the stained walls, peeling paint, and rusty balconies had worsened significantly. No one had mowed the grass in a while. Cars with flat tires or the burned husks of them littered the street. In the distance, a young girl was walking with what looked like a limp.

The girl kept walking toward me. I didn't move. Her multi-colored shirt was dirty and covered in little cartoonish animals with big heads. They were all crying. Then I noticed the little girl's face. There was blood gushing out of some sort of head wound. Dark red flowed down the left side of her face and covered her shoulder and arm. She paused in mid-stride and smiled at me. She had a chipped tooth in the same spot as Anita.

It pinched my heart, but I took a step forward to see if I could help her and slammed into the wall. The street was replaced by the hallway.

I was losing it. I'd never even made it outside.

That night, I couldn't sleep.

I thought about my mother, passed out on the sofa or spending the day in bed, occasionally moaning some unintelligible fragment from the conversation going on in the chemical dream riding her veins. Maybe the angels she saw would become real if I filled my veins with smack. Maybe heroin would help me see Anita again. Maybe the right combination of drugs would make the world melt.

Brian came over the next day. He'd made it to Anita's funeral, the only friend of mine who showed up. At the cemetery, he stood near his car and never said a word, but seeing him there meant a lot. When I called him I said I wanted to try stuff. He was there in a couple of hours. We smoked meth together. It smelled like burning plastic and made me feel like someone was pulling at my teeth's roots from inside my skull. But the agony vanished for a while and I felt strangely energized, so we smoked some more.

Ten hours went by. Brian talked about movies and business. He ranted against the government and spoke of countries with socialized healthcare. He talked about some babushka being the second shooter in JFK's assassination. I listened and felt jolts of electricity running down my legs. The concept of sleep vanished from my mind. We stayed up, talked, watched movies, and smoked some more. I wanted to run and punch things. Then I went to take a leak and walked by Anita's room.

I noticed some of her laundry still folded in the basket. On the top was her favorite outfit, a white sundress with little blue dots and whales. I picked up the dress and let my fingers trace the embroidery. There was a loose string along the hem that Melisa hadn't gotten around to fixing. I tried to tear the string off, but more and more thread started spooling out. A sob caught in my throat, and I had the urge to take a knife and dig into my flesh. Instead, I went back to the living room and told Brian I hated the way I was feeling. He laughed at me. With the gaping holes in his smile and the thin green veins visible around his bloodshot eyes, he looked like a corpse.

I didn't want to turn into him. I was sure he could see the disgust in my eyes. That's probably why he sat down next to me right before he left and said he was trying to get clean.

He had a baby on the way. His girlfriend, Stephanie, who had somehow managed to get clean while living with him, was seven months pregnant. He said he couldn't imagine my pain and didn't say anything else about Anita. There were tears in his eyes. Whether they were for mi angelito muerto or caused by the fear of bringing a life into this world is something I'll never know. Then he stood up and gave me another photo with an address and a new gun.

"Thought you might be interested in this," he said. "You don't gotta kill him, though. Up to you."

I stayed wired for hours after he left. I looked at the books over the TV and picked one up. Cormac McCarthy. The writing punched my brain. I read the whole thing in one sitting. I couldn't remember any of it as soon as I turned the last page. That bothered me. I opened the book to a random page and read a line from it. "You are either going to have to find some other way to live or some other place in the world to do it in." I closed the book and placed it back on the shelf.

After I killed that first guy, I almost wanted someone to come looking for me. I kept waiting for the knock on my door that would lead to a ride in the back of a police car, the cuffs biting into my wrists and reminding me of how we all feel pain. A week went by. The events of that night played in my head like a movie: Hiding next to the van. The blast splitting the night in half. Gore dripping down the door. The worms squirming under the skin.

Driving back to Austin that night, I'd forced myself to go at normal speed even though part of me wanted to run off Congress Bridge and end it right there. Instead, I threw the gun out the window into Lady Bird Lake and kept going until I reached the hospital.

I'd only done it to get money for Anita. Now I was just a shitty wife-beater waiting for the cops that never came. I thought again about driving off some bridge, ending it all.

CHAPTER 6

T hose pinches cabrones are gonna pay for what they did to
my brother!"

The guy screaming about his brother was hunched, probably
trying to wrap his body around his anger. Spit flew from his
mouth like fat white bullets. They landed all over the bar.
Usually I'd move away from people like him, but he was paying
for drinks, so I decided I'd put up with him for a while.

The small television hanging from his wrist and the thick
gold chain around his neck spoke of dirty money and a passion
for throwing it away. I liked that. No te lleves nada a la tumba;
gástatelo todo. Death doesn't care if you show up rocking an
Armani suit and a Rolex or if you show up naked. Neither
should you.

I was holding my fifth beer of the night. The ranting man
had bought it for me, just like the previous three. I ordered and
he kept throwing crisp twenties at the bartender, a thin Black
guy with a massive head full of dreadlocks and a scrunched-up
face who looked like he'd had a gun in his mouth that morning
and didn't have the balls to pull the trigger. I understood
how he felt. If he asked politely, I would pull the trigger
for him.

The screaming cholo had gravitated toward me because everyone else at the bar was already in conversation. El loco told me he was from Guanajuato. I told him I was from Zacatecas. That was a lie. My dad was born there and ended up crossing la frontera because the devil was looking for him. At least that's what he told everyone. *Yo me fuí porque me andaba buscando El Chamuco.* I think he was telling the truth. He vanished one hot afternoon when I was six. Years after he disappeared, my mom said they'd found him in a garage with some things stuffed in his mouth and missing his hands and feet, so I guess El Chamuco finally got ahold of him. I wasn't surprised. The devil gets us all in the end.

My mom was a different story. She came from Puerto Rico. She had moved to Florida to go to college. The first one in her family. She began dating a bichote from the island who had houses to hide in all over Florida. He got her hooked on blow and then heroin. When he died in a car accident, she returned. This time, she had me, and my father, whom she'd met after escaping the bichote, was already out of the picture. The return only lasted about five years. She never stopped using, and her mother grew tired of that shit and threatened to turn her in to the cops and get custody of me. We left. I left my heart there. It was easy because my mom never stopped talking about the beaches and singing "Preciosa." She had a decent voice. That song always fucked me up. *"Preciosa te llaman las olas del mar que te baña, preciosa por ser un encanto, por ser un Edén..."*

Eden is a club that doesn't accept junkies or their father-less kids, but I'd managed to get a taste of it and lived wanting more.

My mom and dad met in Houston. She was trying to get as far as possible from the bad influences in Florida and he was running from the devil. They got married in a tiny church because my mom was an easy road to citizenship for my father and he apparently had a talent for making money. They had me less than a year later, a little brown kid with veins packed with old ghosts, colonization, pain, desperation, and whatever else they were both running away from.

I don't recall enough of my father to say I feel one way or another, but I loved my mom with all my heart. She had believed education was a surefire way to a better life and had passed that belief on to me. She ended up a junkie on a dirty sofa and living off scraps and claiming she could hear angels. I ended up in a bar waiting for a junkie who was going to give me a job. Whoever invented that story about education being the way out of the gutter deserves two bullets to the back of the head.

That's the story of my life, but I wasn't going to share all that now. Plus, when a drunk Mexican buys you drinks, you play the raza card al máximo. Shit, if he kept paying, I'd sing "Cielito Lindo" with him if that's what he wanted.

The man leaned forward again and growled something about hitting the gym and repeated he was gonna get back at the crew who fucked up his brother in Florida. Something about "a lot of mota" and "a huge misunderstanding." The weed explained the money he was throwing around. I wondered how much he'd gotten from whatever business led to his brother's thrashing. He interrupted my thoughts by pulling out his cell phone and showing me pictures of a guy with a tarantula inked on his neck and a face that apparently had done its best to stop a freight train. I shook my head. He patted me on the shoulder and disappeared into the crowd like a stumbling ghost. I was left alone in a sea of people and sound.

I was meeting Brian. Over the past few months, I'd killed four more men. Bad men. Men who deserved to die. Men who had crossed other men. Men who had touched kids in the worst way imaginable. Men who owed too much money to the wrong person or knew too much. Brian always gave me some vague details, but I didn't care. Their souls were garbage. Like they say, they were guilty of something and killing them was the only thing that would numb the pain.

Brian called a few days after my last job. I thought he would hand over another photo, another address, another gun, and another envelope with cash for me. That wasn't the case. He said he wanted to offer me a different kind of job. He told me to go to this bar and wait for him. He couldn't go over details on the phone. "This gig is gonna be different," he said. This one was going to make us real money. "I'm talking retirement, amigo, no more nonsense, no more running around like fucking cockroaches in the middle of the night with shitty guns."

While I waited for Brian, I took out my phone and checked Melisa's social media. I knew her, how private she was, so I knew she wasn't going to be posting anything anytime soon, but her profile pictures were there, along with images of the three of us in a distant, infinitely happier past.

There was a band on the tiny stage playing Rick James while I looked at Melisa's photos and remembered when we met, two bored individuals in a poetry reading where the readers performed with the passion of tired grandparents after inhaling chloroform. Around me, white people were trying to ignore the stick in their ass while jerkily moving around the bar's sticky dance floor, but in my head, Melisa and I shared sandwiches and talked about movies, fell in love, got through school, learned to survive poverty with love and callousness.

Brian apparently was taking care of important business, so I went to the bathroom. If he showed up, he could wait for me. Pendejo.

I entered the bathroom and saw a Black man standing next to the counter. His skin was so dark it seemed to suck the scant light from the overhead bulb. His blue shirt and weird headgear told me he was from some corner of Africa or at least was pretending to be. He smiled at me, all teeth. A shiver ran down my spine. He looked familiar. He looked like bad news. I tried to ignore the feeling and walked to a urinal.

When I finished and turned, the man stood just a couple of feet away from me. The toothy smile was still plastered on his face. The whites of his eyes were a dark yellow like they were made of bloody yolk. He had a silver tray in his hand with some products on it. He pushed the tray toward me.

"You need towel, ore? Some candy? Deodorant?"

His accent was thick, his voice a wet, rumbling thing that belonged in a horror movie. Sweat made his skin shine. I shoved my hand in my pocket, pulled out a few crumpled dollars, placed them on the tray, and told him to fuck off.

"E se. Some advice as a thank-you: be careful, ore."

Ore. I thought I had heard wrong the first time, but he said it again. Ore means friend in Yoruba. When my mom and I had lived in the worst trailer park of the many we lived in while in Houston, we had a neighbor who called me ore. He was a man with a haunted past who had too much love for his gods and too much hatred for everyone else. He was Puerto Rican, but he never talked to my mom or any of the adults much, and that made them nervous. I knew he was decent, though. He heard me talking Spanish and when I said we had moved back to the US from Puerto Rico, he told me how Nigerians had been stolen from their land and brought to the island by the Spaniards. He said their anger still lived in our veins, that we were a mix of evil conquistador blood, Taíno Indian blood, and African slave blood. Then he told me about how his ancestors had dressed their gods in the garb of the Spaniards' gods and filled the veins of all Puerto Ricans with a bit of their ancient blood. I knew he was a good man because he left milk and cans of tuna outside his trailer's door for the army of stray cats that roamed the place. One day he stopped coming to sit outside. Cops found his naked body bent in unnatural ways and stuffed in his trailer's small shower after someone reported the smell. Whoever killed him had taken his eyes as a souvenir.

The man in front of me had probably been born on a ravaged chunk of land similar to that of my old neighbor. The thing about poverty is that it obliterates geography; poor people have the same haunted look all across the world. We all share something that makes us part of the same breed regardless of color or language. This man may have looked like my neighbor, but I didn't have time for him, so I walked out without another word. Didn't even wash my hands.

I reached the same spot I'd had at the bar before going to the bathroom and pulled out my phone. The white numbers read 11:32 p.m. Never trust a gringo when he tells you he'll "see you in ten." That's what Brian had told me an hour before, and I was still waiting on his pale, twitchy ass.

A figure appeared next to me. Guanajuato guy. He threw an arm over my shoulders and shoved his phone in my face.

"Hey, man, say hi to my little brother, Emilio!"

A man with a fistful of sliced ham for a face waved at me from the screen. He looked confused and ashamed.

"That's my brother, man! Mi hermanito. Voy a matar a los pinches culeros que fucked him up, you hear me? Los voy a matar bien muertos a esos cabrones."

He smelled like booze and body odor battling alcohol-heavy perfume. Between the loud music, the chunky white ladies shaking their ass on the dance floor, and the mamón screaming at me about revenge while shoving his too-bright phone in my face, I was ready to split. Al carajo todo esto. If Brian didn't show up in the next five minutes, he could take this job and shove it.

The man on the phone mumbled something I couldn't hear.

The drunk Mexican yelled something about revenge. His voice cracked. He removed his arm from my shoulders and crossed himself while mumbling a prayer. Then he yelled at his brother, again promising he was going to kill the men who hurt him. "Te lo juro, hermanito," he said while making a tiny cross with his thumb and index finger and kissing it. "Their fucking blood is going to run in the streets of Miami when I get there. Te lo juro." It made me think of how religion and violence walk hand in hand, both forever flirting with death. We all know who always wins in the end.

The Mexican was again sucked into the sea of moving bodies. I sent up a prayer of my own: Dear God, the ocean always returns to us that which it takes, but please keep that man for a while.

Brian showed up a minute later and occupied the space the Mexican had vacated.

"What the fuck took you so long?"

Brian said something, but the noise around us swallowed it. Plus, he always talked as if he had a few pebbles in his mouth and was trying to keep them from slipping through the gaps between the teeth he still had.

Brian was a bit taller than me, maybe six feet flat. He had greasy blond hair that fell on his face and covered the kind of features most women would consider attractive in someone with fewer years of bad living messing everything up. He looked like the trailer park white Jesus you see painted on knickknacks at the dollar store. Well, sans the beard. He was always late to everything and so dumb it was sometimes hard to believe he was still alive.

"What did you wanna talk about, B?"

"I told you, man, I have something juicy lined up for us, something that's gonna pull us outta the damn hole forever. Shit, it's gonna pull us out so far we're gonna forget the damn hole, the worms, and even the stupid shovel." He took a deep, shaky breath and looked around. "I don't wanna talk about it here. Let's go home. We're meeting someone. The dude should be there by now."

A normal person would ask you to meet them at home if that was where they eventually wanted to end up, but not Brian. No, he told me to go to a bar, made me wait for an hour, and then showed up to tell me he didn't want to discuss business there. Algunas personas nacen para joder a los demás.

Instead of picking a fight with him, I nodded. Brian turned. I followed him to the door.

My ears were buzzing when we exited the bar. The air outside was a few degrees cooler and smelled better than inside. I was grateful for both changes. I started walking down the parking lot as the door closed behind me, muffling the music. Brian had apparently parked in the same row because he walked in front of me, in the same direction I was going. He walked fast, with that strange, jerky energy tweakers have.

"Dude, this guy you're about to meet? He's gonna hook us up with some info, man. This is gonna be big. I'm talking lots of dinero." The way he said it, the word sounded more like *De Niro* than *dinero*.

I was going to say something about his atrocious pronunciation, but stopped. The guy from the bathroom was standing next to my car. Was he waiting for me? How did he even know which car was mine? I had more questions than answers but knew one thing for certain: any sudden movement and I was gonna knock his ass out.

"You need something, man?" I asked as I approached my car.

The man looked at me. His face showed no traces of the smile he'd sported in the bathroom.

"O nilo lati ṣọra."

"Nah, man, English. I know you speak it. Cut the bullshit."

"You need to be careful."

I took a step forward. A cold tightness enveloped my chest and pulled at the back of my neck. Violence was about to take over. Then I noticed his fucking feet were floating about two inches above the asphalt.

"Buburu . . . bad things. They are coming your way, ore. Iwin kekere . . . she sent me."

Messages were something I paid a lot of attention to before Anita's death. The moment we covered her body with dirt, I decided to stop. If you never get the most important message of your life, the rest deserve to be ignored. I took three steps and grabbed two fistfuls of the man's blue shirt. I tried to push him against the car, but it was like trying to move a wall.

"I don't know what the fuck you're talking about, but—"

"You cool, Mario?"

I turned to look at Brian. He was parked six or seven cars down. The man I was holding grabbed my wrists and squeezed. I looked into his eyes. He was definitely my old neighbor from Houston. He hadn't aged a day. The man could have crushed rocks with that grip. My hands opened up, uncoiling slowly, like wet paper. He removed my hands from his shirt and held them in his vicious grip. I looked down. His feet were still off the ground. I looked up at his face, thinking I never wanted to forget him, but there was no face to look at. His eye sockets were covered by skin and the space where his nose and mouth had been were just shallow craters. I pulled my hands away and he released me. Brian's feet pounded the asphalt behind me. I turned to him. He stopped before I could tell him to.

"What the fuck, man?" His eyes were wide. Brian's hand shot up, his index finger pointing shakily. "What the fuck is wrong with his face?" My eyes darted back to the man. They found empty space.

"The fuck was that all about? Where did that guy go?" Brian's voice was a few decibels too loud and had turned into something you'd expect to come out of a squeaky toy.

I looked around and kneeled to look under the cars. The man was gone. He'd vanished. I grabbed my car's side-view mirror and pulled myself up. Brian stood next to my trunk. His pasty complexion now looked like he needed to be in the hospital instead of standing in a parking lot.

"Dude, he just vanished! He fucking vanished! Did you see that? Did you just fucking see that?"

"I saw it, Brian. Just forget about it. Get in your car. Let's get outta here."

"Forget about it? The man vanished into thin air, Mario!"

I turned to Brian and gave him a look he didn't deserve. He brought his hands up, trying to placate words I hadn't said.

"Okay, okay. Let's go."

I got in my car and turned the engine. This, too, was going to be ignored. If someone or something wanted to talk to me, tough luck. They should have done it when Anita was here, when a message would've helped me keep my life together, my family intact. I would've listened then. Now my ears were closed. The time for angels and devils whispering in my ear had come and gone. I had business to discuss with a gringo loco and whoever we were going to meet. Every bone in my body wanted me to pray to La Guadalupana, to ask her for forgiveness and protection from whatever I'd just seen, to ask her to bring me Melisa back so my life would start resembling something normal. I wanted the growing regret in my chest to go away. But La Guadalupana was dead to me. Silent gods are dead gods. Then I realized that, faced with fear, my instinct had been to pray. An image of my mom on her sofa came to me. Stringy hair plastered to her forehead. A mint-green robe wrapped around her emaciated body. Her smile a radiant thing emitting light that filled the entire living room despite her yellow teeth. I heard her voice in my head: "There are angelitos over your head, mijo. They're talking to you." My anger at La Virgencita, my anger at God, didn't mean I had to stop praying. I now had my own Virgencita, my own angel in the sky . . . and maybe my old neighbor watching my back.

CHAPTER 7

We parked in front of Brian's place, a two-bedroom joint that served as house, place of business, and occasional junkie motel. He was standing beside me before I'd had a chance to turn around and close the car door. Methheads are fast, but eager or scared ones move faster than coked-up cheetahs.

"Man, I'm telling you, this dude knows what he's talking about," Brian said. "It'll be easy money. A fucking lot of easy money. With what we're gonna make, you can do whatever the hell you want and I can give the worm a good start in life. Steph will have to stop bitching about all the money we need to buy baby crap. She's always going on and on about cribs and diapers and clothes and a bunch of other shit. This will keep her happy and quiet. Man, we might even leave this shitty city behind, you know? Move to a place where there's, like, more trees and mountains and shit instead of so many houses and buildings and flat land. Someplace nicer where we can get a clean start. There are too many hipsters and too many damn festivals in Austin nowadays. This isn't the city I moved to fifteen years ago. It was fun back then. Everyone was on drugs. Did I ever tell you I was in a band? It was a punk band. We were badass. The Worse Angels. We had some crazy shows. It was more about the show than the music, you know? Anyway, that's all gone now. And I'm struggling like a motherfucker to pay my property taxes. I wanna go to a place where there are seasons and the trees change colors and you can walk outside and take pictures of your kid playing in a pile of leaves and shit, you know? I wanna go somewhere where I can enjoy life without worrying about my property taxes. I think when—"

"Hey, B, pónle un corcho, man. Stop. Your mouth is going a mile a minute. Relax. Let the man inside tell me whatever it is he's going to tell me and then we can talk about all the plans you already have for the money that's not in your pockets yet, deal?"

Brian nodded like my words made all the sense in the world and started walking toward the house. He was not a bad guy, but his brain didn't work properly because of the chemicals he kept putting in his body. Don't get me wrong, he was a somewhat functional junkie, but only because his job was mostly sitting at home and selling drugs to people like him. That's why his excitement meant nothing to me. I'd seen him excited before, even back when he still had the office job, and the ideas he was crazy about on Monday would prove themselves stupid by Tuesday morning or were simply forgotten by Wednesday. Selling pirated DVDs. Delivering groceries. Refurbishing TVs and DVD players from Goodwill and reselling them to hipsters online. He was a well of mediocre ideas. Dumb and high is a dangerous combination, and that was the state he was stuck in.

As we approached the house, I thought again how weird it was that he was still alive. He used his place as headquarters for everything. That meant he and his girlfriend, Stephanie, ate, watched TV, fucked, and slept in the same place he used to sell dope and, when the junkies had nowhere to go and needed to shoot up, where some of them crashed on the two large couches in the garage as they spent a few hours in the land of warm dreams. And now Brian had a baby on the way. Smart dealers know: no se mezcla tu casa con el panal de abejas. You can only sleep in a bed full of snakes for so long before one of them decides to sink its fangs into you.

We climbed the three steps up to the door and entered the house. The last batch of meth Brian had smoked in there was cut with something that made it smell like charred plastic soaked in stagnant water and hair products. The aroma mixed in with old-carpet stink, the ammonia stench of ignored animal pee, and body odor.

"Steph, we're here," said Brian.

There was a small kitchen to the right of the doorway. Stephanie was in there, getting something from the fridge, a thin yellow rectangle pulled from a 1970s time capsule. She closed the door and smiled at us. She was a gorgeous woman. Her wild mane of light brown hair always framed her face and she had the kind of smooth white skin you only see in movies. Now, eight months pregnant, she glowed like a round angel.

Stephanie wore a blue maternity dress and her enormous breasts were pushing their way toward her neck. Even bloated to the point of bursting she was sexy. Every time I saw her, I thought the same thing: she could have done things, gone places. I knew she was smart, but everything about her current situation spoke of the kind of intelligence that vanishes when the time comes to make decisions. At least she was smart enough to stay away from the meth her boyfriend was so fond of. Still, I couldn't imagine a bright, happy future for her, and that felt like someone sticking a finger in my still-bleeding wounds.

"Hello," I said to Steph. She replied with another smile that reminded me of Melisa, and a dozen blades twisted inside my chest. I saw Melisa when she was pregnant in my head. Round and gorgeous, eating nachos, saying our baby daughter would come out breathing fire from all the spicy stuff she was consuming. There were rough days and nights where she couldn't get comfortable and went to the bathroom twenty times, but she rarely complained. Some people are born to be parents, and she was one of them. I focused on Steph again, the tightness in my chest reminding me some holes fill up with the kind of pain that turns into concrete and forever prevents you from putting anything else in there.

"How've you been, Mario? I haven't seen you in a while," she said.

Normally, I know people don't give a shit when they ask how you're doing. Asking is part of that thing people call the social contract. In Stephanie's case, however, something in her eyes told you that she really wanted to know, and that if you started telling her a sad story, she'd listen. I appreciated the fact that she didn't mention the obvious or ask me how I was "holding up." If Brian had mentioned to her the jobs he'd thrown my way, she either didn't care or recognized her state as the soon-to-be mother of a junkie's child as one that prevented her from passing judgment on others.

"I'm good," I said, because lies are always easier than the truth. "Here to see if what B has in mind is worth my effort, you know?"

"If it's anything like what he told me, it's worth all your effort. This could be the last stupid thing we ever have to do." She placed her right hand on her swollen belly. I thought about the creature in there, floating in warm, cozy liquid, caught in a world between worlds, oblivious to the shitshow he or she would be thrown into.

I looked back up at Stephanie's face. The smile was still there, but the light behind it had dimmed and now spoke of angry ghosts she had a hard time keeping chained to the basement of her life. A life full of bad decisions will do that to a person.

Looking at her did something to my heart and I had to look away, so I looked at the microwave that sat on the counter. The top of it was covered in bottles. A big red box had THYREX written on the middle of it in blocky white letters. There was a bottle of generic aspirin next to it and a small orange prescription bottle with some white stuff inside it. There was a big bottle that said PRENATAL 1 on the label, and it featured a half of a pink woman on it. The woman had pink hair over half her face and was holding her bulging belly. She kinda looked like Stephanie. The prenatals Melisa had used came in a brown bottle and had MULTI + DHA written on the front. That's how I identified them. Never learned what DHA is ...

Brian tapped me on the shoulder, jerked his head to the side, and kept walking into the house. I smiled at Stephanie once more, slapped the doorframe as some sort of goodbye, and followed Brian into the stinky bowels of the house.

We reached the end of the entrance hallway and hung a right to reach the living room. The place was always a mess, but Brian had apparently cleared off the sofa so that the man waiting for us could sit.

He was short and sat on the edge of the sofa, his hands intertwined. He lifted his head, his eyes darting from Brian to me and back to Brian. He looked spooked, ready to jump at someone's face or dart out through any available opening like a scared cat. He had close-cropped hair and shifty black eyes over a nose that had been broken a couple of times and left to heal naturally. His brown skin wasn't as dark as mine, which meant more Spaniard and less African in his blood. His arms and neck were covered with tattoos, some of which were only a tad darker than his skin.

"Juanca, this is Mario," said Brian.

Juanca, which I guessed was short for Juan Carlos, nodded at me but didn't stand up or offer his hand. He immediately looked back down. I took the chair closest to the television. Brian remained standing and offered us something to drink. We shook our heads.

No one spoke for a few seconds. In the heavy silence, I looked around. Ratty brown couch. A few boxes in a corner, their sides and corners bent out of shape. Dirty beige carpet with strange stains here and there. Everything seemed to be a shade of brown or gray. The palette of poverty.

When the silence become too much, Brian took a hammer to it.

"Okay, so listen, I think it's time we all get down to business, yeah?"

I nodded. Juanca did the same. Brian continued. "Juanca here knows some ice routes. You know, from Mexico. They come in driving big trucks full of liquid ice from Juárez, make their deliveries in Houston or Dallas, and drive back with bags full of money. That's how the big cartels do it now, and he knows when and where, right?"

Juanca's eyes landed on me. They said he trusted me as much as I trust doctors. The feeling was mutual.

"¿Quién es este güey, Brian?" It sounded like *Brayan*.

Juanca had no idea who I was. He was sitting on Brian's moldy, stinky sofa, allegedly willing to offer information about a lot of money to a pinche twitchy gringo and a complete stranger.

My eyes were adjusting to the gloom of Brian's house and I could make out the tattoos above Juanca's eyes. He had the word HOOD tattooed over his right eye and the word MADE over his left, both in thin, loopy letters that ended in curlicues. The thing on his chin turned out to be a couple of letters, *B* and *A*. Barrio Azteca. I knew the gang from my Houston days.

Brian kept scratching his forearms like someone who accidentally fell on top of an anthill and then took a nap. His nerves were enough to put me even more on edge. Brian had probably met this guy while getting a shipment of meth or while selling some of it and was stupid enough to start discussing stealing a truck full of money from a Mexican cartel. Now Brian needed me here as a translator. Or maybe he just needed an extra gun or someone willing to eat a bullet. Lucky me. Pinche mamón. The sooner I figured out if this was a waste of time, the sooner I could get back home. I switched languages.

"Brian me dijo que tenías información que compartir. No estoy aquí para hacer amigos o jugar juegos. If you don't have anything to say to me, then I'm outta here." My Spanish was perfect. It was the only language my mother used to talk to me. It was my grandmother's language, and she didn't speak anything else during the years we took refuge in her house in Puerto Rico before moving back to Houston. It was what Melisa and I spoke to each other and to Anita. In fact, the only person in my life who never spoke it was my father. He never spoke a word of it because he feared being identified as an outsider. His accent gave him away. His attempt at hiding made him more noticeable. My mother hated the fact that he never spoke Spanish, even at home. I don't remember much from the few years he was around, but I do remember his smell, his scratchy beard, and his accent. My Spanish came from my mother. The only downside to that was that I didn't sound like a Mexican. I was always conscious of my words, my Puerto Rican accent. Spanish is a language, but Mexican Spanish and Puerto Rican Spanish are two different variations, just like Dominican Spanish, Colombian Spanish, Ecuadorian Spanish, Cuban Spanish, or Argentinian Spanish. Growing up in PR and then Houston had made me fluent in both Rican and Mexican Spanish.

"Wait, man, what are you saying? Don't talk so damn fast," Brian said. Nothing makes a monolingual gringo as nervous as not knowing what those around him are saying. Not all white people have the same level of privilege, but they all share an aversion to being forced to step momentarily into otherness.

"Brian, this guy wants to know who I am, which means you haven't told him. I don't like the fact that you kept me a secret until now, and if you two are talking about what I think you're talking about, you can both go to hell. I'm not fucking around with cartel money."

"It's not cartel money until the cartel gets it," said Juanca in accented English. His demeanor had changed a bit. He'd been aggressive but now looked at me with softer eyes. Maybe my spiel had made him realize I wasn't there to mess with his time.

"What's that supposed to mean?"

"There are a lot of trocas coming in and out with different drugs," he said, moving his hands as if they could pull the right words in from the space in front of him or draw maps of the border and the roads in the air. "There are many guys working for los carteles. It takes a long time for the carteles to realize when something goes wrong. You know, when money disappears. Los cachan en la frontera nomás, antes de que entren o salgan. You know, la Fronteriza. They throw them in jail. La lana no llega o el hielo no llega; se lo queda todo la pinche Fronteriza o los cabrones milicianos. The drugs come in, but the money sometimes doesn't come out, you know what I'm saying? Sometimes the men run away, stay here in the States. The carteles know the deal. They take their families and . . . los amenazan. If they don't show up, they kill the families. But some of these men don't care.

"Shit happens. It's part of the business. Plus there are so many eyes on the border that they are sending more batches to make up for the ones that don't make it."

"You're saying the carteles are gonna think something bad happened and call it a day? Like losing a truck full of cash is just overhead to them? That's stupid. They don't play around," I said.

Juanca looked at me like I'd said something nasty about his mother. Before he could reply, Brian jumped in.

"The plan is to make it look like the crew that was supposed to take the money back to Mexico decided to keep it," he said. He was smiling. All the English had helped him. He knew what we were talking about and that gave him confidence. Strange how switching languages can make someone who is not used to it feel like an outsider. Since Neither Juanca nor I spoke, Brian went on. "Listen, what we need to do is let them make the transaction in Houston and then collect the cash on their way back." He made it sound as easy as going to the grocery store to pick up milk and bread.

"Collect the cash? And how are you planning on doing that, B? You're gonna ask them politely? Calmly suggest they fork over what they're carrying?"

"Well, they have to return to Mexico, right? Juanca knows what route they'll use, what tunnel or whatever. Seriously, this dude has all the info. All we have to do is stop them before they get there and take the money. Then we...make them disappear. Done deal. The cartels will go looking for the sons of bitches that never came back, not us."

"Exacto," said Juanca. "Los desaparecemos. De esa manera lo primero que los jefes van a pensar es que los cabrones se volaron con la lana, you know what I'm saying? They're gonna start looking for them, not us. No le puedes pedir dinero de vuelta al vacío del desierto ni a la incertidumbre, cierto?"

"That's not a fucking plan, man. Those guys are soldiers. There could be a dozen of them in any given truck and they will shoot us the second we approach them, no questions asked."

"We're gonna get some help for that. A secret weapon, you

know what I'm saying? Va a ser facilito. Neta. Trust me. If you're waiting for them, it's not that complicated."

Juanca's words threw a bucket of cold water on the conversation. *Los desaparecemos. We make them disappear.* There it was. Kill them all. The big solution. I looked at him and wondered if he was serious. He was rubbing his hands together again, but his eyes were on mine, unwavering. He meant it. He meant every fucking word. The meth. The money. The killing. Bad men working for worse men who wouldn't hesitate to kill their families. I couldn't imagine putting a price on my wife and daughter, and being reminded that we were dealing with the kind of men who have no qualms about killing women and children made me want to get the fuck out of Brian's house as quickly as possible and never talk to either of them ever again.

"How do you know so much about all this, Juanca?"

He looked at Brian as if asking permission to speak. I kept my eyes on him, trying to read him, trying to see if he was lying to me. I guess Brian nodded or he stopped caring and carried on.

"I used to be a driver with them. There is chaos en el cartel because they are splitting down the middle. You know, Zambada against Los Chapitos. They are getting sloppy, even more violent than before. They are sending more and more trocas, more and more liquid ice. The other carteles know, they smell the blood, and they're trying to get in on the action, you know what I'm saying? Sending more drugs, buying more guns, killing more people. With all the attention at the border, it's hard. Lots of money goes missing. Lots of ice and weed and coke and everything else gets confiscated. Now is the time to do this and get lost. Trust me, güey. No hay pedo. Go in, get what we want, and ghost."

I'd seen images of cartel mercenaries running around with guns and riding in the back of a pickup truck with a machine gun attached to it. I'd read about one of El Chapo's sons getting caught by the authorities and then being released because they couldn't deal with the number of soldiers and firing power the Sinaloa Cartel brought to the streets. Any hope that Sinaloa was a place where the government and the law still ruled evaporated that day. The world watched it happen online and on TV and forgot about it the day after it ended because the idiot at the White House said something more stupid than whatever stupid thing he had said before.

"So what, you just quit and they let you walk away?"

"Yeah, I stayed home after the last trip. Los pinches hijueputas no me pagaron lo mío. Some jefes de grupo hold your lana until the next job comes along. It's a way to make sure we show up again and again. But fuck that. I wanted out. I want to help my amá move to a better place and lay low so I don't end up with flies crawling over my eyeballs. La Huesuda finds you sooner or later, but the more you tempt her, the faster she gets there. Todos tenemos fecha de caducidad, pero no hay por qué empujarla pa'lante."

Now it all started making a bit of sense. Juanca had decided to stop working and wanted enough money to disappear forever.

"How much money are we talking about here?"

Brian leaned forward. He was eager to become part of the conversation again. "If all goes well, about two million bucks."

That's a lot of money. Too much. The kind of money that has death tied to it.

"Okay, stop right there," I said. "You two are talking about taking on a truck full of cartel people with guns, driving away with two million dollars, and quietly slipping into oblivion for the rest of our lives as if no one will come looking for that money? Whatever movie you two were watching before I got here seriously fucked your brains up."

"Listen, man, you gotta hear Juanca out," Brian said.

"We're not doing this alone; we'll be working for el Cartel de Juárez, y Don Vázquez nos va a ayudar. Like he said, we'll have a special little weapon he's gonna let us use. All we have to do is go pick it up and bring it with us. If all goes well, the mess we're gonna leave behind will make those who find it too shit-scared to come looking for us."

I didn't know what I was going to say next, but hearing that name stopped me. Don Vázquez was the highest-ranking member of the Juárez Cartel. No one knew much about him, but when Vicente Carrillo, the head of the organization, was arrested in 2014, Vázquez took his place. I knew this because I'd taken three courses on money-laundering prevention while working at the insurance company. The cartels loved to give folks in the US money to take out a life insurance policy, wait a few months, and then fake some good news or an inheritance and try to pay the whole thing up front. After that, they wait a couple of weeks and ask for their money back for a variety of reasons. Insurance companies keep 15 percent as a penalty fee and the cartels get a nice, clean check from an American company. The 15 percent is just overhead for them, the price of getting their money cleaned. This was one of the biggest rackets in the seventies and eighties. It made insurance companies millions of dollars. Even Colombian drug lord Pablo Escobar did it back in his day. Then the feds caught on. Now companies have to ask policyholders to show where the funds came from before they can send large amounts of money into the company. That was my job. It kept me somewhat updated on cartel business because we regularly received reports on most organized crime and the new ways in which they were trying to trick the system into laundering their money for them.

What Juanca was saying was extremely dangerous, a death sentence probably, but if he was right about turmoil in the Sinaloa Cartel, then maybe we had a chance. A tiny voice was whispering in my ear that there might be something here, some way to pull it off and make enough money to get the fucking insurance company and the hospitals off my back and then get out of Austin forever. No more emails. No more deleting texts of "Hi, Mario. Our records indicate that you have an outstanding balance..." No more PAST DUE and FINAL NOTICE letters. No more owing money or dealing with reminders that in this fucking country, losing a loved one always comes with a bill. Hell, maybe I could even get Melisa back...

"Okay, Juanca, here's what we need to do: I'm gonna shut my mouth, Brian is gonna shut his, and you're gonna lay this whole thing out for us. The only things I know so far are that you wanna hijack a cartel truck loaded with two million dollars somewhere in the fucking desert, kill everyone like it's the O.K. Corral, and then drive the stolen truck back to Juárez and deliver it to...I don't even know where. Nah, that doesn't work. Gimme some details. Fill in those blanks and we'll take it from there."

Brian was looking at me and nodding. His right hand was busy scratching imaginary bugs under the skin of his left arm. He was probably happy that I'd more or less taken over. Junkie de mierda. Juanca looked at Brian and then back at me. Then he looked sideways. I followed his gaze. Stephanie had entered the living room at some point. She had a blue glass in her right hand and seemed to be trying to guess who would speak next. Juanca broke the silence and awkward staring.

"Si quieres detalles te doy detalles, cabrón. If you and Brian do this, everything's okay, we go and we get it done. The only reason I'm sharing this with you is because Brian told me he knew a guy that was down for whatever, man. I guess he thinks you're some kind of ghetto Rambo who will drive ten hours to go kill some motherfucker you don't even know with a shitty gun you've never even tried shooting before. But maybe he's wrong about you. If you two are . . . pinches cobardes, then all you have to do is keep your fat mouths shut. En boquitas cerradas no entran moscas y a Don Vázquez no le gustan las lenguas sueltas, you know what I'm saying?"

"I hear you loud and clear, man," I said. "If we don't take the gig, our mouths are shut. Forever. Now break it down for us and take it easy so Brian can catch everything you're saying. Start from the beginning. I wanna know how you know all this and how you plan to make us walk out clean and not spend the rest of our very short lives looking over our shoulder."

If my comment made Brian feel insulted, he didn't show it. Instead, he had his eyes glued on Juanca's face, waiting for the plan that was going to make us all rich. Juanca took a deep breath and started talking.

CHAPTER 8

Two million dollars. A couple of days. A few dead men. A different future.

The more Juanca spoke, the more I realized his English wasn't as bad as I'd first thought. He understood me perfectly and communicated efficiently. It was the accent that was throwing me off. It was much thicker than mine. Spanglish is a thing for everyone whose first language is Spanish instead of English, but in his case it seemed practiced, almost like he knew that switching back and forth was the perfect way to engage me while keeping Brian slightly confused. He'd been testing out the waters. Or maybe the hesitancy and confusion at the beginning had not been an act and he was, like many of us, someone who had a bit of a hard time communicating in a language not his own because it meant he had to think of everything and translate it before it came out of his mouth. Nerves always made that worse. Whatever the case, he was smarter than I had first thought. He had no problem telling a story. He knew exactly when to look straight at me and pause for my reaction. That scared me. I needed to know more.

"How do you know about *this* trip?"

"There was a guy in Juárez who was helping hide the hielo inside the trocas after it came in from Culiacán. He worked for a shop in town. De mecánico. They get the trocas in the shop, mix the liquid hielo with water, and then fill one gas tank with the mix and put a little bit of gasoline on the top in case they check on it at the border. Once they get it to where it needs to be, they boil that water off and get the hielo back. One of his bosses was holding out on him, so the man complained. He had a wife and kids. Mouths to feed, you know what I'm saying? Anyway, they beat the shit out of him and left him for dead out in the desert so the animals could eat him. But he survived. He lost a fucking eye from the beating, but he got his ass up and made it all the way back to Juárez. He knew he couldn't take on those cabrones himself, so he asked Don Vázquez for money to move his family to Monterrey in exchange for info about the last troca he helped prepare. Don Vázquez promised him the lana. He got the info and then fed the cabrón to his cocodrilos. Don Vázquez hates chivatos. Anyone who talks to you about someone else will talk to someone else about you, you know what I'm saying? The troca he talked about is the one we're gonna hit."

"Cocodrilos? Don Vázquez has crocodiles?"

"Yeah, they help him save time. No one wants to be moving all those bodies and digging all those holes out in the desert. At night . . . well, there are bad things out there, things that feed on the living as well as the dead. If you take too long digging a hole, they come for you. And the bodies stink like shit when you burn them. The smell brings the things from the desert to wherever you are. Vazquez's new partner, well, she thought it'd just be easier to feed people who need to disappear to los cocodrilos."

"See, Mario?" Brian said. "I told you Juanca knew his shit. This dude's hooked up, man. He knows the border like the palm of his hand. We get the money and he'll have us in and out in no time. Then we come here and split. Goodbye, shitty life!"

Juanca nodded at Brian. I focused on his face. If it made him uncomfortable, so be it. I wanted to read his movements, to find a lie making his face twitch.

"Who's the partner you mentioned and how are this woman and Don Vázquez going to help us get the job done?"

Juanca smiled for the first time since we'd been there. He looked at me the way a predator looks at his prey. His smile sent shivers down my spine.

"The partner is none of your business, Mario. Your only business here is to decide if you want to do this thing or not."

"Fair enough. Will I get answers if I say yes?"

"You'll get answers if you say yes and you mean it. You say yes just so I tell you more and then decide to walk away . . . I might have to shoot you, cabrón."

The smile was gone. He meant it.

"I don't like getting shot. However, I need to know one more thing, and this is something I hope you can answer because it's really fucking important. How—"

"Doscientos mil cada uno."

Doscientos mil cada uno. Two hundred thousand dollars each. Cash. For one gig. Fuck.

Brian and Juanca had mentioned the money. Both said it was a lot, but this was the first I'd heard of how much each of us would pocket. Two hundred thousand dollars for killing some drug mules. Two hundred thousand dollars stolen from criminals who were flooding the streets with poison. Two hundred thousand dollars was more money than I'd ever had. It was more money than I would ever manage to put together with decades of shitty jobs and long hours. Two hundred thousand dollars was enough to leave Austin behind, offer Melisa a new start, and get a little house in Maine or Vermont or any other of those places full of nice streets lined with trees that show up on postcards and TV shows. Two hundred thousand dollars was more money than I'd ever dared dream about. Being broke is not a financial status; it's a state of mind. It breaks you. Every setback pushes you closer to believing you don't deserve better, that you're struggling because you deserve it, because you're worthless. Melisa deserved better. I deserved better. Anita had deserved better. Two hundred thousand dollars made a shitty idea sound good to me because it was enough money to be able to fucking breathe for a while and get the better we deserved.

Or maybe it would be the opposite. Maybe it would be two hundred thousand dollars for a bullet to the head.

"Okay, let's say I want that money. Let's say I go with the plan. It's you, Brian, me, and who else?"

"Brian, you, and me. That's it. You don't want to have to share any more of your cut, right? Once we're back from giving Vázquez his money, we each take our cash and bail. Toman la lana y se hacen los fantasmas mudos por el resto de sus vidas."

"Wait, I didn't get that last part," said Brian.

"He said once we get our cut, we need to vanish and become mute ghosts for the rest of our lives."

"Shit, with that money in my pocket I can do that and much more. You want a ghost, I'll give you a ghost. I can also play a witch, a zombie, a vampire, and a fucking werewolf that plays the maracas as I waltz my way the fuck outta this town."

"I'll have everything packed," Stephanie said. Brian walked toward her, kissed the side of her head, and wrapped his arms around her shoulders.

Crossing the border twice seemed like a bad plan; having three men go up against who knew how many, like a death sentence. And I didn't know why we needed to go see Vázquez before everything went down. Whatever weapon we were going to pick up would probably not be worth the trip.

"Is going to Juárez first necessary?"

"Very necessary."

"Why?"

Juanca smiled again. "Too many questions again, güey. You haven't told me if you're in or not."

"I'm in."

"He's in!" said Brian. He let go of Stephanie and came over to slap me on the back.

"Remember what I said, man: you leave me hanging, I'll put a bullet in your head."

After being so close to death as it hounded Anita and feeling like there was nothing keeping me here, having something to look forward to gave me a sense of...something, like being alive wasn't a waste of time. That feeling pushed me to reply to Juanca's threat with one of my own.

"I heard you the first time, and I don't doubt it. However, if you try to play me and make me do the work and not pay me, I'll put a bullet in *your* head. I've gotten pretty good at doing that lately."

Juanca's lips curled up. "I like this motherfucker, B," he said, pointing at me. He took a few steps forward. I thought he was going to pull out a gun and kill me then and there. Instead, he stretched his hand out. We shook.

"Las cuentas claras conservan amistades."

It was something I'd heard all my life. The translation would be something like *clear accounts preserve friendships*, but there is an idiom that approaches its true meaning better: Good fences make good neighbors.

"We leave Friday. That should give you enough time to... prepare or whatever. I'll pick you guys up early."

I looked at Brian. He was nodding, looking like he was ready to go. In a way, so was I. I didn't trust Juanca, and this could all be a suicide mission, but I'd held on to less in the past, and this time I didn't care as much about possible consequences.

Two hundred thousand dollars. Fuck, that was a lot of money. It was enough for me to start a life far away from the things that haunted me. Maybe somewhere where there's snow in the winter and people say hi to each other in the streets. My brain again showed me a nice little house with a white fence and a huge tree in front of it. The fucking American Dream. The house had a little porch where Melisa and I could sit drinking coffee, watching leaves spiral down to the green grass.

I pushed Melisa, the leaves, the coffee, and the house away. That was a dangerous place to go. I needed to focus on the task at hand and forget about everything else. If La Huesuda took me for one last dance, so be it. The tiny arms waiting for me on the other side were not an outcome I'd ever regret.

That thought stopped me. Would I go to heaven to be with my baby after killing people? I knew regret could help erase sins, and I sure hoped so because I regretted elbowing Melisa more than any other of my stupid decisions. Would killing without regret shut heaven's doors in my face? There was no way to know. I decided I didn't care. I killed motherfuckers who deserved to die, right? Plus, my mom used to say that suffering is a surefire way to earn an entry ticket to heaven, and I'd suffered something I wouldn't wish on my worst enemy. The worst part of saying you no longer believe in God is knowing that God is still there, listening to you. That's why the praying sneaks back in when shit goes south. That's why not believing is just standing on the opposite side of the same room you've always been in.

"I see you thinking, Mario. You excited or scared or what?" Juanca asked, looking at me and ignoring Brian, which meant he already knew the tweaker was excited and eager to hit the road.

"Just thinking about some stuff I gotta do before Friday."

"Fuck yeah!" said Brian. "The Three Amigos, ladies and gents!" Juanca and I looked at him. Silly gringo.

"Órale pues. Be here at six or so. We have a lot of driving to do."

I got up and turned around. Brian jumped up and patted me on the shoulder again. For a methhead dope dealer, he sometimes acted like a kid. Stephanie was looking at us. She had been standing in the same spot since entering the living room. The blue glass in her hand was empty. She absentmindedly rubbed her bulging stomach in slow circles. I'd seen that distracted protectiveness before. The gesture broke me in half so hard I thought I heard something snap inside me.

"We need to celebrate this," said Brian. He shoved his hand into his pocket and pulled out a small bag. He shook it in the air, the joy in his face reminding me of an eager puppy. I didn't want any part of it, so I mumbled something about being too tired to party and said I'd see them Friday morning.

I was halfway down the hallway when I heard footsteps behind me. Stephanie was following me. I opened the door and turned around. She leaned into the doorway a bit.

"Thanks, Mario," she said. Then she lowered her eyes and dropped her voice a few decibels. "You know Brian would probably fuck this up royally without your help, so thank you."

Something like a warm balloon grew in my throat and made it hard to breathe.

"Don't mention it."

I wanted to say I was doing it for the money, doing it because killing bad men made me feel less awful about everything for reasons I wasn't smart enough to comprehend. I wanted to say that my sick mind had turned stealing a truck full of cash from some cartel members into a future with Melisa in a little house in an alternate dimension where I never pushed her into our kitchen table. Instead, I looked at her in silence, focusing on the hand still protectively placed over her belly. That's when I realized I was doing this for her and the little creature in her belly as much as I was doing it for the money. Shit like that would surely weigh heavily on the other side of the scale if I ate a bullet. Good people go to heaven even if they do bad things. I turned and walked to my car, already thinking about the sharp, cold silence that would slice me open the second I got home.

CHAPTER 9

They tell you that with enough willpower and effort a person can change their essence, alter their mood, transform their reality. They tell you positive thinking is a powerful thing, that praying is sometimes the only solution. That's all bullshit. Melisa always read self-help and lit more candles at church than anyone else. None of it worked. When our daughter's life was quickly sucked away by a disease we couldn't see, our wishing, positive thinking, and endless prayers never did a goddamn thing.

Sometimes things go wrong and there's nothing you can do about it. And yet, we mostly refuse to give up. Instead, we invent gods to help us push forward. Pain invades us and we find reasons to carry on. Death approaches, bony arms outstretched, and we fight it with that inexplicable desire to keep living.

The majority of people always want to think life is worth living, that we must do everything in our power to keep going, to stay alive. They don't grasp that the value of their life is much lower than they imagine.

Think about it.

How much is your life worth? I'll tell you: the value of your life is less than the craving of a desperate junkie who breaks into your house to steal your shit and finds you there. Your life is worth less than a jealous husband with the wrong idea and a gun in his trembling hand. The value of your existence is much less than that of your life insurance in the eyes of a dejected spouse. If you're Black or brown, the value of your life is less than the fragile masculinity of a cop who wants to feel superior or a racist who wants you out of the way so they're not forced to face someone they don't understand. El valor de tu vida es lo que vale el segundo en que alguien aprieta el gatillo, el segundo en que alguien pone toda su ira en su mano y te clava un cuchillo.

Not enough? Think harder. The value of your life is zilch to most people. That's why they sell you food that will kill you. That's why they put poison in the water and don't care if you get cancer. That's why they allow you to rely on our shitty health system and allow insurance companies to deny you coverage based on a ridiculously long list of preexisting conditions, one of which is probably being alive.

Your life is precious to you but disposable to others. That's the rule of the game, the only one that matters. Once you accept it, everything is okay. At one point, my life mattered to my wife and my daughter. That was no longer the case. Now I would kill and pocket a lot of money. Maybe even enough to have a reason to get up in the morning again. That or I would die out there, under the stars that watch so many good people die on their quest to escape a nightmare and come to this country to fight with all they have for a slice of the American Dream.

I was ready.

The night before we left, I'd fallen asleep on the sofa with the TV on. At some ungodly hour, my upstairs neighbor decided to take a shower. The angry song of old pipes woke me up.

I blinked. A woman was on the television screen, shaking

badly and holding a gun up as tears ran down her face. It made me think of Melisa. I missed her smell, the array of products she always had on the bathroom counter, the way she folded laundry impeccably but always left the towels and sheets for me to take care of. I missed the way she'd blow raspberries in Anita's belly and call her mi enanita. I missed the way she'd tuck loose strands of hair behind her ear or do some other small gesture that revealed to me the quiet, shattering beauty of femininity. I missed her cold feet seeking out my heat at night. I missed a collection of moments, of movements, of body parts and gestures, of things she did and said. I had no idea if the sum of that was that I missed her as a whole, missed her as a person, but I craved the parts that made her who she was.

The woman on the screen pulled the trigger. The camera focused on her face, zooming in. She tried to make her eyes scream in horror but only managed to look confused. They cut away to a commercial without showing whomever she'd shot. She was alive and that's why she mattered. The final girl. The dead person was not a thing of the world any longer . . . except for those left behind.

I got up and walked to the kitchen to get a glass of water. After drinking, I placed the glass on the counter and turned to exit the kitchen. With the old table gone, it was dark and empty. I could see a shape move on the threshold. I started reciting un Padre Nuestro.

"Padre nuestro, que estás en el cielo, santificado sea tu nombre; venga a nosotros tu reino; hágase tu voluntad así en la tierra como en el cielo. Danos hoy el pan de cada día——"

Then came a word, a small explosion next to my ear that killed the prayer pouring from my mouth.

"Ore . . ."

The voice came from behind me, so I turned, my heart

jumping from my chest to my throat, punching the side of my neck from the inside.

Then the image of the huge Black man from the bar, the one who looked like my old neighbor, popped into my head, but there was nothing but a wall behind me. *Ore.* The fucking messenger was back. He was the shadow figure in front of me. He was the word whispered behind me. He was the thing trying to get my attention that I was going to ignore.

"She is not strong enough yet, ore, don't take that ona. Only irora awaits."

The voice was coming from everywhere and nowhere at once, but I didn't want to listen. I kept praying, asking La Virgencita to make the apparition go away.

"Dios te salve, María. Llena eres de gracia: El Señor es contigo. Bendita tú eres entre todas las mujeres . . ."

After a few seconds, that's exactly what happened. One second the shadow was there, the next it wasn't.

Shaken, I walked back to the sofa and sat down. I hated God, but I needed him. I resented my mom for passing on her stupid devotion to me. Sometimes, I think faith is like a disease in our genes, something we can't escape despite knowing we should. However, I couldn't help but feel that what had happened, and my response to it, meant there was someone looking out for me.

CHAPTER 10

My alarm went off at 5:00 a.m. I was actually sleeping for a change. I'd started watching a show about people living near the Arctic Circle, and all that whiteness had put me at ease. The people in the show hunted and fished for a living, and whoever had directed the thing was obsessed with the sound of boots crunching in the snow. That sound had lulled me into a dreamless sleep.

I showered, dressed, and wondered if I should pack a small bag. We'd be spending at least a couple of days on the road, so an extra set of clothes sounded like a good idea. In the bedroom, I opened my two drawers and grabbed a few T-shirts and two pairs of jeans and threw them into a black rucksack I kept in the closet for short trips.

The Texas heat made the inside of my car feel like a prepped oven when I sat down, despite the early hour. The AC would take a few minutes to start working, so I lowered all the windows and started driving as fast as possible to keep from melting into the seat. On the radio, a reggaetón beat played, the bass so loud it turned the lyrics of the song into an annoying, irregular buzz.

Brian was sitting on the steps in front of his door smoking

a cigarette when I pulled up to his house. He looked up at me from the steps as I got out of the car, but made no effort to stand. His usual dopey smile that curled his mouth into a perfect example of why meth is an awful drug never appeared. Instead, he looked at me the way you look at a stranger who walks a little too close to you. His eyes were red and a greasy coat of tweaker sweat covered his face and neck.

"Hey, B, you okay?"

He blew out a stream of smoke that quickly disappeared into the morning air.

"I'm . . . I'm good, man. Woke up a few hours ago and wasn't able to go back to sleep."

"What, you worried about this?"

"Nah, it had nothing to do with this."

"Then what was it about?" I asked, sitting next to him on the stairs. He looked up at me with haunted eyes.

"The worm, man. I . . . I worry all the damn time now."

"That's normal. If it makes you feel better, the worrying will never go away."

The front door opened. I stood up. Steph came into view. She was wearing a white robe. One of those they give you at the hospital. It flapped silently even though there wasn't even a light breeze that day. Everything behind her was dark despite how bright the hallway was. Her eyebrows were pushed together, tied into a knot at the center of her forehead. It was the kind of look women give men when they fuck up. She had ugly purple bags under her eyes. Not dark like you get when you're tired or when women go to bed with makeup on. This was the kind of purple you get three or four days after someone punches your lights out. It was old-blood kind of purple.

Brian didn't even acknowledge her; he just kept sucking on his cigarette. Once when I was growing up in Houston, I'd seen someone put out a cigarette on their forearm as a dare. I remembered the kid had howled in pain as it blistered into a crisp halo.

I thought about searing the cigarette on Brian's face like an avenging angel. Then my mind flashed to elbowing Melisa and I suddenly had the urge to put the cigarette out on my own arm.

As I stepped toward Brian, he curled the side of his mouth and blew out more smoke. Thick and impossibly white. It solidified in front of me, quickly taking on a rectangular shape. I felt relaxed.

I glanced back at Stephanie. She took my hand, turned around, and pulled me behind her down the hall. She hadn't said a word to me since I'd gotten there, but I knew there was a story, and that was making me even more nervous. She opened the door to the second bedroom. It was empty except for something that looked like an aquarium and a rocking chair. Steph pulled me by the hand and made me get closer to it. Inside was a creature twitching on top of a white pillow. It looked like a skinned rabbit, but the leg bones jutted out like a bipedal animal. There was a tube in its mouth and a strip of gauze covering the eyes. Steph let go of my hand and walked closer to the aquarium, reached inside, and ripped off the gauze with a sound that reminded me of someone gutting a deer. You know, when they cut right between the white layer under the skin and the muscle and then pull on the skin covering the meat. I saw two pink flaps of skin glued to the gauze. I looked down at the creature in the tank and realized its eyelids had come off with the gauze.

Then Stephanie reached down into the aquarium again and lifted the thing, cradling it to her chest as she made her way to the rocking chair. Steph collapsed with a sigh and her robe opened. Her breasts were engorged, with veins reaching down to her torso, the nipples huge and bloody. She placed the creature to her breast and sank back into the cushion, closing her eyes. "Mario, this is my son."

Her voice sounded like it was coming from a galaxy that no longer existed or something, like you'd imagine the voice of a ghost if it was calling you long-distance from an old phone. I looked at the premature baby or whatever the fuck it was. It was definitely a boy. His penis was almost the size of his legs and his skin was transparent, kinda like a salamander. He had tiny greenish veins crisscrossing his bald head and chest. His small fingers ended in pointy yellow nails that looked dirty. The slim digits twitched as the tiny creature suckled.

The thing detached from Stephanie's breast and opened its mouth slowly. It ran its tongue along a line of sharp little teeth. Then it screamed.

The sound built like an approaching siren. It grew louder and louder until it became impossible to bear and I had to cover my ears. Steph just sat there as if she couldn't hear it. Then the walls started shaking. The aquarium shattered. The sound was pressing against me from all sides. Then everything stopped. The creature shut its mouth.

I blinked back. Stephanie was standing in the doorway, a hand reflexively cradling her huge belly. The smell of smoke heavy in the air. I didn't want to think too much about what another waking dream portended.

Brian put out the cigarette on the porch, stood, and wrapped a hand around Stephanie's waist.

"You boys be careful," Stephanie said, leaning into Brian but looking directly at me before going back inside. When the door closed, I sat back down on the steps.

"Shit, man, I don't know how she keeps her cool," said Brian. "I've been panicking since she showed me her pregnancy test.

It gets worse the closer we get to her due date. I picture them handing me a newborn at the hospital, and all the things I don't know or I'm not sure about come at me like a fucking knife rainstorm. I start wondering if I'm gonna be able to afford all the shit a baby needs. I worry about going to the pediatrician and . . . well, you know, I look the way I do, man. It's not a good look when you're carrying a baby. I . . . I just don't know how I'm gonna do this, man."

I had nothing to say to Brian. It was obvious his brain was working through some issues, but I wasn't the right person to help him tackle them. When Melisa was pregnant, I went through phases like that. One day I'd imagine my baby coming out of the womb with a horrendous, disfiguring purple bulge on her face. Other times I thought about her turning four or five and still refusing to talk because there was something wrong with her brain. When she was born and everything was fine, I breathed for a second and then started worrying about a bunch of other things. In the middle of the night, I would wake up and go check on her because Melisa had made me read a bunch of articles about SIDS and they had messed me up. All those worries hung around like spiders in the corners of my brain. There was no way I could start telling Brian everything would be okay. I was not the man for that job, so I looked at the houses across the street and kept my mouth shut. I hoped my silence and company somehow made him feel better.

"How long you think this is gonna take?" Brian asked.

"I have no idea. Couple days at least. You sure you're down?"

"Fuck yeah, I'm down. I can't bring a baby into this shitty house. I don't want my son to grow up around all this shit. My dad was never around, and I plan to be the opposite of everything that bastard was."

I looked at him and my eyes apparently spoke for me.

"I mean, yeah, I'm a junkie now, but I'm gonna use some of

the money to get straight. I think I can pull off rehab before the worm shows up. Welcome him all clean and shit, you know? I watch dads on TV playing with their sons and ... I don't know, man, I want that. Life ain't perfect and I know it, but there's more to it than this; there's better things out there. This baby? This baby is what I needed to get my head straight. I'm ready for that. I'm done selling and doing and hustling and everything else. If we're gonna have this kid, we're gonna do things right, you feel me?"

Again, what Brian needed was a shrink.

We sat there for a while. From time to time, Brian would say something about his father or about being a good father. I merely nodded. I'd had a taste of what he was talking about. There is a strange, ephemeral sweetness to domesticity. As a man, I wanted to go out, to sleep with beautiful women, and to recapture that stupid sense of indestructability that I remembered feeling in my late teens and early twenties. However, there was something great about making love with Melisa and then not thinking about getting the hell out of there. There is a bond that grows between two people when they go through hell together, and it stays there forever. If you can enjoy it, it keeps you alive. If you lose it, like I did, it slowly kills you. The same goes for fatherhood. Some men run away like cowards. The bottle or the pills or the pussy or the streets call to them more than their kid's smile. That never happened to me. As soon as Anita was born, I knew making her happy and keeping her safe were my only two jobs, and I did them with pleasure. Sure, there were sleepless nights and frustration and cold showers at three in the morning to bring a fever down, but a smile from her, one low, sweet "Love you, Daddy" from her lips, was enough to make it all disappear. Hell, it was enough to make the entire world disappear. Brian didn't need any of that from me. He'd have time to figure it out by himself. At least it seemed like, despite the fear and chemical haze, his heart and head were in the right place.

I ran my hands down my face and realized I had tears in my eyes. I coughed to push the pain back where it belonged.

Finally, an old, black Pathfinder pulled up in front of us. The bass of whatever was playing inside the car was making the windows vibrate. Juanca killed the engine and stepped down.

"Pinches mamones, we haven't even started yet and you two look like you could use a nap."

There was a smile on his face. He seemed like a different man.

"Come on, rayitos de sol, grab whatever you need to grab y vámonos. Vázquez needs us to pick something up in San Antonio."

Brian went into his house, probably more to get a fix before we left than to pack a bag. I got up with a grunt.

"What's in San Antonio?" I asked. I didn't like the idea of another pit stop.

"You believe in God, right?"

The question took me by surprise. I didn't know what to answer and wasn't in the mood to explain my faith to Juanca. I believed in God. I believed God didn't love me. I believed forgetting God was the right thing to do, but I knew there was something there, and denying God would be denying the man whose house my little angel now played in.

"Brian told me you're Rican. That means you probably believe in a bunch of shit. You pray to old gods, Black gods, our Guadalupana . . . you island motherfuckers are all over the place."

"That's a different story. And it's none of your business."

Juanca laughed.

"We're going to drop a milagrito in San Antonio before we head out," Juanca said.

"At La Guadalupana?" I asked.

76

"Yeah, you know her?"

"I do."

When Anita was still alive and doing that clinical trial, before she started staying at the hospital, we'd visit La Virgencita, La Guadalupana, at Tepeyac both on the way to the med center in Houston and back. It made the trip longer, but we thought it was worth it. Melisa would place a milagrito in her chapel while I waited in the car with Anita, who always fell asleep the second we were on the road, her little body curling in on itself in her car seat.

It was all bullshit. I knew that, but it felt good to be at least getting a blessing before doing this thing.

Juanca looked down at the bag in my hand.

"Did you bring something to defend yourself, pistolero?"

"You mean a gun? Nah, I get rid of every gun I use. Plus, I thought the whole reason we were going to Juárez first was to get weapons. Did I get that wrong?" I asked.

"No, tienes razón, sicario. I was just wondering what was in the backpack."

I moved to the side, opened the back door of the SUV, and threw my backpack down on the floor.

"Me lo imaginaba. You can say whatever you want, man, but you have the whole sicario thing down."

He looked at me and smiled. I didn't feel like replying.

We heard Brian coming down the steps. His body language made it clear he had given himself a chemical dose of energy.

"Gonna use your bathroom real quick, B," said Juanca.

Brian came up to me. He had a little gray backpack of his own. I was sure it contained much more than a couple of clean shirts. For the second time, I wondered how he was going to pull this off, how he was going to stay sharp with all that ice in his system.

"You wanna ride up front?" I asked him.

"No," he said. "Maybe when we get closer to El Paso. You can take the front now. Maybe I'll sleep a little. Too nervous right now to do anything else. This whole thing about going to San Antonio first...I don't know, man. I don't like it. I just wanna get it over with."

"Relax, B. We're just making a little pilgrimage to the Virgin of Guadalupe. We'll probably just light a candle, ask her to protect us, and then be back on the road."

Brian didn't look convinced, but it was hard to tell with his bloodshot eyes. Juanca came out of the house and trotted down the steps.

"You guys ready?"

We got in the car and Juanca turned the ignition. The song that had been playing when he pulled up erupted from the speakers for a second before Juanca silenced it with a quick stab of his finger.

We drove down quiet East Austin streets, where dilapidated houses and new developments stood side by side, the difference between them a visual reminder of the effects of gentrification. The second Juanca turned left and then went under I-35 to get on I-35 South, he reached out and stabbed the radio with his index finger again. A heavy beat exploded out of the speakers. Everything rattled. Then the music stopped. Someone cocked a gun and fired a few times. The beat came back and a man started rapping over it in Spanish. He talked about killing his enemies and becoming rich in the streets. I turned to look out the window.

"So where exactly are we going, Juanca?" Brian asked.

"Don Vázquez wants us to go to see El Milagrito. Extra protection for us."

"And what exactly is El Milagrito?"

Juanca looked at Brian as if El Milagrito was common knowledge and he was the last asshole in the world to hear about it.

"If you've never seen El Milagrito, you're in for a treat."

Brian didn't say a word, so I looked back at him. His head was against the window and his mouth was open, looking like a tiny cave full of dark tree stumps covered in brown moss. His arms were wrapped around his thin body the way Anita used to on those long drives. The shithead had fallen asleep before he even got his question answered, but between his emaciated body and unhealthy skin, he looked more like a corpse in the back seat than someone napping.

Juanca was one of those guys who either like to tell stories or feel that the sound of their own voice is infinitely better than uncomfortable silence. As Brian slept, Juanca talked about life on the streets and started telling me a weird story. I stayed quiet. As soon as Juanca was done telling me a story about the guy who allegedly killed six men with his bare hands and vanished into thin air forever, he jumped into a strange tale about some Colombians who had tried to move in on some territory in Texas that belonged to el Cartel de Juárez. Juanca and some friends had been paid generously to round them up and then kill them all by cutting off their arms and legs and letting them bleed to death. They were given instructions to record everything on their phones and then send the recordings to a few high-ranking members of the cartel. Those guys then sent the video to whoever was calling the shots. That's part of why there aren't many Colombians doing business in Texas.

Juanca kept talking. Every story was more or less the same. He'd killed a guy. He and a friend had killed a guy. He had made some money. The cartel had asked him to do something. Guns. Drugs. Money. Death. After a few more stories, we reached the outskirts of San Antonio and traffic got denser and slower. A few minutes later, Juanca pulled off I-35 and drove on the service road for a few miles. Eventually, we stopped at a place called La Cocina de la Abuela. He parked in front of the door and turned off the car.

"You guys want some breakfast? I'm starving. Let's go. I'm buying, pendejos."

The groan that came from the back seat was Brian's agreement. I said nothing, but the acid churning in my empty stomach suddenly became a presence, as if the mere mention of food had somehow summoned it.

Juanca climbed out of the car and shut the door. I looked back to check on Brian. He was scratching his eyes.

"Where are we, man?"

"San Antonio. You heard Juanca. We're gonna get some grub and then go to light a candle. You okay?"

"I'm tired as fuck. I should probably eat something now before..."

He stopped there. I knew what he meant.

"Let's go, then."

We got out of the car and stretched our limbs. Juanca was standing by the door, waiting for us. His face belonged to a man on his way to the movies or the mall, not to someone in the middle of a mission that had the stench of death all over it. His smile made him look young, and it contrasted with the ink on his face and arms. Under the bright Texas sun, the collection of images and words that covered his skin was brutally clear.

We walked into the place. The décor made it clear that time had stopped moving inside the joint sometime in the late seventies. A young, ridiculously skinny girl with a long black ponytail came up to us.

"Buenos días y bienvenidos a La Cocina de la Abuela. ¿Mesa para tres, señores?"

Juanca smiled at her in response. I said yes. The girl told us to follow her.

She pointed to a small table near the back. We pulled chairs out and sat down. Brian and I sat on one side, Juanca across from me on the other side. As soon as our asses hit the chairs, the young woman was there again, setting down napkins and cutlery and asking about drinks. We asked for water. Juanca and I also asked for coffee. The girl smiled and walked away with a bounce in her step that reminded me youth is wasted on the young.

The menus were stuck between the salt and pepper and a bottle of salsa. We all grabbed one and studied it in silence for a minute.

Desayuno completo.

Chilaquiles.

Huevos rancheros.

Huevos divorciados.

Huarache.

Machacado.

The menu was short and simple, but they got breakfast right. When the young lady came back, a tray full of glasses with iced water on her arm, we ordered. Huevos divorciados for everyone. I was sure I was the only one who went with that as a sad joke and not because of the two salsas.

As soon as the waitress walked off, Juanca planted his elbows on the table, brought his hands up to his face like he was about to pray, and leaned forward. The underside of his right forearm featured a tattoo of Satan posing in front of a lowrider, a bottle of booze in one hand and a large gun in the other. The piece was surrounded by crosses, guns, a woman in a bikini with angel wings, and a tattoo of the Virgin holding two guns. On his left arm, a grinning Catrina floated in smoke next to the face of Jesus. He also had some words in cursive I couldn't make out, two hands together as if in prayer, just like his were, and some fire near his wrist. There was a lot more going on, on both arms, but he started talking and I focused on his face.

"I expect both of you to follow orders. I need two soldiers, not two kids too scared to pull the trigger if shit goes bad."

"You know it's all good," said Brian. "I told you we're in, man. We're not gonna let you down."

"Good," said Juanca. "Good. From now on, we ride con Diosito," he said and lifted his left forearm to show us the tattoo of an agonizing Jesus, his face covered in blood, right above a large gray cross with a cloth wrapped around it that read EN LAS MANOS DE DIOS. He finished while pointing to the Satan tattoo I'd already seen on his other arm. "Then, when it's time for things to get ugly, we ride con El Chamuco. You know, because sometimes God is your copilot, but it's the Devil who takes you home."

CHAPTER 11

Half an hour after devouring our breakfast, we pulled up in front of a one-story wooden house in the Eastside Promise Neighborhood.

"Where are we?" I asked.

"*That*"—Juanca stabbed a finger in the direction of the house while parking—"is our church."

The place had been white at some point, but paint had been peeling away from the slats for years. The two windows in the front of the house had sagging, rusty AC units hanging underneath them like plump metallic tumors. It was a house I'd never seen and yet a house I'd seen a million times before in barrios all over Austin, Dallas, Houston, San Juan, Carolina, and San Antonio. It was a house that spoke of poverty and old folks rotting away alone in front of old TV sets and surrounded by photos of family that rarely visits. It was a house that spoke of kids with no fucking chance of going to college and of angry mothers having to walk a couple miles to the bus stop so they can go to their shitty cashier or cleaning jobs. Yeah, it was a busted house that was part of the country's DNA.

"That's a hell of a strange church," I said.

"For where two or three gather in my name, there am I with them," said Juanca, turning off the ignition.

"I thought we were going to La Virgencita de Guadalupe, though." It felt like something was caught in my throat.

"Hey, could you leave the AC running, man?" Brian chimed in from the back seat.

Juanca turned around.

"You're not coming?"

Brian shook his head. "I'm not feeling too hot."

"What's wrong, gabacho? Scared that you'll get too close to God and he won't turn out to be White Jesus?"

There was a smile plastered on Juanca's face, but it was more like a mask than a smile.

"Nah, man, I'm just tired is all."

Juanca stayed silent for a few seconds, his eyes locked on Brian's sweaty face. The plastic smile withered into a straight line.

"Cool, man. This was your one chance to be in the presence of something special, something holy, but have it your way. And no on the AC. I'll roll the windows down a bit, but I'm not leaving my car running in this fucking barrio while you're passed out back there. They'll steal it and be a hundred miles away before your ass wakes up."

Juanca and I stepped out into the blistering heat and closed our doors. The heat coming from the pavement and sidewalk made me think of a dog's breath. Some gnats buzzed, wrapping around my face and arms. I swatted them away. Their sound stayed in my ears.

Back in the car, Brian sank lower into the back seat, wrapped his thin arms around him like a blanket, and closed his eyes. The move reminded me of Anita again. However, she'd been soft and healthy, while Brian looked like he'd been making out with La Huesuda under some bleachers in the middle of the day.

Juanca leaned toward me and spoke, his voice barely above a whisper. "I think he's trying to do this thing clean. Está fatigado, cansado. Parece que dejó el hielo. Luego hablo con él. I think he should stay on the shit if it's gonna keep him sharp, you know what I'm saying? Se ve mal el cabrón . . ."

We walked up to the door and Juanca knocked three times. The floorboards beneath our feet groaned under our combined weight. After a minute, the sound of slow footsteps came from behind the door.

"¿Quién llama?"

It sounded faint and annoyed; the voice of an old woman who's done screaming at life and wants to be left alone.

"Es Juanca, Sonia. Vengo a recoger el encarguito de Don Vázquez."

Locks clacked and a chain rattled. Finally, the door opened with a groan. An old woman with gray hair piled into a messy bun on the top of her head looked at us, her mouth a stern rictus. She was on the shy side of five feet and stood a foot from the threshold, looking at us with deep, shiny black eyes that belonged in a face fifty years younger. Her face was covered in deep lines, tiny dry riverbeds of experience.

"¿Y este quién es?" the woman said, looking at me.

"Sonia, this is Mario. He's gonna be working with me to get Don Vázquez what he needs. Mario, this is Sonia, La Protectora. She takes care of El Milagrito."

Sonia didn't reply. Her eyes drank me in with the interest folks usually show while reading the nutrition facts on bottled water. Sonia wore a blue robe with white flowers on it and chanclas. Both things reminded me of my grandmother. Under the hem of her robe, her thin legs protruded like crooked white branches. Sonia made a sound with her throat, something like a Neanderthal approval, and stepped aside. She brought up a gnarled hand and waved us in.

The interior of the house was dark. There were no lights on and the windows were closed and had heavy blue curtains drawn tight. The space we walked into was made up of what apparently doubled as living room and sleeping quarters for someone. There was a pillow on one corner of the couch and a white sheet bunched up next to it. The couch looked ancient but the television was huge and flat. Between the TV and the sofa, a small rectangular coffee table was covered in lit velones de santos. They bathed the space around the table in a dancing orange light.

In front of us was a small kitchen with modern stainless steel appliances that were as out of place as the eyes on Sonia's weathered face.

Sonia closed the door behind us and clicked four locks into place. Then she turned to us and lifted her knobby hand again, palm up, and used it to signal us down a hallway that opened up next to the kitchen. Juanca didn't move, so I stood there with him. Sonia walked in front of us and we followed.

The hallway was darker than the entrance, but some of the light from the candles crept into the space around us. Sonia walked slowly, her head bent as if the floor was calling to her. The hallway's walls were covered in photos. Weddings from various decades, their ages suggested by various hairstyles and the size of the men's lapels. Graduations. Babies in diapers holding on to sofas and tables. Kids posing for school pictures with gap-toothed smiles. Family reunions. A stern-looking man with haunted eyes in a Navy uniform. Sleeping babies in front of those elaborate backgrounds you only see in mall photography places. It was something I'd seen a million times before: hundreds of crappy photos that were like fingerprints, simultaneously unique and universal.

There were no open windows in the rest of the house. Every room, corner, and hallway dark. The air smelled like soiled bedsheets, disinfectant, and mothballs. The first door on the right was a darkened, windowless bathroom. A large red candle with a white image of Santa Muerte was next to the sink, and the flickering flame made the shadow of Santa Muerte's scythe dance on the wall.

Sonia waved us toward a second door.

The walls in that room had the strangest wallpaper I'd ever seen. Then I realized it wasn't wallpaper; the walls were covered with enough crosses to convince anyone that it was a store of religious paraphernalia and not someone's home. Crosses of all sizes, colors, materials, and textures covered every inch of all four walls from floor to ceiling. Crosses with a loinclothed Jesus, bleeding from under his ribs, his eyes looking up in pain, his mouth open in a silent plead for mercy. A cross with a masked luchador replacing Jesus. Crosses with photos of people nailed, tied, or otherwise glued to them. Crosses with strange dark stains that looked too much like blood to be anything else. Crosses with words on them.

LA PASIÓN DE CRISTO
INRI
JESÚS ES EL REDENTOR
SANTA MUERTE, PROTÉGEME
MISERERE MEI, DEUS
BENDITO ES EL FRUTO DE VIENTRE, JESÚS
CRISTO SALVA
BLESS US, FATHER
ÉL MURIÓ POR NOSOTROS
BENDITA SEA SU SANGRE

That level of devotion isn't healthy.

The room's only window had been covered with black plastic and there was only one ceiling lamp in the room emitting a dim yellowish light. I could make out that there was a bed in the middle of the room. A thin kid lay on top of it, apparently sleeping. Next to the bed was a massive brown man sitting on a chair and a small table covered with various bottles of pills and what looked like some creams. The kid on the bed was lying on his right side, facing us, his eyes closed. A diaper was the only thing covering his body.

My eyes were still adapting to the gloom, but I could see the kid's bones looked like they were trying to escape the thin prison of his skin. The kid had a huge forehead and messy black hair sticking out at odd angles. He opened his eyes while I was looking at him, but he didn't acknowledge us. Drool fell from the side of his mouth and pooled on the already soaked pillow. His arms and legs were bent as if he'd been frozen in the middle of a seizure that had made his body cramp up.

A gnat flew around me, its persistent cry hitting the back of my brain as my eyes continued adjusting to the darkness. I looked at the kid's curled hands, which he kept close to his chest. Both hands were missing fingers, either the whole digit or part of it. I looked down. The same thing had happened with his feet. The upper half of his left ear, which was the only one visible, was also missing. The rugged scar tissue poked from underneath the hair like a pale mountain range emerging from a black ocean. I thought of a hundred movies where war heroes showed off their battle scars and horror movies where someone disrobed to share the aftermath of some horrible torture. This was like that, except it wasn't fucking pretend. There were large scars on his arms, legs, and torso that looked like someone had tried to scoop out chunks of his flesh or carved him up with a scalpel. Some of the scars were white, their ghostly pallor betraying their age, but others were an angry, fresh pink that spoke of recent pain and spilled blood.

I needed to get the hell out of there.

The man sitting near the bed was a mountain of brown flesh so big that I couldn't see the chair he occupied. At least I assumed there was a chair there. All I could see was his rotund form hunkered down in that corner, his legs bent in a way that made it clear he was sitting. His eyes were droopy and he had large patches of darker skin under them. He was wearing jeans, a white ball cap, and a black T-shirt big enough to make a tent for two and have enough material left to cover the floor of the tent with it. The shirt read ERES UN PENDEJO and underneath, in quotes, "YOU ARE MY FRIEND." I'd seen them before at the Mercado in San Antonio. The big man's arms were covered with ink just like Juanca's. I couldn't make out any of it in the darkness. His hands were on his lap, the right one holding an Uzi the way some people hold a book or place their hand on a napping cat. A small brick of gold and diamonds adorned his right pinky and a huge gold cross hung from his neck on a thick gold chain. Whatever these people were doing in this decrepit house with the fucked-up kid, they apparently needed serious security. The fat man looked at us with dead eyes and exhaled like a wounded animal finally giving up the ghost.

"¿Tienes el dinero?" Sonia asked, standing at the foot of the bed.

Juanca shoved his hand into the right front pocket of his jeans and pulled out a bent white envelope. It was thick. He handed it to Sonia. She grabbed it, considered its weight for a second, and threw it to the fat man. It landed on his massive belly and slid down a few inches before stopping. The man switched the Uzi to his left hand, picked up the envelope, and placed it on the table next to him. No one counted the money.

"You know I don't like Don Vázquez. He's the devil. Don't bring his money my way again. I don't like whatever he's doing over there with his people . . . or with that witch I heard he has now. He's bad news and you should know that. People who get near him, they don't last too long. Ese hombre hace tratos con El Chamuco. Tiene un infierno negro donde debería tener el corazón. I'm only doing this because it's you, but it's the last time. Espero que tengas eso muy claro."

"You got it, Sonia. Esta es la última vez que te pido algo para Vázquez. You have my word. Te lo prometo."

Sonia exhaled. It turned into a phlegmy cough that bent her over even more. Her chest rattled like an old car trying to do eighty on the highway with a trunk full of rocks.

When the coughing fit subsided, Sonia cleared her throat and spoke, "Osvaldito, tráeme las cosas."

The mountainous man placed his hands on his knees and pushed himself up into a standing position with a grunt. He was at least a foot taller than me. Juanca and I stepped out of his way as Osvaldito sucked in his prodigious gut to squeeze by us. He pulled his arms in and hunched his shoulders to go through the door.

Sonia moved to the head of the bed, lifted the mattress a bit, and pulled a white plastic bag from underneath it. She shoved her hand into the bag and pulled out a white-and-blue piece of fabric. It reminded me of the pads rich people put on their floors so their beloved pup can take a shit in the house instead of having to go outside.

Sonia did things with a quickness and agility that matched the youth in her eyes instead of the decrepitude of her body. She moved to the bottom of the bed with the pad in her left hand and used her right to bring the kid's feet together and lift them. His legs moved more like sticks than human limbs, and I could see clearly now that the small toe and the one next to it were missing from his left foot. Only the big toe was left on his right foot.

Sonia reached into the bag again and took out some gauze, alcohol wipes, and a white packet with some blue lettering on it, and set it down on the bed. QuikClot. A blood stopper.

The fat man sauntered back in, breathing as if he'd just

run ten miles in the Texas heat. He approached Sonia and handed her a huge gym bag with a hideous flower print that reminded me of a plastic-covered sofa my mom and I had once taken from the side of the road while living in a trailer park in Houston. The damn sofa wouldn't fit through the door, so my mom pushed it against the side of the trailer and left it outside. It rotted quickly. I often threw rocks at the rats that lived in it.

Sonia placed the bag with the flower print on the floor and dug in with both hands this time, shaking out something long and red. When she stood straight, she was holding compact bolt cutters.

"What the fuck is going on here?" The question was out of my mouth before I realized I was speaking. There wasn't a single scenario in my head in which bolt cutters and medical supplies meant anything good, especially not in a tiny dark room in a dilapidated house with a fat bastard holding an Uzi. My eyes darted to Osvaldito. The Uzi no longer looked like a toy in his massive hand.

Juanca put his hand on my shoulder. "Relax, man. We're just getting what Don Vázquez needs. It'll be quick. We'll be outta here in no time."

"But—"

Juanca squeezed my shoulder. Hard. His eyes opened wide, the white in them a silent warning.

"Cálmate," he said.

He split the word into three syllables. *Cál-ma-te.* It said much more than calm down. It was a warning wrapped in the promise of violence.

A voice at the back of my head whispered, *Fuck no, fuck no, fuck no,* but I stood by like an idiot, a silent witness to an unfolding nightmare.

Sonia nodded and Osvaldito got up with another grunt and

approached the bed. He grabbed the kid's legs, hooked his arm around them, and held them against his belly, cradling them like a baby. He did it all without letting go of the Uzi.

Sonia ripped one of the alcohol wipes open and used it to clean the bolt cutters, focusing on the black blades at the end. Then she put the tool down and wiped her hands and then the kid's foot.

The kid's eyes were empty. It made something crack in my chest. He wasn't moving except for the rhythmic expansion of his withered rib cage. I allowed my eyes to roam his collection of scars and missing parts again, trying to understand.

Sonia grabbed the third toe on the kid's left foot, which was really the first because the other two were missing, and pulled it up. She gripped the bolt cutters and used her hand to guide the implement under the kid's foot. She then wiggled the toe into the tool's metallic V-shaped mouth.

"What the—"

Osvaldito looked straight at me. His eyes were dark pools of hatred, his stare a warning: keep your mouth shut. The Uzi was also looking at me. I swallowed my words again.

"Agárrale bien las piernas, Osvaldito, que voy a hacer fuerza," said Sonia.

The fat man leaned on the legs a bit and readjusted his grip as Sonia applied pressure. The bolt cutter's handles approached each other, stopped. The blades closed around the toe, digging into the skin.

Sonia inhaled, repositioned her right arm, and applied her weight to the top handle.

The blades closed a bit more.

Then there was a loud crunch as the blades slid against the kid's skin and clicked together.

The toe thudded as it landed on the pad, followed by a trickle of blood.

Bile rose in the back of my throat.

Sonia pulled the compact bolt cutters away from the kid's foot.

For a second there was a tiny circle of bone and gristle where the toe had been, but blood quickly blossomed and covered all of it, the new wound vomiting blood copiously.

That's when the kid reacted.

His eyes got so big they looked like they were going to pop out of his skull. Veins erupted in his neck and temple. His shriveled arms tensed, twitched, started flapping with the desperate, short moves of a wounded bird staring at a predator's mouth.

Finally, the kid opened his mouth and a sound like a sustained *N* erupted from his throat, but it was far from a scream. He jerked his limbs some more, as if trying to unfreeze himself, to uncoil his body to fight the pain.

I looked into the kid's open mouth. It was devoid of teeth. His tongue was a scarred lump pulsating between his gums. I turned away and stared at the crosses on the walls while Osvaldito held on to the kid's legs, blood dripping on the pad in an arrhythmic song of pain.

Sonia finished wiping the bolt cutters with the same alcohol wipe she'd used to clean her hands and dropped them on top of the gym bag. Then she grabbed another wipe, ripped the packet open, and applied the rectangular piece of disinfecting cloth to the wound. The kid kept making the strained sound. Tears had pooled in his eyes and were rolling down his face, falling on the puddle of drool on the pillow. I thought about the other missing fingers, the scars, the flesh that looked like it'd been scooped out. Sonia and Osvaldito were monsters. Real monsters. I felt cold, the kind of cold you only feel when you're truly afraid.

Sonia held the wipe against the wound for a few seconds and then grabbed the QuikClot and placed it against the wound. She told Osvaldito to hold the sponge in place. "Ojalá que deje de sangrar con esto," said Sonia. "No quiero tener que quemarlo otra vez."

Quemarlo. Burn him. Otra vez. Again. Burn him to cauterize a wound. Burn him after chopping off a piece of his flesh without anesthesia. Burn him.

The kid kept jerking his body and moaning. His movements slowed down a bit, but the sound stayed the same. It was going into my ears and making me feel cold despite the heat.

While Osvaldito held the sponge in place, Sonia ripped a few pieces of medical tape and applied them to the kid's foot to hold the QuikClot in place.

"Listo, corazón," said Sonia, patting the kid's leg. "Ahorita te doy algo para el dolor." Then she looked at us. The horror in my face must have been obvious. "We'll clean it good and put an antibiotic ointment on it in half an hour or so when we're sure it's not bleeding anymore." Then she turned to the wall and prayed.

"Dios te salve, María, llena eres de gracia, El Señor es contigo. Bendita tú eres entre todas las mujeres, y bendito es el fruto de tu vientre, Jesús. Santa María, Madre de Dios, ruega por nosotros, pecadores, ahora y en la hora de nuestra muerte. Amén."

The sound of her words and the strangled noise coming from the kid's throat melded together into an unholy song. Sonia inhaled deeply and started again, louder this time.

"Dios te salve, María, llena eres de gracia, El Señor es contigo. Bendita tú eres entre todas las mujeres, y bendito es el fruto de tu vientre, Jesús. Santa María, Madre de Dios, ruega por nosotros, pecadores, ahora y en la hora de nuestra muerte. Amén."

As Sonia started her prayer again, a new sound joined them. I thought it was insects at first, a thousand tiny legs on wood or a thousand wings clashing against each other. When it got louder, I realized it was neither; the sound came from the crosses.

They were rattling against the walls.

Sonia kept repeating the same prayer, now a monotonous penance that was a mere whisper under the sound of the crosses slapping and scratching against the walls.

"Dios te salve, María, llena eres de gracia, El Señor es contigo. Bendita tú eres entre todas las mujeres, y bendito es el fruto de tu vientre, Jesús. Santa María, Madre de Dios, ruega por nosotros, pecadores, ahora y en la hora de nuestra muerte. Amén."

There are two kinds of religious people in the world. The first are the truly devout. They make God a presence in their life at all times and try their best to live according to the laws of whichever religion they belong to. That was me for a while, a man pushed into the imaginary arms of a protective deity since childhood. Recently, however, I'd been sliding into the second category, the "Oh shit!" religious person. These folks only turn to their deity of choice when things go south. Then they turn to their god with prayers and promises.

The rattling crosses made me do just that: I closed my eyes and asked La Virgencita to get me safely out of that evil house, as far away as possible from Sonia and her fucking bolt cutters. The fact that Sonia was praying to the same Virgencita was not lost on me, but in my head, the two couldn't be the same. What compassionate Virgin looks on and pours blessings on the head of someone who spends her life cutting a helpless kid into pieces?

Sonia finished her prayers and the moment she stopped talking the crosses stopped clattering. The kid's lamentations became longer but lower in volume. Sonia returned to the bed. With the wound bandaged for the moment, she told Osvaldito to put the kid's legs down. I guess he had held them this long to keep the bleeding under control. While he did so, she walked to the small table next to the chair and opened a drawer right below where the fat man had placed the envelope with the money. A moment later, Sonia turned back to us with a white handkerchief in her hands. She lifted it to her forehead and closed her eyes.

"Padre celestial, Dios todopoderoso, Señor absoluto de los cielos, te ruego que este pedazo de tu santito proteja a estos hombres en cualquier cosa en la que tu sagrada protección sea necesaria. En tus manos lo dejo todo, Dios bendito."

When the prayer was over, Sonia went to the wall and started walking around the room, holding the handkerchief close to the crosses, slightly brushing it against them. When she was done, she returned to her spot next to the bed and used the handkerchief to pick up the severed toe. She wrapped the white cloth around it, crossed herself with it, whispered something, kissed the tiny bundle, holding it against her lips for a few seconds, and handed it to Juanca.

"I don't know what Vázquez has in mind, mijo, but this is some serious power you're taking to him. Whatever it is, if you're involved, take care of yourself. Cuídate mucho. You know there are never any guarantees even when dealing con El Milagrito, ¿entendido?"

Juanca moved the hand with the toe in it up and down a few times.

"Con esto no vamos a tener ningún contratiempo, Sonia. Mil gracias por tu ayuda. Te prometo que tendré cuidado."

Sonia looked at him and narrowed her eyes. Then they shifted to me. Something in them was glinting impossibly bright in that dark room. Behind her, the kid was making a different noise, something between a moan and labored breathing.

"You're welcome. Now get the fuck out of my house and let me take care of mi niño hermoso. We need to pray extra hard today. We can't have another infection. Osvaldito, show them out."

Osvaldito left the side of the bed and we repeated our little ballet to let the big man lead the way. As we left the room, I looked at El Milagrito, the little miracle, one last time. Now I could read every missing piece, every upraised scar. How long had he been suffering at the hands of these people? How much money had they made chopping him into pieces?

The thing about humanity is that it's always worse than the worst you can imagine. We are base, vile creatures rutting in the muck we've created, our eyes looking up at a poisoned sky we've populated with ghosts to help us sleep at night, to allow us to come up with reasons to do the things we do. I immediately knew my silent inaction in that small, dark room would haunt me.

None of us are as brave as we think we are.

Osvaldito opened the front door and stepped aside. Juanca stopped next to him, asked, "You're new. What happened to the other guy?"

The big man said nothing.

"¿Qué pedo, güey? Cat got your tongue?"

Osvaldito opened his mouth. Sitting inside it was a short, pinkish lump near his throat. His tongue had been cut out.

"No mames . . . " said Juanca with a chuckle. "Estos huevones están todos locos," he added, walking out. Osvaldito looked at me. His eyes made me think of a taxidermy mount. He moved his arm to the front of his body and used the short barrel of the Uzi to scratch his balls. I followed Juanca.

I don't know what I was expecting when we walked outside, but I wasn't expecting the world to be there, brightly lit and looking the same. I wasn't expecting the car to be in the same spot and for everything else to look like things that belong in a world where kids get mutilated in small, dark rooms.

In the car, Brian was still wrapped in himself. He looked even paler than usual and had droplets of sweat on his forehead and nose. He was completely unaware of the bloody nightmare that had gone on inside that house. I almost envied him.

Juanca and I got back in the car. He'd put the severed toe away at some point and plucked his keys out from wherever he'd been holding them. He stuck the key in the ignition and the car roared to life, waking Brian up.

"You . . . you guys done?" he asked.

"Yeah, we done," said Juanca. "You should've been there, man. Mario kept his cool. I thought he was gonna freak out, but this motherfucker acted like a professional. Haha!"

Juanca's laugh was out of place, an alien sound in an impossible situation. It made me uncomfortable.

Juanca turned on the radio and clicked a few buttons. He smiled. "I have the perfect song, compas," he said. A guitar twanged. Juanca turned up the volume. A second later, the sound of an accordion exploded from the car's speakers. Then, a voice, somewhat unclear and hidden by the strident accordion and the state of Juanca's speakers. The man started singing about someone crossing the desert to make it to Tijuana. The thing about crossing made me pay attention. The song told a story of two narcos carrying weed in a coffin. Juanca sang along with the radio, a smile on his face.

"You know this is about real cabrones, right?" he asked.

"What are you talking about?" asked Brian from the back seat.

"Rosaura Santana and Juan Escalante. They were real. Los cabrones got tired of being poor and tried to bring a hundred kilos de yerba across the border in a fucking hearse, man. They tried to go through Tijuana thinking it'd be easier. You know, because of traffic and all. When the pinches oficiales made them open the coffin, Rosaura and Juan pulled out the metal and started firing. Fourteen people died that day, including them. I listen to this corrido Chalino wrote for them every time I go on a run. It reminds me that shit can go wrong . . . and that bullets should fly if that happens."

Brian made a sound from the back seat, something between a gasp and a moan. I said nothing. Juanca stepped on the gas. We were pushed back onto our seats. The sensation embodied what I'd been feeling: I was a victim of inertia.

CHAPTER 12

No one said much as we drove out of San Antonio on I-35 and then joined I-10. I looked out the window and read the names of the places we passed and the names of the fast-food joints we left behind. It was a way to try to push my thoughts away from what I'd just witnessed. It almost worked as a coping mechanism. Almost.

El Milagrito's toe was in the car with us. Not being able to see it didn't help much. My mind kept going back to the bolt cutters closing down, the crunch of bone under steel.

I wanted to ask questions but knew I wasn't ready for the answers, so I kept staring out the window, listening to the sound of the wheels rolling over the road, trying to push myself away from what I'd experienced by burrowing deeper into myself.

Soon I was thinking about Anita. Her smell. Her smile. The softness of her skin. She had been loved. She was still loved. We'd failed, but Melisa and I had tried to protect her from everything. Her childhood had been a nice one, full of giggles and toys. The poor kid in that bed, El Milagrito, had a life that was the exact opposite. All he'd known was suffering and pain. I'd failed to save Anita and now I'd failed to help El Milagrito.

I had to think about something else, so my mind turned to Melisa. Her smell. Her smile. The softness of her skin. The same three things I'd been remembering about Anita, yet three things that were worlds apart. The love we can show two people can be immense and yet incredibly different. I loved a woman a certain way and loved the girl she'd given me an entirely different way. Both loves had now morphed into cancers of the soul that went with me everywhere.

Maybe the money would mean a second chance. What people with money don't understand is that most poor people's problems *can* be solved with money. There are problems that won't go away no matter how many bills you throw at them, but for people like me, for folks whose nightmares have names like hunger and eviction, money is a wonderful thing that can make tribulations disappear in a matter of seconds.

Melisa and I met during a time when both of us were a step away from being hungry every day. We were fighting to finish our degrees, fearing the day we had to start paying our student loans. The hustle to leave that space made our love stronger, but that same hustle, that continuous state of stress where making ends meet was the thing that mattered most, had also hurt our marriage even before Anita's illness. Poverty pounds away at your will and happiness until you're left with nothing, just stumps. Having money, real money, came tied to the possibility of getting Melisa back. Her smell. Her smile. The softness of her skin.

"Yo, man, I'm hungry," said Brian. "Any chance we can stop to get some grub soon?"

"Not yet, gabacho," said Juanca. "I wanna get out of the San Antonio traffic. You can get a snack when we stop for gas in a couple miles."

Brian had interrupted my thoughts. It was a good thing. I didn't want my two ghosts haunting me all the way to El Paso, so I sat up straighter and read every sign we drove by and listened to the music. Juanca had a mix of Chalino Sánchez corridos playing. I'd never been a fan, but I knew enough about Chalino's music to know that it wasn't my cup of tea. His voice wasn't that great and the strident sounds of narcocorridos never appealed to me. My musical taste came from my mother. Salsa, mostly. However, I paid attention to Chalino because I wanted my mind on something other than Melisa and Anita. A song ended and another one began. The sound quality was mediocre at best, but I got the gist of the first lines and they hit me hard. They were about how nothing is the same after you're dead and then there was something—which I couldn't get entirely—about a cold grave waiting for me. By the time the song mentioned the end being near, I had tuned out. The words I'd been able to make out reminded me of Héctor Lavoe, my mom's favorite salsa singer, who used to say that everything has an end and nothing lasts forever because there's no such thing as eternity.

Fuck.

I had picked the worst time to start paying attention. The words—the ones I'd just heard and the ones that lived in my memory—cut through me and found the fear I'd been trying to ignore. I tuned out and looked out the window again, at the cars and the drivers' faces. I wasn't in the mood for omens.

Eventually traffic thinned out a bit. The Chalino mix ended and Juanca played with his phone to change the music. Reggaetón came blasting from the speakers. Behind us, Brian was nodding off again.

My mind drifted away from the bolt cutters.

Long drives have their own language, their own rhythm, their own reality. They always trigger memories for me. I drove a lot while at the insurance place. They sent me to money-laundering trainings in Orlando, Biloxi, Santa Fe, Baton Rouge, Oxford,

Dallas, and other cities. I always drove. It kept me out of the office longer and was more fun. I loved being home but also loved being behind the wheel, music blasting.

I loved stopping in places where the history of this country, past, present, and future, converges in a succession of abandoned houses full of secrets, dilapidated cemeteries, boarded-up stores, shitty diners, and gritty gas stations in the middle of nowhere.

I lived for glimpses of towns past their expiration date where cracks, ghosts, and memories outnumber residents. That's the real America. The soul of this country lives in the gap-toothed smiles of gas station cashiers, the matted fur of small-town dogs, the buzzing of neon signs in small dives where a layer of dust covers every surface, the shattered spirit of drive-through employees in nowhere towns, the weird smells and carpet stains in cheap motels where the windows look out at empty parking lots.

I enjoyed stopping at gas stations that had machines in the bathroom that offer off-brand cologne for a quarter and wondering what chemicals galloped in the veins of the wild-eyed truckers passing through. I loved nameless diners and Waffle Houses with dirty cutlery where the server had a gold tooth that outshined most people's souls.

When we drive, things that were tangled in our heads begin to detangle or to be revealed as inconsequential.

Those drives had the power to make me feel like a lost whisper in Austin's traffic or a bird gliding effortlessly over the Atchafalaya Basin; a fake tourist on the Biloxi coast or a lost memory in the endless straight roads of the Florida Panhandle.

Those drives also triggered memories of Puerto Rico.

My grandmother telling me to let dogs lick my wounds when I fell down because their saliva was holy.

My mother cooking and dancing in the kitchen to the sound of Héctor Lavoe singing *"Tu amor es un periódico de ayer..."*

My grandmother's crooked fingers caressing my face.

The ocean lapping at my feet.

A bright, almost liquid green covering every mountain.

A sky so impossibly bright and blue that it made me blink to make sure I wasn't dreaming.

My grandmother's soothing voice telling me that my blood was sacred, the result of the mix of Taíno, African, and Spanish blood.

Red explosions at the end of the long, thin branches of flamboyán trees.

My mother, in one of those stretches of time in which she managed to stay sober, smiling at me as I wolfed down arroz con habichuelas in my grandmother's minuscule kitchen. My mother's smile was always a rare sight, except for those years we spent on the island. Her smile was a supernova. Her smile was my world, my balm, my dream.

The quebrada behind my grandmother's house, its murmuring water always cool.

The sound of the coquí putting me to sleep with its repetitive soundtrack.

We were only on the island for about eight years, but it was the happiest time of my life. Long drives will forever bring that back no matter where I am, and I will be grateful for it no matter what I'm doing.

Brian coughed from the back seat. The sound shattered something inside me.

I needed to listen to someone talk. The voice of Chalino coming from the speakers again, talking about guns and death, wasn't helping.

"What's up with El Milagrito, Juanca?" I asked, looking

out the window at a sign that notified me we were passing Roosevelt.

"What about him?" asked Juanca.

"You have a fucking toe in your pocket right now, man. Cut the shit," I said.

Juanca laughed. "¡No hay pedo, hombre! Relax," he said. "El Milagrito is sacred, man. Diosito touched that kid. He made him special."

"Special how? He didn't look special to me. He can't even take care of himself."

Juanca looked at me like I'd dropped the words *your, mother,* and *whore* in the same sentence.

"Nah, huevón, not special like that," he said. "His mom died. She was Sonia's daughter. She was a junkie. Sonia says she was in and out of the house at all hours. She didn't even tell nobody she was pregnant until she couldn't hide it any longer. Cuando ya no podía esconder la panzota she told her mom. She didn't know who the father was. Alguno de los cabrones que se aprovechaban de ella, seguro. Pinches hijos de puta. The thing is she never stopped using. She died from an overdose right there in the house. Sonia found her in the bathroom with a needle still in her arm. Sonia started crying on top of her and felt the chamaco kick. The little man was still alive. Sonia panicked. She had to get the kid out, so she ran to the kitchen, got a knife, sliced her dead daughter open, and pulled the kid out. She's been taking care of him ever since."

"That's a hell of a story, man, but it doesn't explain how things got to . . . you know, what they are now," I said, frustration creeping into my voice.

"Ah, ya entiendo," said Juanca. "El Milagrito was always special. He was already like that when Sonia pulled him out. You know . . . encogido. They kept saying el chamaco was gonna die, that Sonia had pulled him from the hands of La Huesuda at the last possible moment and that she was gonna come back for him. You know how people are. They said you can't keep a kid alive that was supposed to die, that it goes against God's wishes. Sonia didn't care. She took him to a brujo who worked on him a bit. Le hizo una limpia. Lo protegió contra el mal de ojo. He said the kid had walked with La Huesuda and lived. Dijo que era un niño sagrado. A few months after he was born una vieja del barrio vino a casa de Sonia. She said she'd had a dream about the kid, that he was a child of God that could protect people and that was why God had kept him alive. She said he was a milagrito, a little miracle, you know what I'm saying? The lady asked Sonia for a nail clipping. Sonia thought that shit was weird, but she had a soft spot for the old lady, you know? She gave the vieja a nail clipping and that was that. About a month later the lady came to visit Sonia. Her son was working a corner and pissed off the wrong cabrones. They came to get him. Llenaron la casa de plomo. Her husband and three sons died. She was sitting in front of the TV and nothing happened to her. Bullets flew around her and not one of them touched her. She told Sonia that was proof that the kid was holy. Word spread fast. No hay correo más rápido que el chisme en el barrio. Folks from el barrio started coming around regularly, asking for a nail clipping or some hair or whatever. Sonia realized it was the perfect way to pay the medical bills and buy formula and diapers and all that shit. The opportunity to make some money just landed in her lap, you know what I'm saying? She started charging. People paid without a word. Shit, they were happy to pay. I guess the church has made people think that salvation and protection are always available for a price. Anyway, brilliant hustle, right?"

A racket. A lie. A kid who'd been turned by drugs into something useless somehow turned into a religious treasure. However, we didn't have hair or nail clippings. We had a fucking toe. And Juanca had apparently paid a lot of money for it. Sonia was brilliant, but also a monster. That made us something even worse. I remembered the scars on the kid's body, the missing parts. Those weren't small things. They meant a lot of people and a lot of money. Everyone who had taken a part of him, and those who allowed it to happen, deserved a fate worse than his.

I thought about Anita, her tiny body subjected to all those tests and injections, and whatever was left of my heart shattered all over again.

"We don't have things like that. Nails or hair. We have a whole fucking toe. When did it escalate?"

"Oh, you know how it is, man, word gets around," Juanca said. "The ladies had sons, and those sons didn't want to end up dead. Eventually even sicarios started coming. They'd heard there was a niño milagroso in that barrio, that if you had something of his then bullets wouldn't find you. Sicarios are always filling the space between them and all the bullets out there with prayers and sacrifices and shit, so they were willing to pay big money, but they wanted more than nails and hair.

"Sonia had been struggling. Bills. Food. Rent. Gas. The sicario offered a lot of money for a tooth. The kid had five or six in his mouth by then. The sicario wanted to wear the fucking tooth around his neck, encased in gold. Sonia said no, so the sicario pulled a gun on her. She took the money. El cabrón got the tooth himself using the butt of his gun. Takes a special kind of motherfucker to hit a kid in the face with the butt of a gun, right? Anyway, that's when she got security. The whole milagrito thing kept growing. The sicario, some guy named Martín, became known as El Fantasma. He was taking out cabrones left and right and no one could touch him. You were always hearing rumors about how he'd get shot and bullets would go through him like he wasn't there. It all started to add up. More people came. Now she has her own church and everything. People come by on Sunday to pray to El Milagrito. Powerful people here and in Mexico buy from her. In this fucking business, protection is very important, you know what I'm saying?"

I imagined the amount of pain the kid had gone through and the pain that was still ahead. A pain he couldn't fight or even speak out against.

I imagined Anita being subjected to something like that. I pictured assholes like Juanca and me coming into her room, paying for a chunk of flesh, and leaving with a piece of her body. It was inhuman. I'd done none of the cutting, but I stood by while Sonia chopped off his toe. I was complicit. I was as guilty as her and Osvaldito, who held the kid's feet up like she'd been doing nothing more than clipping his toenails. Living with that, if I lived, was going to be hard. I decided to report it as soon as we got back.

"Are we gonna stop anytime soon?" asked Brian from the back seat, his voice an amphibian croak.

"Pretty soon," said Juanca. "Next stop: Ozona. We need gas. And I need coffee."

CHAPTER 13

We stopped at a gas station on the side of the interstate. Brian climbed out of the car and held on to the door.

"I'm hungry," he said. He looked like he was having a hard time standing up straight. Droplets of sweat covered his forehead and his hair looked like chunks of old carpet glued onto a sick dog.

"You okay, man?" I asked. Ahead of us, the doors to the minimarket swooshed open and Juanca walked in.

Brian walked forward two steps and leaned in a bit, like a man bent over by the weight of a secret.

"It's...it's the ice, man. I'm trying to go clean. I wanna come back clean from this. For the baby. Once I come back with the money, Steph and I can just pack our shit and hit the road to somewhere better, but I know that's only gonna work if I'm clean. She told me right before we left. I did a bit this morning, much less than usual, though. That's it. Been craving ever since." He dug around in his pockets and brought out a bent cigarette and a lighter. He lit up, sucking on his cigarette like it had an answer to something inside.

I didn't know what to say. Addiction is a monster. I'd seen that monster haunt my mother, steal her youth and smile away,

109

collapse her veins until she had to shoot up in her feet and then her neck.

"It's all good, man," Brian said. The right side of his mouth curled into a reasonable facsimile of a smile as he blew out smoke. "I'll be okay. I just need to eat something."

He killed his cigarette under his shoe, and we walked into the minimarket together. I grabbed the types of snacks that would have made Melisa frown and a coffee in a can that promised to taste like a vanilla latte.

We paid and headed back to the car. Juanca was filling up and checking his phone. Brian got in and curled back up on the back seat. I walked a bit toward a green area next to the last pump. An old man walked a dog. He coughed violently and scratched his balls. It reminded me of Osvaldito.

Somewhere far away, something large bellowed. The sound, long and deep, made my blood run cold. I looked at where it had come from, but there was just thick black smog, like smokestacks at a factory. I couldn't see anything beyond the end of the street.

The smoke thinned and I noticed something dangling from a lamppost, gently rocking back and forth, moved by a breeze I couldn't feel. I took a few steps and stopped. The mournful sound came again, too loud and organic to be a machine, too big and rumbling to be good news. I kept walking and looking at the thing hanging from the lamppost. It looked like a big doll.

Fear squeezed the back of my neck with its icy fingers.

I broke into a run, the kind in which you move forward at a desperately slow pace. Right before I reached the lamppost, my knees cracked against the pavement. I looked up at the doll.

Its hair was blowing in the breeze.

Its white dress had tiny blue dots on it.

I knew they were whales.

The figure hanging from the lamppost was Anita.

"Hey, Mario, I'm done."

The image vanished. My girl gone, the doll gone. The old man was back. The dog had its head down to the grass, its ears falling forward onto its face. I needed to get my shit together, and fast.

When we hit the road again, Juanca didn't turn on the music. Instead, the sound of the AC, the wheels rolling on the pavement, and our breathing filled the car with a strangely hypnotic hum. Soon Brian fell asleep and his breathing changed. There's something about tension that makes you tired, and his body was dealing with a combination of stress, fear, and the demons of his meth addiction. I felt sorry for the bastard.

Juanca drove with his right hand on top of the steering wheel. His eyes were on the road, but I could tell they were somewhere else as well, somewhere far away.

I leaned my head on the window and watched the world go by. I could feel Anita and Melisa like two planets orbiting my thoughts, not in the center yet but too big to be ignored, their weight so great they affected my inner tides with their gravity.

Anita was gone and no amount of running would put any distance between her ghost and me. Melisa was a different story. She was somewhere out there, maybe thinking about me, maybe finding the things she deserved in the arms of someone else. The thought hurt, but I felt like it was the right one, exactly the thought I deserved.

We'd been dating for about three months when I met her parents. They were stern, hardworking people. Church people. They wanted someone who was somebody for their daughter. A doctor or a lawyer. I was neither. I was broke. I went to their house for dinner wearing an old pair of shoes. It was the only pair of shoes I had. Melisa's parents had a gigantic pit bull that kept making eyes at me while I chewed on a milanesa Melisa's mom had overcooked and picked my way around a salad made with lettuce that had started going brown. I responded politely to all their questions. Where was I from? What did my parents do? Did I go to church? Did I have any kids from a previous relationship? I thought it'd gone well. The next day I met Melisa for coffee. She told me her father had asked her if I needed money for new shoes the moment I left.

I felt a hollowness in my chest so absolute it made it hard to breathe. At the corner of my right eye, I started to work up a tear, but I wiped it away with my knuckles and blinked a few times. I closed my eyes to collect myself and saw Anita's smile, heard Melisa say "I love you." I tried to find a calm place inside me, but everything good that wasn't a memory was gone. I was empty. Pain, anger, and memories were all I found. I'd never felt so alone. A sob escaped my throat. I dressed it up as a cough. The car remained silent, but the sick scream inside me was drowning the world.

CHAPTER 14

The connective tissue between large Texas cities is brown nothingness. Buildings sprout from the flat ground in the distance when you get close enough to a city, their tallest structures reaching up to the sky like the blocky dark fingers of some buried giant from an alien race, but before you get there, the only thing around you is dirt, a few weathered shrubs, and an endless blue sky that sometimes makes you think it's close enough to shatter if you throw a big rock at it.

It's like whichever deity was in charge of the terrain just gave up and copied and pasted the same mile over and over again all the way along I-10.

The funny thing is that it always reminds me of Puerto Rico, a place of green mountains where all you have to do is jump to catch a glimpse of the ocean. Our moods are often shaped by the landscape we're in. In the car, with Brian once again sleeping in the back seat and Juanca humming along to another mix of narcocorridos, the blankness of the land around me made me wonder if we would ever get anywhere or if we had somehow entered a nightmare dimension in which all that was left of the world was straight stretches of blistering pavement and an occasional small house with its roof caved in, another ghost structure screaming silently at the empty blue sky.

I was thinking about pulling out my phone, opening the Facebook app, and checking Melisa's profile. Maybe she'd posted something recently that would answer at least one of my questions, all of which I more or less had already answered in my head: What was she doing? I knew whatever she was doing, she was doing it without me . . . and I deserved that.

Facebook was a coward move. I knew I had to call her. I had to try. The way I'd thrown her off me, knocked her down, came back to me all the time. That look in her eyes. She didn't deserve that. I had to live with being the person who did that, but I could also change into someone who would never do that again, someone who would be more patient, more loving. Promising her that would be a good start. The only reason I didn't call was that the possibility of a yes was far more appealing, and less painful, than a final no. She could hang up or tell me to fuck off forever. I knew that, and the thought haunted me. Wanting her back and deserving her were two different things. I knew locking myself in the bathroom and letting her vanish had been almost as bad as pushing her, so her not wanting me would be normal. That's why I hadn't called her. Maybe now was the time to do it.

Before I could make up my mind, Juanca moved his hand and flicked on the signal light. A few seconds later he swerved right and eased the car onto a dirt road that curved a bit and died in a dry patch of dirt in front of a shack that promised barbecue.

After so many hours on the road, stepping out of the car was an uncurling process, a resetting of bones and waking up of muscles that made me tense up and yawn. We waited a bit, feeling the circulation go back to full tilt in our lower bodies, our legs aching to walk, to obey the natural swing that's kept bipedal beasts moving forward for millennia despite the black abyss yawning before us.

There were three other cars on the patch of dirt that worked as the parking lot. None of them looked new or clean. None of them were memorable. The middle of nowhere is incredibly consistent in terms of being unremarkable. The sun was high in the sky, threatening to burn us to death if we stood around long enough, so we moved to the door.

The inside of the place was gloomy and my eyes had to adjust to it after being subjected to the blinding light of the parking lot. The temperature was much cooler than outside and the overpowering smell of barbecue hung heavy in the air, a mouthwatering mix of sweetness, charred meat, and spices.

As with most middle-of-nowhere joints across the South, this one looked like someone had hit the stop button on a remote control in 1972 and nothing had changed since then. A handful of tables took up the inside of the place. Only two of them were occupied. The décor was a mix of a failed attempt at hill-country chic circa 1970 and neon signs for the kinds of beers folks buy at gas station convenience stores on their way to places they wish they could escape.

A heavyset white woman with a messy blond bun on top of her head and a soiled white shirt appeared from the left, grabbed some plastic menus off a small table, and told us to sit wherever we wanted.

Juanca moved to a small table with four chairs near a window. We followed, pulled chairs out, and sat while our server, still silent, threw the menus on the table and cleared her throat like an angry teacher waiting for silence.

"I'll be right back with your waters," she said.

The table had a checkered red-and-white tablecloth under a sheet of plastic so old it had cigarette-burn marks on it from when you could still smoke in restaurants. A big bottle of barbecue sauce sat in the middle of the table, a red dried crust decorating its top and falling down its sides like candle wax.

Brian picked up a menu and started studying it like it contained the answers to all of his life's questions. I picked one up and looked at it while Juanca played with his phone.

"Pulled pork sandwich with a side of potato salad," said Brian. "I gotta hit the john."

He placed the menu back on the table and stood up quickly. He looked better than he'd looked since we left San Antonio. The proximity of food and the smell of cooking meat had apparently injected some life into him.

Brian walked toward the back of the place and entered a small hallway that, according to the sign on the wall, led to the bathroom. As soon as he vanished from sight, Juanca glanced up from his phone.

"Escúchame," he said, his voice lower than usual. "Keep an eye on him. El cabrón quiere lana. He has a baby coming, knows he's gonna need the money. He might be thinking there'll be more to split if you're not around, you know what I mean? Nunca sabes lo que va a hacer un hombre por dinero. Ese gabacho está desesperado. La distancia entre un desesperado y un muerto puede ser un puñado de dólares."

The distance between a desperate man and a dead man can be a fistful of dollars.

That line bounced around my skull like an injured bird. Around it, the rest of my brain decoded Juanca's words with a small delay, as if the message was intended for a sharper mind. I had ignored the guy from the bar—my dead neighbor. I had ignored the dreams. I had ignored the dark promises in Chalino's song. This was different.

"Not sure I know what you mean, Juanca. Are you saying—"

"No te hagas el pendejo. I'm saying there's more cake when the party's only two people. You don't have to trust me, güey.

I don't expect you to. No me conoces de nada. Pero ese . . . "
Juanca lowered his voice and leaned forward a bit more. "Ese
cabrón está comiendo hielo en el baño ahorita. Si yo fuera tú,
tampoco confiaría mucho en él. Quiere un chingo de lana para
empezar una vida nueva. Sin ti en el medio, los dos cobramos
más. Maybe you think he's your friend, man, but you have to
understand you're just a body coming between him and a lot
of money."

"So are you. If he's thinking of taking me out, what makes
you think he won't do the same with you?"

"That's exactly why I'm keeping an eye on him."

"Why not take him out then? You could still get someone else."

"Two reasons. First, it's too late to get anyone else. We're
gonna be outnumbered out there as it is. Second, some of those
men we're gonna kill out there? Those are the last men I will
ever kill. My quota is full. I know that now. If I kill anyone
else—before, during, or after—La Huesuda is gonna come for
me. It's just how things work. I need someone to carry some of
those ghosts on their shoulders, you know what I mean?"

"Okay," I said, drawing out the vowels, unsure if Juanca was
playing some fucked-up mind game.

"Look, you ever go to see that unblinking visionario in
Austin?" Juanca asked.

I'd never heard about an unblinking visionario, so I shook
my head.

"Man, that guy was good. White guy. His name was Isaac.
Everyone went to him before a job. It was like he could talk to
God and the devil on the same day and tell you what was gonna
go down."

"So why the hell didn't we pay him a visit instead of that shit
in San Antonio?" I asked.

"Well, that man didn't give people what El Milagrito was
able to give us. Plus, he disappeared. Se lo tragó la tierra. After

GABINO IGLESIAS

so many years of dealing with the underworld, he must have pissed off the wrong guy. I heard six cabrones showed up at his business, all with big guns. They walked in there and lit up the fucking place. Someone heard it go down and called the pigs. The shooting stopped before the pigs showed up. They stayed outside and hollered, you know how they do, but no one came out. Finally, they went in and found six dead cabrones, all with their eyes gouged out and stuffed in their mouths. The whole fucking place was full of holes, but there was no blood on the floor except for the blood that had come out of the skulls of the sicarios. They never found the visionario."

"What's your point?"

"My point is I went to see him a week or so before he vanished. He said my sack was full. I had to stop killing for money. If not, I was dead."

"And this time it's dif—"

"Don't worry about this time. This time is okay. These cabrones deserve it. After that, I'm done. Any extra bodies on top of the men we're aiming for would push the scale to the wrong side."

The idea that he would kill only those who he thought deserved it was easy to understand. The men I'd killed deserved to die, but they didn't haunt my dreams. Melisa, on the other hand, was an anvil of guilt crushing my chest.

Silence is sometimes the only option, so I nodded at Juanca. Growing up in PR surrounded by people of all religions, I knew that death was serious business and no one wanted to collect more angry ghosts than they could handle. I had no reason to believe Juanca and start thinking Brian was going to put a bullet in me the second we secured the money so his cut would be bigger. Then again, I had no reason not to. The same went for Juanca. Brian and I knew each other. We'd spent time together here and there. He'd gone to watch me put my daughter in the ground. None of that meant we were friends. I was now spending time with Juanca, and that didn't mean we were friends. None of it meant either of them thought my life was worth more than my cut. Maybe Brian was washing his face and thinking about staying strong for his baby. Maybe he was eating ice and thinking about killing me to build a future with my chunk of the money. Life is what happens between the things we think we know and the things we learn about too late to do anything about it.

"Fucking wetback."

The words came from somewhere behind me. They cut through the noise in my head and stopped my thoughts cold. Something about racial slurs has that effect on me. It's like someone yelling *fuck* at church. The idea that someone can think being a certain color or from a certain place makes you better or worse than anyone else is a level of stupidity I can't wrap my head around. Sadly, it's also the kind of profound stupidity I'd been surrounded by since coming back from Puerto Rico.

I turned to the patrons sitting at the other tables. An old man with a blue plaid shirt and a John Deere hat sat alone at a table across from us, bent over his plate, shoveling wet coleslaw into his mouth with a fork. His long, curved nose and posture made me think of an old bird. At the other occupied table sat three men. They were all big boys. Two were fat and looked like brothers with matching brown beards and receding hairlines. The third one was skinny and had a weak chin that somehow turned into a neck. They were all dressed like they worked construction: long-sleeved shirts, big boots covered in dirt, paint, and cement, and jeans that resembled camo from all the different kinds of stains.

"Relax," said Juanca.

I looked at him and suddenly his face tattoos were impossible to ignore. So were the images covering his arms.

When you spend time with someone who stands out, the prolonged contact with their uniqueness makes it fade, and their differences, so obvious when you first meet them, blend into your reality. It happens to everyone. It had happened to me. Juanca looked like a poster boy for gang violence, but I had stopped noticing the way his accent, his constant switch to Spanglish, and the collection of tattoos that covered his arms, neck, and parts of his face made him a walking cliché pulled from some shitty action movie where the good guy is a muscular white man with a heart of gold.

"They're not even talking to you, man," said Juanca. "You're not a wetback, right? Brian said you're Boricua—a spic." His smile was genuine; he was just a brown man recognizing a different brown man's unique otherness.

"Yeah, but those m—"

"Ignore them. It's all good. Esos güeyes se pueden ir a chingar a su madre. Nosotros tenemos cosas más importantes que atender. Tenemos—"

"Do you know what you're having?"

I looked up at our server. She was holding three plastic glasses with ice water in one hand and was using the other to set down utensils wrapped in paper napkins. I blanked and looked back at the menu.

"Pulled pork sandwich with a side of potato salad for the gentleman in the bathroom and . . . I'm gonna have the two-meat plate, smoked turkey and lean brisket, collard greens and potato salad for my sides," said Juanca.

"And you?" Her voice wasn't pleasant.

"I'll have what he's having," I said, nodding toward Juanca. She didn't write any of it down before walking away.

Brian returned to the table. His hair was wet. He looked like he'd finally woken up from a fitful sleep. A shiver ran down my spine. He was no longer Brian; he was a man who maybe wanted me dead.

"Guess y'all ordered?"

"We did," said Juanca.

"Cool. So, from here we go to . . . your house?" Brian asked.

"Yeah," said Juanca. "My mom's actually. I'll tell you all about it after we eat. I don't really want to talk about our plans here, you know what I'm saying?"

Brian nodded slowly. Juanca went back to his phone. I pulled mine out and looked at the screen. There was a new text from the hospital reminding me I owed them money. I deleted it and clicked on the Facebook app. I scrolled through photos, articles, and a variety of updates that simultaneously said nothing and everything you want to know about people. The scrolling helped the world slide back and evaporate. My first stop was Melisa's profile. I went to her profile pics folder and scrolled. Seven or eight profile pics ago, she'd used a photo of her standing in front of a koi pond with Anita in her arms. Anita was eight months old or so, all rosy cheeks and bright eyes. We had gone on a little museum trip to Houston and ended up at the Japanese Garden. I remembered that photo well because Melisa's smile was brighter than the sun. But when we were packing up the car to leave, two men in a sports car pulled up next to her in the parking lot. One pointed and yelled, "Look, a Mexican with a baby girl. That's what I call a cleaning kit with a replacement!" They took off. I looked around for a rock to throw. I wanted to murder them. I would have happily stabbed the man who insulted my angels and watched him bleed to death on the sidewalk with a smile on my face. I did my best to convince Melisa it was an isolated incident, but she'd been through things like that before and knew she would go through them again. I held her and told her some people were trash, but the good ones far outnumbered the bad ones. When someone we love is hurting, lying is the easiest thing in the world. So is violence.

I couldn't handle more memories, so I went back to scrolling through the lives of other people as a tiny voice at the back of my head reminded me I was a coward for not calling Melisa and apologizing. Someone had baked bread. A nice woman got a new puppy. Trump had said something incredibly stupid again. Some people tried to be witty and others wasted words talking about things they hated. The three of us sitting at that table were on our way to do something that could change our lives, something that would bring us as close to death as you can get without falling into her arms. And no one knew or cared. The world would go on. Death is a small interruption that only affects those tied to whomever La Huesuda takes home with her.

A figure next to me made me snap out of it. It was our server again, this time holding plates. I shoved my phone back in my pocket and decided not to chastise myself for looking at more of Melisa's profile pics. Whoever said it's better to have loved and lost than never to have loved at all was probably an asshole who never lost anything they actually loved.

We ate in silence, pushing food into our hungry mouths with the intensity of men who don't want to accept that they could be eating their last meal. For me, being on the move and feeling like I was doing something that could put me in a better situation was enough.

Money.

Melisa.

A new start.

Fuck death.

After a few minutes, the three idiots at the other table started cracking jokes. One of the bearded guys was doing most of the talking. They raised their voices a couple notches to make sure we heard them.

THE DEVIL TAKES YOU HOME

"Hey, Frank, what do you call a bunch of Mexicans running down a hill?"

"I don't know, man. What do you call 'em?"

"A mudslide."

Their laughter was lifeless, the sound of hyenas before a meal.

"That's a good one, bro."

"I have one for you, Chris: there are four Mexicans sitting in a car. Who's driving?"

"I don't know, Frank, who's driving?"

"Immigration."

They laughed again. Their words landed on our table like dead moths. Brian focused on his food like his life depended on it. Like a lot of white people, his whiteness turned into confusion wrapped in shame in the face of blatant racism.

I felt sick looking at Brian. The weakness of so many others was embodied in the man sitting next to me. I looked away and my eyes landed on Juanca. Something in his face had changed, a subtle hardening of his features that spoke of tectonic plates of hatred shifting under his skin. His eyebrows hung lower, the words HOOD and MADE now closer together. HOODMADE. His mouth moved mechanically. Open. Close. Chew. Swallow. Repeat. On his arms, skulls floated in smoke. The Virgin looked sad, the way all mothers who have lost a child look. A money sign surrounded by tiny stars spoke of his love of money. The face of a beautiful woman made up to look like death looked at me. Satan occupied a large space. The black-and-gray image of Santa Muerte appeared bigger than before. Closer to his right elbow was the head of a man with a mustache I didn't recognize. The tattoos had nothing to do with each other, but something told me they were the story of his life. When my eyes drifted up toward his face, he was looking at me.

"Hay una pistola en la guantera."

His voice was low and hard. His eyes communicated one thing

clearly: he was letting me know there was a gun in the glove box, but this wasn't a conversation and I didn't have to ask anything or reply. He was thinking the situation would escalate.

We were almost done eating when the three men stood up, threw some money on the table, and walked to the door. I wasn't facing them, but they were big enough that their actions were clear in my peripheral vision. When they reached the door, one of the bearded guys turned back and strode across the restaurant. His heavy boots clomped on the old wooden floor. He came up to our table.

He stood next to us for a second, looking at Brian as if trying to figure out what a white boy was doing breaking bread with two brown men with accents. We all looked at him, caught between confusion and a mix of anger and anxiety.

"I hope y'all are on your way to El Paso," he said. There hadn't been much humor in his voice to begin with, but the minuscule amount that had been there was gone. He brought his hand up and ran it down his beard, closing his fingers into a fist under his chin and pulling on his facial hair. None of us said anything, so he went on. "When you get to El Paso, I want you to keep fucking driving, you hear me? I want you to keep fucking driving, cross back to your shithole country, and never bring your ass to this side of the border ever again. Is that clear?"

The second bearded man showed up.

"Let's get a move on, Chris."

"Not yet, man," Chris said. "I'm telling these fucking wet-backs to go back to their country. This is America. You can't come into a restaurant and start talking Spanish. You do that in your own country, *comprende?*" He lifted his hand again and pointed at Juanca. "And this son of a bitch right here? He's probably in that M-13 gang or whatever the fuck it's called, his face tattooed like that. Motherfucker belongs in prison. He's gotta be a rapist or a drug dealer. Just look at his face!"

Juanca nodded but stayed quiet. He wasn't looking for a fight. He was trying to enjoy his meal and get to bigger things in El Paso. He placed a hand on top of the table and for a second I thought he was flashing his gun, but he just counted off three twenties, folded them, and carefully placed them under the box containing the sugar and sweeteners.

"We were just leaving," said Juanca.

The man who had sauntered over to get Chris put his hand on Chris's chest and gently tapped him. "Let's go, brother."

The men took a few steps back with their eyes on us before they finally turned to go. As they reached the door, Chris mumbled something about breaking his foot off in our asses if he ever saw us again. They pushed the door open. An explosion of light filled the restaurant for a few seconds and then disappeared. As soon as the door closed behind them, Juanca stood up and almost jogged to the door. I followed him, convinced his speed was because of anger, because he couldn't wait to get the hell out of there.

I was wrong.

As we approached the door, Juanca reached back with his right hand, lifted his shirt, and pulled a gun from his waistband while pushing the door open with his left.

Heavyset men aren't usually quick on their feet, much less with a belly full of meat and ice tea. The men were about ten feet from the door, standing around fiddling with cell phones and cigarettes. That Chris guy had been the last to exit and was closer to the door. The skinny one was on his left and the third guy was a few feet in front of them, digging in both pockets at once.

Juanca lifted his hand without breaking stride and brought the butt of the gun down on the side of Chris's face. The man yelped and staggered sideways. He brought his hands to his face. Juanca walked up to him, grabbed his shirt, and placed the gun under his chin. The big man gasped and went up on his tiptoes.

The other two yelled something but moved back as soon as they saw the gun.

"What the fuck do you think you're doing?"

Chris's right cheek had a deep red gash under his eye. It was opening slowly, blood pooling in the wound before starting to trickle down his face and disappearing into his beard.

"Shut the fuck up and kneel, bitch," said Juanca.

"I'm not fu—"

Juanca's right leg flew up. He nailed the fat man in the groin with his knee. Chris groaned and bent over. Juanca let go of his shirt, grabbed the back of his head, and pulled him down toward the knee that was flying up again. The big man's face crashed against Juanca's knee with a thud and a crunch. Chris crumpled sideways. His body hit the ground so hard it bounced a bit. Air escaped his lungs with a loud *oomph*.

"I said kneel, motherfucker!" Juanca's snarl had transformed his face into a demon mask. His ink made him look otherworldly. "Kneel right this fucking second or I swear on my amá I'm gonna shoot you in the face and then kick your head until your brains run from your nose, *comprende?*"

With a groan, the big man put one hand on the ground while keeping the other one on his face, then got on his knees. Juanca turned around and aimed his piece at the other two. Both were stunned, silent. Their eyes jumped from the gun to Juanca and then to me. I didn't like how close to me they were. I didn't like that I wasn't holding a gun.

"Come on, say something," Juanca prodded. Neither of them spoke. "No jokes now? You two just gonna stand there like a couple of assholes?"

Juanca switched the gun to his left hand, put his right hand in his pocket, pulled the car keys out, and threw them at me.

"Saca la pistola que te dije y mantén a esos dos pinches cabrones tranquilitos. Si se mueven, mátalos."

That sounded great. The dark thing inside me was back. I wanted to hurt these racist fucks, to scare them. I wanted to let the anger flow. Seeing the racist pig on his knees and bleeding from the gash on his face made me happy in a new way. The pain of others had never brought me joy, but now, watching—and making—assholes suffer made my broken soul smile.

I moved to get the gun from the glove box as Brian strolled out of the restaurant, looked at the scene, and decided to join me on my trip to the car. He came so close his arm bumped into me as we walked.

"What the hell is Juanca doing, man? What if the cops show up? We need to get the hell outta here right now."

I looked at him. I had nothing to say. I pressed the fob twice, yanked the passenger door, and opened the glove box. A few papers, a yellow candy wrapper, and an envelope were sitting on top of a black, blocky gun. I grabbed it. Things fell to the floor. I slammed the door and ran back to where Juanca was waiting for us. Some strange instinct kicked in and I raised the gun at the men standing there with their eyes threatening to pop out of their skulls.

"Now listen to me, motherfucker. My man here is gonna make sure those two cabrones stay right where they are, you know what I'm saying? And you and I . . . you and I are gonna have a little talk."

"What are y—"

Chris tried to ask something, but Juanca's right leg flew up once again. His right boot connected with his face. The big man went back and curled sideways.

"Get your racist ass up, pendejo. We're not done."

Juanca leaned over the man, grabbed him by the shirt with his left hand, and pulled him up.

"Get your hands off your fucking face!"

Chris was starting to understand his predicament. Instead of asking something or resisting, he removed his hands. Tears were rolling down his face, mixing at the edge of his beard with the blood and snot that were coming from his nose. Juanca saw the blood and smiled. Then he lifted his gun and brought it down on the big man's nose. There was a wet crunch followed by a gargled yelp. Chris went down again, curling into himself once more and making a wet sound somewhere between a snore and a moan. His repeated trips to the dusty floor had turned him almost entirely brown.

The two assholes I was aiming at kept looking at me and then at their bleeding friend. I lifted the gun a bit more. They took a step back. Guns say a lot without words.

Juanca walked around to Chris's side and kicked the hands that were covering his face. Then he kicked again.

"Call me a wetback now, cabrón. Tell me to go back to my shithole country. Come on, act tough, just like your little president. Say something, hijo de puta!"

Juanca repositioned himself and kicked again. This time, the tip of his boot connected with Chris's temple. It sounded like a melon falling off a table. The big man's arms went limp. He stopped moving for a couple of seconds. Juanca reached down and slapped him. Then he grabbed Chris's hair and slammed the gun against his face again.

"Fuck! Wake up, cabrón!"

Chris moaned again. His eyelids fluttered open.

"Smile for me," Juanca said.

The skinny guy said something I couldn't make out, so I thrust the gun toward him again. That shut him up. I wanted him to rush me. Shooting him would feel great. I wanted to let all the darkness out in the shape of a bullet. The violence around me was energizing me, making me feel good. I pulled the trigger.

The skinny guy's left eye exploded, a hole appearing right where his eyeball used to be. Instead of falling, he stood there, swaying a little. A white tendril moved in the dark, ragged hole. Whatever was in there was uncoiling, getting ready to come out.

I saw Chris on the floor, a tentacled thing squelching its way out of his skull . . .

"Come on, smile for me, pinche cabrón," Juanca said again.

I blinked back. The two men were still in front of me, fear painting their faces white but otherwise unharmed. Something buzzed by my ear.

Still on the floor, Chris looked up and pulled his mouth into a strange shape. He was sobbing. The mix of blood, snot, tears, and dirt had turned his face into a Halloween mask. Juanca slammed the gun down on his face again so hard the handful of hair he was holding stayed in his fist while Chris's head flew back and smashed against the dirt. Half a second later he coughed while turning sideways, gagged, and spat out two teeth covered in blood.

"*That's* what I wanted to see," Juanca said. "Now listen to me and listen to me good, cabrón, because if we cross paths again, I'm going to put so many bullets in your body your family won't be able to identify you. And if those two assholes over there are with you, I'll do the same to them when I'm done with you, you got that?"

Chris nodded between moans and a strange sound I realized was crying. Ugly crying. I almost smiled.

"Now that fucking ugly mouth of yours is missing two teeth. You will never have them again, so you will remember me every time you smile, hijo de la chingada. Remember I did this to you. Look at my face! Remember I fucked your mouth up because you said racist shit. Remember I fucked you up because the only language my amá speaks bothers you." Juanca stepped closer to Chris and placed the gun on his forehead.

GABINO IGLESIAS

"From now on, whenever you see a brown person, you will keep your fucking ugly mouth shut. Whenever you interact with someone named Martínez, García, Vázquez, Rodríguez, Torres, Hernández, Morales, Pérez, González, Sánchez... whatever, you will be nice to them. The pinche frontera crossed us first, pendejo, so don't ever send anyone back anywhere. This land isn't yours; this place is ours. Esta no es tu pinche casa. Next time your little white supremacist bullshit pops into your head, remember your family came here on a fucking boat not that long ago. And then remember a brown man had you crying like a little bitch in a parking lot after knocking out two teeth from your stupid mouth, you got that?"

I was sure Chris was going to growl and then launch himself at Juanca. No man would put up with such pain and humiliation and not retaliate, right? I was wrong. He did none of that. Instead, he sobbed harder and nodded, mucus, blood, and saliva streaming steadily and forming a brownish glop of nastiness that covered his lower face, beard, and chest.

"Good boy," said Juanca. "Now pick up your teeth, wipe them on your shirt, and give them to me." Something in Chris's face changed and his head went a few inches to the left like that of a curious dog. He wasn't sure he'd heard right.

"Yes, you heard me, cabrón; pick up your teeth, get your dirty mocos off them with your shirt, and hand them to me. I'm keeping your teeth."

Chris didn't move.

"Now!" Juanca said, shoving Chris's head back with the barrel of the gun.

Chris winced. Then he put a hand on the ground, reached down, and picked up his teeth. He cleaned them with the bottom of his shirt with shaking fingers and placed them in Juanca's outstretched hand. As soon as he had them, Juanca shoved them in his pocket and turned around.

130

"Here's what's gonna happen now, cabrones. My friends and me are gonna get in our car and get the fuck outta here. If you come after us, we'll kill you. If you call the cops, we'll kill the cops and then come looking for you and kill you. I'm taking a pic of every damn license plate out here. You make me come back here with more friends, this shithole will be on the news for the first and last time ever, you hear me?"

When men look at the business end of a gun, masculinity becomes a sandcastle built too close to the tide. The two idiots I was still aiming at nodded like schoolboys. Their silence was almost eloquent. They were scared. They had given up. They weren't used to that level of violence. On the floor, Chris mumbled something wet that sounded like an apology and then coughed up some blood.

"Vámonos," said Juanca.

I didn't know what to do. Pointing death at someone and then walking away struck me as dangerous. These guys could jump in their car and come after us. Knocking two teeth out of someone's mouth was more than doing someone wrong. It wasn't an insult; it was a bloody attack that would never be forgotten.

Juanca lowered his gun and started walking to the car. Brian left my side and followed, muttering "Fuck" over and over again and looking around, probably worried about the cops showing up. I walked to the car but kept the gun at the ready.

In the car, Juanca turned on the ignition. Music came blasting out of the speakers and my heart skipped a beat.

Juanca stepped on the gas as he backed the car up while turning, sending a cloud of dry dust into the air. He was obscuring our license plate.

We left the barbecue joint behind and climbed back onto the road. Juanca drove with one hand and kept his gun in the other. I held on to mine.

We drove fast. The silence was a thick tension in the car, but our breathing eventually slowed down. The ghost of what we'd done was there with us. A few miles later, Juanca spoke, his eyes bouncing between the road ahead and the rearview mirror.

"They're not following us."

His words calmed me somehow. My lungs expanded. I relaxed my grip on the gun.

"What the fuck was that all about?"

Brian's question hung in the air, ignored and unanswered.

I opened the glove box and placed the gun inside. When I closed it, I remembered the stuff that had fallen out and bent to pick it up.

There was a thick envelope under my left foot. By the size and feel of it, it contained photos. As I brought it up, the flap opened and some of the images slid out. I picked them up and looked at the one on the top.

Dirt.

Blood.

Knives.

Sky.

A drooping cloud.

A mustache.

It took me a second to understand what I was looking at because I was holding the image vertically. The blue of the sky and the ragged cloud that looked like someone had tried to rip out a chunk of blue wallpaper gave it away. My brain told my fingers to adjust the photo before the rest of it had communicated what the image contained.

I turned the photo sideways as alarms went off in my head.

The photo showed a man on the ground. A dead man with a thin mustache with Dalí corners. His feet were missing. Bloody stumps caked with dirt poked out from the bottom of his filthy jeans. He was lying on his left side, his bloated hands tied together with duct tape in front of his body, making him look like a sleeping child. Knives of all shapes and sizes covered the side of his body like trees covering a hill.

Three blades sprouted from the side of his head like the metallic antennas of some strange insect. His eyes were bloodshot, his features deformed by inflammation and bruises. One of the knives had perforated his cheek and held his mouth open, probably lodged in his teeth. The image was gruesome, exuding the kind of unrestrained violence that reaches inside you and pokes your lizard brain with a stick.

"Put that shit back."

I jumped in my seat. I looked at the envelope in my hand. The photos had slid against each other, their identical corners revealing the fact that the rest of the pictures were the same. It looked like a glitched computer screen, the same rectangular nightmare echoing in my hand. There must have been at least ten copies.

"What . . . what the hell is this, man?" My voice was a bird caught in a cat's throat.

"Pon las pinches fotos donde estaban."

Anger tainted Juanca's voice, made it something dark and heavy with the promise of more violence. I put the photo I was holding back in the envelope and added the few others that had fallen out. I tapped the envelope to make sure all that death was contained, neatly arranged. Then I closed it and placed it back in the glove box. The rest of the stuff was still on the floor, so I bent down and picked everything up.

"Those are none of y'all's fucking business."

I said nothing. There had to be a story behind the human pincushion in the photos, but I wasn't sure I wanted to know it. Maybe Juanca was planning on getting Brian and me out of the way once the money was secured, and he had fed me that story at the barbecue joint to ensure I was keeping my eyes on Brian instead of him.

If Brian had seen or heard anything, he didn't show it. He was looking out the window rubbing his hands up and down his forearms. He looked more like a child than someone who'd put a bullet in someone's head.

"You okay there, B?"

The silence was long enough to make me uncomfortable.

"No, I'm not fucking okay, Mario. I'm far from okay. What the fuck was that all about? Those guys could be getting some guns and coming after us any minute now. You don't know these kind of dudes. I do. I grew up with them. They get angry, they get guns, and they all have guns. Big guns."

"Ah, now the white boy has something to say!" said Juanca. "Shut the fuck up, Brian. If you're scared, I can drop you off right here. Good luck getting a ride back to Austin."

"Why would—"

"Just shut the fuck up! Pinche gabacho cagado. You didn't say a single word when that asshole was at our table. You're talking shit about how you know dudes like them, but you were too happy to keep your mouth shut and not get in the middle of things back then, no? Pinche sacatón. Even when we were outside you didn't do shit. You could have punched one of them if you wanted, but you didn't. Instead, you worried about yourself. Culero."

"I don't—"

"Nah, hanging with brown dudes is okay when you're making money, but as soon as someone calls us names the cat gets your tongue."

"Juanca, I don't—"

This tongue lashing Juanca was giving Brian was what he deserved.

"Cállate. Just save it, man. I don't need to hear la mierda que vayas a decir. This ain't my first day as a brown man in this country. Your puto presidente calls me a rapist and your uncle votes for him because he wants a tax break or some shit. People from my barrio are thrown in cages after some asshole pulls their kid away from them and you keep your mouth shut because the folks on TV have told you we're all coming in and taking your jobs, right? I haven't seen a single white person step up to another white person in my whole life on this side of the border. I don't give a fuck about what you have to say right now. When you see some racist shit going down, you speak the fuck up. Your words will mean something... and so will your silence."

Brian said nothing. Years of living surrounded by racism and silence were bubbling to the surface. The new me enjoyed violence, especially righteous violence, and everything that had gone down since we exited the barbecue joint felt right. That included Juanca tearing Brian a new one. He was echoing my thoughts: a silent ally isn't a thing.

We drove saying nothing for a while. My mind drifted and eventually was sucked into the black hole at the center of my being: Anita. I missed her. I missed her energy and the sound of her laughter. I missed the sweaty side of her head resting on my arm as she slept. I missed her tiny hands splashing in the bathtub, her stubby fingers wrapped around a small plastic boat she'd fallen in love with at Savers.

I allowed the pain to come. It pushed the anger away and replaced everything inside me with cold, black emptiness. Then it brought the anger back, a big thing that kicked at the universe and demanded retribution.

The worst part about remembering Anita had always been Anita herself, a shining light at the center of a stupid world. Lately, that had changed. Now she shared that spot with her mother. I would see Melisa burying her nose in our daughter's neck, hysterical laughter exploding from her mouth like aural fireworks. I would see them on the bed, Melisa on her phone while some cartoon on the TV enraptured Anita's eyes. I would see them together and the fragments of my heart would start vibrating with purpose. Inevitably, the thought always came: Anita was gone, but Melisa was still here. Her absence didn't have to be final. Her company, her arms, her warmth—they were all possibilities.

I looked over at Juanca. He'd put the gun away and slouched in his seat. As if sensing my gaze, he straightened his posture and turned. Juanca didn't say anything for a second. I could see his tongue running along the top of his teeth even though his mouth was closed.

"You cool, man?" He was smiling now but his eyes looked blank.

I thought about the envelope and those photos of that man with the Dalí mustache, the bloody stumps in the place of feet, just like that poor kid's toes.

"Fine, just thinking," I said.

I couldn't exactly tell him what I was thinking about, but he seemed satisfied and set his eyes on the road.

Being in the presence of monsters is okay as long as you don't think too much about what they're capable of. The scarier thing is when you realize what you're capable of yourself.

CHAPTER 15

People are usually surprised when they hit the border and realize there's no change in the landscape, no giant dividing line in the sky. The land doesn't care about the stupid lines humans insist on drawing on them, and the southern border is no different. There's nothing there that makes it obvious you're approaching an interstitial space between cultures, nothing that says people of one color live on one side and people of a different color inhabit the opposite side. Instead, there's a short, dark fence next to the road and more empty space, a few bushes, and more dry earth.

My idea of another country has always been tied to airplanes, to traveling for hours and eventually arriving at a different place where the tongues of residents take the shape of another language and the atmosphere and air let you know you're someplace else, someplace different. Sometimes it's also a place where violence is closer to life. A body full of knives found in New York City would make national news, but down here, it was just another victim of cartel violence. Differences like that matter. Houston isn't Puerto Rico. The American South isn't the Caribbean. Tacos, brisket, corn bread, and tamales aren't mofongo, arroz con gandules, and tostones. The

Atlantic caressing and gently pulling at your feet is nothing like the Pedernales pushing against your legs, the round river stones pressing against your soles, their slippery, green-tinged surfaces sliding underneath you. The differences are huge. You can see your arrival as a change of place, a shift in geography and culture.

That doesn't happen in El Paso. Things on both sides of the river look more or less the same and the streets of both sides are packed with brown and white faces, the same food, the same air, and the same Spanish and English words thrown back and forth. That what happens in la frontera is so problematic is shocking. Viewed from the border itself, the conflict is not between two countries; it's an argument between neighbors that occupy the same land but don't share the same privileges, and it's an argument often policed by people who don't even live anywhere near that neighborhood.

Juanca eventually smacked his signal light down and veered right. The car slid onto an exit, and small houses, lampposts, short fences, and trees replaced the wide-open space. Lights were on behind some windows. The darkness that had draped itself above us while we were on the road, and the fear of the unknown that had crept into the corners of my brain, had kept me on edge. I also didn't feel comfortable sleeping next to Juanca now. Yeah, the violence outside the restaurant and seeing those horrible photos had messed up my nerves. The residential area, the domesticity and normalcy of it all, put me at ease.

Eventually Juanca slowed down and parked in front of a squat house made of red bricks with a large dead tree in front of it. A champagne Lumina sat in the driveway, its wheels pooling at the bottom. Juanca killed the engine.

"This is my place," he said. "Well, my amá's place."

We repeated the unfolding and stretching process. Juanca's

car ticked arrhythmically in the quiet street, our deep breaths and the distant sound of cars a few streets over the only sounds on the street despite the relatively early hour.

At the end of the street there was a tall brown wall. Mexico was on the other side of that.

"I gotta pee, man," said Brian with a grunt. Hearing his voice made me realize whatever he'd asked in the car and this short declaration were the only words he'd uttered since Juanca had dressed him down. It'd been nothing more than a short scolding brought on by his silent complicity, but it had changed the atmosphere between us.

"Me too," said Juanca. "Let's get inside. And stay behind me. Mi amá está un poco sorda. She might shoot one of you if she doesn't see me first."

The thought of an old lady with hearing problems sitting inside that house with a gun made me uncomfortable.

I watched Juanca digging into his pocket. I assumed he was looking for keys, but watching him reminded me there were also other things in there as well.

Instead of a key chain, Juanca pulled out a single key as he approached the brown, peeling door of the house. He slid it into the lock, turned it, and pushed the door open. The hinges let out a high-pitched scream. Juanca stood at the threshold and yelled.

"Amá!"

Brian and I came up behind him. Beyond the door was a small living room with a brown-and-yellow sofa covered in plastic and a small table with a huge television on the opposite wall. The TV was thick and, just like a tree, that meant it was old. The sofa's plastic cover was also a throwback. I wondered if Juanca ever sat in front of it as a kid with a pile of rocks next to him, waiting anxiously for some rodent to crawl from under the cushions.

In the weak light coming from the lamp in the middle of the hallway stood a short, thin woman in a robe. Her hair was a frayed halo of gray around her head. It reminded me of the way people look in cartoons when they get electrocuted. The blue robe she wore had huge red flowers on it. Amapolas. It covered her body but hung from her bony shoulders like she'd stolen it from a much bigger woman. She was wearing white chanclas. Something bulky hung from her right hand.

"¿Eres tú, Juanito?" her voice was a delicate vase teetering at the edge of a table.

"Sí, Amá, soy yo."

Juanca stepped into the house and turned to invite us in with a nod.

I walked into the house and the first thing I noticed was a strange smell. It made me think of rain but also of digging with Melisa in the yard. She had a thing for roses. There were yellow roses next to our door. In the back, she took whatever available space she could find to add some plants. She had a green thumb. Thinking of her all sweaty and dirty was oddly comforting.

"Ay, mijito, ven aquí y saluda a tu madre."

Juanca obliged. His body seemed too big for the hallway and the tiny woman disappeared when he embraced her. I heard whispers and kisses. The woman pushed Juanca away and grabbed his face with both hands. The thing she'd been holding in her right hand was a gun. A big gun. Her frail fingers were still stretched around it when she brought her hands up to Juanca's face. A sad smile pulled the corners of her mouth upward while dragging her eyebrows down a bit. Happiness, love, and something akin to pain fought for control of her features. No one won that battle.

"¿Cómo has estado, Amá? ¿Cómo te sientes?" Juanca asked.

"Cansada, hijito. Me pesan los huesos." With that, she looked our way. "¿Quiénes son estos señores, Juanito?"

"Son unos amigos de Austin. Los traje para que me ayudaran con algo."

"¿Vas a cruzar? Me dijiste que ya no—"

"Tranquila, Amá. Es solo una vez más. Te lo prometo. Después de eso te saco de aquí."

The woman nodded and lowered her head. I got the sense that this was a conversation they'd had many times before. After a second, she lifted her head and came toward us.

"Buenas noches, señores," she said as she walked toward us. "Yo soy Margarita, la madre de Juan Carlos. Tomen asiento, por favor. Están ustedes en su casa," she said, lifting a frail hand toward the yellow sofa. Brian and I mumbled a "buenas noches" and a "gracias" and sat down.

"Mira, Juanito, si van a ir, por lo menos déjame que les de una bendición para que la Virgencita los acompañe."

She wanted to give us a blessing. Cold fingers squeezed the back of my neck when she said it.

Juanca sighed. He came to the sofa and sat between Brian and me.

"My mom wants to pray for us. She wants the Virgin to protect us."

This was not the time to argue. If praying for us made her happy, good for her.

Juanca's mother approached us, closed her eyes, lifted her hands, and started praying.

"Querida Virgencita, esta noche te pido que protejas a estos tres hijos tuyos con tu manto sagrado. Acuérdate, oh piadosísima Virgencita de Guadalupe, de que nunca se ha oído decir que nadie que te haya implorado protección, nadie que haya implorado tu santísimo socorro o que haya buscado tu intercesión ha sido abandonado por ti, Madrecita Santa. Animada por esta confianza que todos tenemos en ti, Virgencita, esta noche regreso a ti, Santa Madre, y me acerco humildemente a ti como una hija para que tú, Madre del Verbo Encarnado, no menosprecies mis peticiones, y en tu infinita misericordia me escuches lo que te pido y protejas a estos hombres de todo aquello que les quiera hacer mal. Amén."

We sat there, looking at her as she prayed. When she finished, I inhaled. Without being fully aware of it, I'd been expecting something to happen. The shaking crosses covering El Milagrito's walls were still in my head, occupying that special space where we only keep things that should be nightmares but that happened to us while we were awake.

Brian asked about the bathroom and Juanca silently pointed a finger toward a dark hallway. Brian stood up slowly, like his balance was off, and plodded in the direction Juanca had signaled.

Margarita stood over Juanca and asked him to be careful again. He nodded. "Sabes que no puedo perderte, mijo," she said. "Si te pierdo a ti ya no me queda nada en esta vida."

You know I can't lose you, son. If I lose you, I won't have anything left in this life.

Both of them were hurting. They'd obviously lost someone very close to them. His father or one of Juanca's siblings, maybe. There's a place beyond pain where feelings are so strong there are no words to describe them. I entered that space. Around my neck, the weak, soft ghost of Anita's arms pressed itself against me. Something flared inside me and I wished for the end of the world.

Juanca's mother inhaled a shaky breath. Her rheumy eyes filled with tears. None fell. Her face was full of wrinkles, but it had a soft look to it. Juanca hugged her again, whispering something in her ear. I don't know what promises he was making, but they worked. His mother pulled away, patted her son's arms, and said she was going to bed. She was tired and had stayed up past her bedtime to wait for her son. Juanca told her to get some rest. She grabbed him by the face again and pulled him down. She kissed the right side of his face, his forehead, and then the left side of his face. I looked away. This was a moment between them.

"Que pase buenas noches, señor," she said. Her face was calm. Then it struck me; she reminded me of my abuela.

"Usted también, señora. Espero que descanse."

I meant it. Her eyes were still wet. Under them were pockets of purplish flesh. She came closer. The lines of her face came into focus. She was old beyond her years. I saw the way pain had damaged her, stolen large chunks of her vitality. The pain in those lines was like the pain inside me. I felt like hugging her, like giving in and asking her to hold me. She wasn't my mother, but sometimes the touch of any mother will do.

"¿Usted cómo se llama?"

The question caught me by surprise.

"Mario, señora. A sus órdenes."

"¿Le puedo pedir un favor, Mario?"

A few seconds before, I'd been ready to ask her to hold me, to blend her pain with mine. Now she wanted to ask me a favor.

"Lo que usted quiera."

"Tenga mucho cuidado y cuide a mi Juanito, por favor. Usted tiene cara de bueno, por eso nomás se lo pido. Yo a veces veo cosas, especialmente cuando rezo mucho. Ayer en la mañana vi algo, algo feo. Don Vázquez es un hombre malo. La oscuridad que tiene adentro anda buscando víctima, y no quiero que sea mi Juanito. Yo le dije que no fuera."

I told him not to go.

"Le repito, Mario, solo le pido porque no tengo a nadie. Y como ya le dije, usted tiene cara de bueno. Yo sé de estas cosas. Usted tiene ángeles que lo cuidan."

Cara de bueno. There it was again. She'd said it twice. The

face of a good man. She stood there and asked me to take good care of her son because some evil thing was looking for a victim and she didn't want it to be her boy. An image came to mind: Juanca shoving that Chris guy's teeth into his pocket, thick blood drops dripping from the butt of his gun. The teeth were still there . . . probably next to El Milagrito's toe.

I couldn't even protect my own daughter, señora.

I nodded.

Juanca's mother thanked me and walked away, her chanclas barely leaving the ground, their rhythmic scraping on the floor somehow too loud in the quiet house.

A few seconds after she disappeared into the hallway, we heard her door close.

"She takes a lot of pills," said Juanca. "She'll be out in a minute. She's hard of hearing, so we won't wake her up no matter what we do."

A toilet flushed and the bathroom door opened. Light from inside it spilled into the room, morphing into an irregular rectangle on the floor. Brian stood by the door shaking water from his hands. Then he dried them on his jeans.

"So, what's the plan now? I'm hungry," said Brian.

"Ya estás otra vez con la pinche comida. Listen, man! You'll get food after."

"Okay! Sorry."

"We're going to pick up . . . let's just say, a special weapon."

Juanca reached back and pulled out a gun. He held it by the barrel and pushed it my way.

"I have another piece on me and one in my room. You take this one. It's the one from the car. You looked comfortable with it. Take it and keep it. We're going in the tunnels soon. You might need it."

I grabbed the gun, made sure the safety was on, and placed it in the back of my jeans.

"In the tunnels?" asked Brian.

"We're about to go down," said Juanca. "And, Brian, I need you to be careful and keep your eyes open. That's all."

"Why?" he asked.

Juanca took a deep breath and exhaled with enough frustration to remind me of every teacher I ever had.

"Because there's a chance we might not be alone down there."

CHAPTER 16

I used the bathroom quickly. When I opened the door to go back to the living room, the photos on the wall opposite the door caught my eye. There were two sepia portraits above all the others. They were surely Margarita's parents. Underneath them, birthdays and photos around tables filled the space. Spotting Juanca was easy. His eyes were the same. He looked untouched by life without his tattoos. There were a few school photos and a couple of recent ones. Juanca's ink appeared. Near the end of the wall, a recent photo showed his current look. He stood next to a grinning man with bright eyes. Next to the man was a good-looking blonde with fine features and a yellow dress. She was taller than both of the men. I heard Juanca and Brian talking and moved away from the wall, my concerns flooding back into my head all at once.

The idea of other men in the tunnel was unnerving. There aren't many spaces to run or hide.

Juanca and Brian were sitting on the sofa when I returned. Their asses made squealing sounds against the plastic cover whenever they moved.

"So you're saying there are wild animals down there?" Brian's pale face and bloodshot eyes made me wonder if he was using again.

Juanca sighed. "Just keep your eyes open, huevón. As soon as we leave this house, I want the two of you to be ready for . . . whatever, you know what I'm saying?"

"How the hell do animals get into the tunnel?" I asked.

"They're not animals," said Juanca. "They're . . . criaturas, okay? They live down there. They can be found in many tunnels. They come and go. They're thin, so they dig smaller holes. Between them and us, the whole border is like a chunk of cheese. If they're hungry, they might jump us or something. We haven't used this tunnel in a while, so I want you two to be prepared for whatever, you know what I'm saying?"

I could see in Brian's face that he was uncomfortable with everything Juanca had said, but the tension between them and Juanca's tone were keeping him from saying more.

"Now let's stop this bullshit and get to Don Vázquez's, yes?"

Brian looked at me. His eyes were red like he'd been crying, or he'd snuck some ice. Either way, I didn't have the energy to deal with him now.

Juanca led us out of the living room and into the kitchen. He rested his hands along an island table topped with black granite and looked at us expectantly.

"Okay, so where's the tunnel, Juanca?" I asked.

"You're standing on it."

CHAPTER 17

"Mario, come give me a hand with this," Juanca said as he started pushing the table.

"The access to the tunnels is in your fucking kitchen?" asked Brian.

"Yeah, it's always been here. Kind of a family thing, you know what I'm saying?"

"How did you get into all this, Juanca?" I asked as we moved stuff around. He seemed on the verge of opening up a bit, and I wanted to know as much as I could about his past. I didn't trust him. The photos from the car kept flashing in my head. So did his warning from the barbecue joint.

"Mi familia es de Ciudad Juárez. I was born and raised there. My father worked on this side of the border and would send money home. He picked limes, oranges, watermelons, cucumbers, whatever. Sometimes he wouldn't get paid and when he complained, the assholes said they'd call la migra on him.

"He got tired of working the fields for next to nothing and hooked up with work carrying drugs for a local dealer in El Paso. Se convirtió en mula. That gig paid more than picking fruit under the sun, so he started sending us money regularly. My amá hated what he was doing, but things got better. We

148

had good shoes and there was always enough to eat. We even got a few things for the house. It's easy to ignore bad shit when you have a full belly, you know what I'm saying? Then they killed him."

Brian had stopped moving around and was leaning against the counter, listening to the story. I was doing the same, standing there like an idiot. Juanca looked at us and kept going.

"I was still un pinche escuincle. The next day, my amá took most of the money she had managed to save up and paid a coyote to bring us to El Paso. It wasn't like you see in the movies, stuffed like sardines in the back of a truck or some shit. My amá knew some people. They brought us here using a tunnel. After we moved, my mom got a visit from some of my dad's old friends. They crossed the border back and forth like it was nothing, man. They had connections. They had these tunnels. Before I knew it, we had a little house on a street called Broadway, like the famous place in New York. We became marionetas. There was a false floor covering the entrance to a tunnel in the kitchen, just like this one, and two of the rooms were filled with bags of dirt from when they dug it out. It was a good cover, a nice lady with three kids. No one suspected anything. She looked like any other Mexican mom in El Paso. She was nice to the neighbors. She went to church. People were sure she cleaned houses or some shit."

The image of the beatific old lady I had in my head came crashing down.

Juanca took a deep breath. I wondered if this was a story concocted to give the impression that he knew what he was talking about. His eyes had that glazed-over look some people get when their bodies are left in the present but their minds go back in time. He ran his hands over his thighs and kept talking.

"My brother Guillermo started helping people bring stuff in and out. He was just a kid, only four years older than me, but he knew he was the man of the house. He wanted to make enough money to get us outta there. You know how it is, poor kids always want better things. He was no different. He wanted a big house with a pool and for our amá to stay home and not have to work. He knew the streets were the quickest way to get money and thought he could get out before he got in too deep, but he fucked up before that happened."

Juanca had stopped working as well. He had his foot up against the wall and he was looking at us as he told the story.

"I don't know what went down, pero se lo chingaron. He left on a trip one night and never came back. His bones are probably out there. Or maybe not. A lot of the carteles work with stewmakers, you know? Guys who dissolve bodies so that no one finds anything. Maybe Guillermo ended up in a pit somewhere."

Juanca paused for a minute, a little ball moving down his neck as he swallowed. I thought about Juanca's mother, how she'd asked me to take care of her boy, and her final words to him: *Si te pierdo a ti ya no me queda nada en esta vida. If I lose you, I won't have anything left in this life.*

"But, you asked about me, not him, right?" croaked Juanca. "Anyway, I was doing deliveries in El Paso by the time I was sixteen. I rolled with Barrio Azteca." He brought his hand up and tapped the letters inked on his chin with his index finger. "They were the kings of El Paso back then. In 2008 we made una alianza con La Línea, los duros del Cartel de Juárez. I was a good driver, always kept my cool and shit, so they let me keep doing that, but there was more work, you know what I'm saying? The trips got longer and the shipments got bigger. It was usually seven or eight cabrones armed to the teeth for each trip. La Línea thought they were going to be able to keep controlling the area, but el Cartel de Sinaloa took over.

Homies started dropping like flies, man. Every day there was killing. The streets ran red with blood. Every morning I woke up to another homie missing or dead. Everyone had a father or a brother or a friend or a cousin who got killed. We started giving money to the gringos locos that patrol the border so they could find safe routes for us. We dug new tunnels and changed a lot of things, but los cabrones de Sinaloa kept it up, siguieron chingando. Everything became about sending the message that they were in control, you know what I'm saying? Killing wasn't enough; they had to chop off people's heads or cut off their balls and shove them in their mouth or cut people into pieces and put everything in the back of a troca or whatever."

My mind darted back to the photos of the man with the mustache hacked to pieces. Juanca was clearly capable of sending a message himself.

"That's enough of that shit. Let's get moving. Look at the corner," Juanca said, pointing at the floor. Unlike the rest of the house, which had ash-colored tiles, the kitchen had laminate flooring. On the floor, bunched up against the corner, was what looked like a white ball of braided nylon twine. I bent over to pick it up.

"You want to wrap it around your hand so it won't slip," said Juanca. "When you have a solid grip let me know. We're gonna go toward the fridge. Pull hard. The wood panels are heavy. When we pull, the floor is gonna lift. When it's almost straight, we have to grab it and bring it down on this side of the kitchen carefully, got it?"

I nodded while wrapping the twine around my right hand.

Juanca moved back a bit and we pulled, but nothing happened. I stopped pulling.

"Sigue jalando, cabrón. No te rajes."

I pulled again, harder this time. After a second, something

gave and the floor started moving up. There were about a six feet of floor coming up. It was like watching the kitchen bend in on itself. It got heavy. We pulled harder. I dug my feet in and leaned back. My arms felt the strain. The twine bit into my flesh. The floor kept rising. The piece we were lifting was about eight by six feet but weighed more than I thought it would.

When the piece of flooring became vertical, Juanca jumped forward.

"Grab it, grab it!" he said.

I moved to it, my hands up. Juanca pulled a tad more and gravity took over. The floor smacked against my palms, heavy and solid.

"Okay, now bring it down slowly."

We scooted back. Right in the middle of the dirt patch we'd uncovered was a large, dark hole about three feet in diameter.

"Is that . . . is that the tunnel?" asked Brian.

"No, pendejo, that's the entrance to the underworld," said Juanca. "El Chamuco is waiting for us. Come on."

The hole looked about as inviting as an angry bull.

Juanca pulled out his cell phone and turned on its flashlight. The light coming from the phone illuminated a rusty ladder on one side of the hole.

"I'll go first. When we get down there, there's a box with flashlights. We'll each grab one and leave it at the other end."

"How deep is that thing?" asked Brian, his face contorted like he'd just seen maggots writhing on a pile of roadkill.

"About fifty feet," said Juanca.

"Fifty feet? You have a hole in your kitchen that goes fifty feet into the ground? That's impressive, man, not gonna lie."

"Nah, this is minor stuff. Only reason we had to go that deep is because of the river and some of the construction. Other tunnels that were less deep collapsed or would get flooded when we got heavy rain. This one is small but it gets the job done. The one we're gonna use to come back? Yeah, that one is impressive. You'll see. Now let's get going."

Juanca sat down on the floor, his legs dangling into the darkness. He switched off his phone's flashlight app and shoved the device into his pocket. Then he placed both hands on the floor, turned around, found the ladder with his feet, and started moving down.

The weight of his body made the ladder groan. I didn't like that sound.

As soon as he disappeared from view, Brian looked at me.

"You go next," he said.

"You scared, B?" Even if he wasn't planning to kill me, I kind of liked watching him squirm.

"Fuck this, man. A damn hole in the ground . . . and there are some kind of creatures down there, remember? Why can't we just drive there? This is about thirteen kinds of fucked."

Fear is like steroids for stupidity. I said nothing. Instead, I sat right where Juanca had, found the ladder with my feet, held on to the cold, rusted steel, and fed myself into the waiting earth.

CHAPTER 18

Climbing down was relatively easy. The ladder moved a bit and groaned like a tired beast, and the smell of wet earth smacked my nostrils the farther down I climbed. My brain plucked a hundred horror movie clichés from its archives and showed me something dark and tentacled pulling me down into the abyss. It showed me a creature with a mouthful of glistening teeth slithering around at the foot of the ladder, waiting to latch on to my ankle. Then I heard a click. Soft light came from below me. Juanca. He had found the flashlights.

At the bottom, Juanca was waiting a few feet away from the ladder because there wasn't enough space to stand next to it. He gave me two large, black flashlights that were incredibly heavy. I fussed with one and clicked it on. The circular light came to a stop right in front of me. The tunnel was only about four feet wide and the walls had a sheen to them that struck me as unnatural. Everything smelled of stagnant air and decay.

"We're going that way," said Juanca, shining his light down the narrow tunnel in front of us. His light penetrated the darkness for about ten or twelve feet, but the black veil behind that was impenetrable.

I shone my light up the ladder and hit the brown bottom of Brian's boots. I moved toward Juanca to make space for Brian.

When he got to the bottom, I passed him the other flashlight. Brian flicked it on immediately.

"It's fucking hot in here," he said.

"Okay, let's move," said Juanca as he started walking.

I allowed Juanca to get about six feet in front of me so we wouldn't fumble into each other. There was nothing to measure progress because everything looked the same. The tunnel could've been six hundred feet long or six miles long and we wouldn't know the difference.

Soon I could feel drops of sweat running down the sides of my face and down my back.

"So, this Vázquez guy is a pretty bad dude," Brian's voice trailed off into a question mark.

The light from my flashlight fell on Juanca as Brian said this and I could see a slight tensing of his shoulders.

"Look, Vázquez doesn't care much for killing; he cares about money, and last time I checked that's why you're here too." Juanca's voice was low and steady. "Now shut up. Wouldn't want those criaturas you're so worried about to wake up because we're gossiping."

My flashlight landed on a dark shape on the wall. It seemed to press itself against the dirt. It looked like a thin, black starfish.

Juanca had apparently not seen it, but it made me pay attention. After a few more feet, the light landed on the dark shape again.

"Hey, Juanca, what the f—"

The thing darted. This time we were closer and I heard a wet squelch as it moved.

"What?"

I flashed my light and scoured the wall. The thing was gone.

"Nothing."

From time to time a drop of water fell on me and my heart raced like a runaway horse tripping downhill. Eventually Juanca slowed down.

"We're here. I'll go up first. There's a box right there," he said, his circle of light falling on a small wooden crate to the right of a ladder. "Wait until I get up there and open up. Then you can come up one at a time. This ladder isn't too solid, but make it quick."

Juanca started climbing, each step asking too much of the old ladder, whose rust had eaten away at its integrity. The creaking sound was replaced by a high-pitched wail that drilled into my eardrums.

"Fuck," said Juanca. He was almost at the top but hadn't opened the hatch yet. "You have to wait till I open. The ladder can't support more than one person."

Over the noise, I could hear Brian mumbling "fuckfuckfuck" as he shone his light into the tunnel. The yellowish light bathed the wall nearest to us, but we couldn't see anything beyond it.

Brian put his foot on the first step and the ladder groaned under the weight.

"You need to wait," Juanca yelled down. "The whole thing will collapse."

I pulled at Brian's shirt and he stepped down as the wailing pierced through the tunnel again. I felt hot breath on my shoulder. Something was behind me.

Metal slid against metal and then there was a loud *thunk*. Juanca pushed whatever was up there open and artificial light exploded in a round hole.

Whatever had been behind me scudded away and I heard the sound of its feet scraping the earth.

"Okay, one of you can come up now," Juanca called down.

Brian rocked from side to side, the light from his flashlight jerking around and across the walls and down to the floor. I let him go first. He grabbed the ladder and started climbing so quickly, I knew what we'd heard had planted unspeakable horrors in his brain.

Brian was quick. I kept my flashlight on and moved it between his ascending body and the impenetrable darkness in front of me. As Brian reached the halfway point of his ascent, an angry hiss came from the darkness in front of me. My heart stopped for a second. There was something there, and it was apparently angry. I placed my hand on the ladder.

When Brian reached the top, his body blocked most of the light. I turned, clicked off my flashlight, threw it in the box along with the two that were already there, and started climbing as fast as I could.

CHAPTER 19

Instead of a kitchen, the hole on the Mexican side of the tunnel opened up into what looked like an ordinary meeting room. It was big, with fluorescent lights and a false ceiling. Plastic chairs were stacked along one wall and there was a piano in a corner with a black tarp over it. A few random boxes were scattered near the wall in front of us. A white door at the end of the big room seemed like the only way in and out.

Juanca pulled out his phone and texted someone.

"Where the hell are we?" asked Brian.

"Iglesia Gracia de Dios Soberano," said Juanca. "A church. We're waiting for a friend of mine, Padre Salvador. We're borrowing his car."

"So there's a priest here that works for the cartel? That's fucked-up."

"No, there's a priest that takes care of his people," said Juanca. "He and Vázquez set up an orphanage here for kids whose parents were killed by cartel violence. Vázquez gives them money all the time. They have food and shoes because he gives the orphanage money and people like Padre Salvador take care of them. When was the last fucking time you made a donation to a church, B? You got a problem with what they do? The last thing I'm in the mood for is a fucking junkie telling me—"

The door at the end of the room swung open. A man in his fifties with salt-and-pepper hair and a beard that eclipsed his neck and hid his mouth walked in. He wore a white button-down shirt and black trousers.

"Hello, gentlemen," he said in perfect English.

"What's happening, Salvador?"

The man approached, gave Juanca a hug, and then shook our hands while introducing himself.

"I know you are in a hurry, so please follow me."

Salvador turned and led us out of the room. We exited onto a dirt courtyard and crossed it behind the priest. We walked around the building and then through a gate that led to a parking lot. Salvador stopped and turned to us.

"You're going to be using the blue Honda over there," he said. He pulled a set of keys from his pocket and handed them to Juanca. "You can leave it in front of El Imperio and La Reina will pick it up later. And be careful. I've been hearing things about this new woman Vázquez is working with."

"Gracias, Padre. I'll be careful."

"Don't mention it, Juanito," replied the priest. "How's your mother?"

"She has good days and bad days. Lately there are more bad than good days, but you know she rarely complains."

"I will pray for her. I will also pray for you, Juanito." Padre Salvador sighed. "Perder un hijo es algo muy doloroso. Ninguna madre debería pasar por eso. Perder dos hijos es demasiado. Eso es algo que te puede destruir el espíritu. Perder tres es algo que la mataría." The priest looked up at the night sky. Maybe he was praying for us. Maybe he was wondering was there really something up there. His words echoed in my head. *Losing one son is something very painful. No mother should ever have to experience that. Losing two sons is too much. That's something that can destroy your spirit. Losing three will kill her.*

Padre Salvador spoke again. "That your mother still has her faith intact speaks volumes about her relationship with God. She shouldn't have to deal with more loss. You need to get this over with and take care of her, you hear me?"

"Sí, Padre. I'll take care of her myself. I'll come back and take care of her after. This is the last one. You know that."

Juanca had mentioned Guillermo back at the house, but no one else. Why hadn't he said anything about another brother?

"And use some of the money to erase that stuff on your face, please. I know it will bring your mother joy. Deja que tu pobre madre mire a su hijo a la cara sin tener que ver cosas que le recuerdan a la suciedad que le robó dos hijos."

Let your poor mother look at her son's face without having to look at reminders of the filth that stole two sons from her.

Juanca nodded.

Two sons. There it was again.

Padre Salvador sighed once more. He slapped Juanca on the shoulder and then looked at us.

"Good luck to you, gentlemen. Men who do bad things for the right reasons are always forgiven in the eyes of the Lord, especially when they do so with a pure heart. God is called 'God of vengeance' in Psalm 94, and that's because there are sins that merit punishment. Remember Colossians 3:25, 'For the wrongdoer will be paid back for the wrong he has done, and there is no partiality,' and Exodus 21:24–25, which is a favorite of mine, 'Eye for eye, tooth for tooth, hand for hand, foot for foot, burn for burn, wound for wound, stripe for stripe.' I know Juanito wouldn't ask you to join him in this if he didn't think highly of you. God be with you all."

Padre Salvador was kidding himself if he thought any of us were pure of heart. In my head, I saw Melisa staring at me from the floor. The table shattered. I'd done that. I was a fucking monster. Prayers and guilt would do nothing to erase what we were going to do.

Salvador gave Juanca one last pat on the back. "Pronto los hombres que mataron a tu hermano van a pagar por lo que hicieron."

Juanca threw the keys he'd received a couple feet in the air, caught them, and started walking to the Honda. "Let's get this done."

Something turned in my brain. *Eye for eye. Soon the men who killed your brother are going to pay for what they did.* My breath caught in my lungs. This wasn't just about the money. Juanca wanted revenge. And if he could keep a secret like that, he could do much worse.

CHAPTER 20

Juanca drove out of the church's parking lot and found a wide two-way street. He turned on the radio. Banda music came pouring out, but the speakers were busted and most of it was a buzzing sound that vibrated against the side of my calf and around my ears.

The streets were dark and the world had shifted to night mode. There weren't many businesses around. Huge, desolate patches of dirt behind fences made up most of what I could see on our right. More than a residential area, it reminded me of the kind of warehouse place where trucks are much more common than cars.

We were turning left onto a larger avenue when Brian spoke.

"Are you really going to take that ink off your face, Juanca?"

"I will. My amá will love it. I got the Barrio Azteca letters on my chin when I was sixteen. She didn't talk to me for weeks. She always hated the streets. They have taken too much from her, you know what I'm saying? Ninguna madre debería enterrar a un hijo, y ella ha enterrado a dos."

I was surprised he replied to the question so quickly and that he'd given us so much. Some people are open like that and some are more private, keeping their world close to them and away from everyone else. Juanca had struck me as the second type. Something about being home, about seeing his mother, had softened him.

"Juanca, what happened to..." I let the question hang in the air.

Juanca held up his phone. On the screen was a photo of him and two other men. They had their arms around each other's shoulders, their proximity speaking of familiarity and love. Their faces were three drafts of the same painting. His brothers. One of them looked familiar, but I couldn't figure out why. He had a thin mustache that was starting to curl up comically at the corners.

"Guillermo is on the right. The one on the left is Omar. He taught me everything I know about... everything. Mi viejo no estaba, así que Omar se convirtió en mi padre."

The smiles in the photo were not the sadistic smiles of killers or the masks of criminals trying to look respectable—they were the smiles of men who loved each other, who had stories to tell and had experienced horrible things together. Their smiles were genuine and warm. I bet this photo was one Juanca's mother loved.

Juanca pulled his phone back and turned on the radio. "We're almost there." There was no anger in his voice, but I didn't want to push my luck after seeing what he could do with a dozen knives and a piece of flesh. He was right about one thing, though: no mother should bury a son... or a daughter.

I thought about Melisa. I hoped she was sleeping. Her pain had to be like mine. No, it was probably bigger. She'd carried Anita inside her for nine months and then pushed her out into the world. They shared the bond forged in that strange, gory, loud, bloody, painful ritual we call childbirth. I was merely an idiot standing by, ready to hold her hand and give her coconut water whenever she asked, but I had done nothing. I often wondered how our pains, immense as they undoubtedly were, differed because of that connection every mother has with the children they bring to life.

Outside my window, a different world from the one we'd left was flashing by. I read the signs and took it all in. An Oxxo gas station. Restaurante La Nueva Central. Motel La Villita. Motel El Refugio. Restaurante La Avenida. Taquería La Golondrina. Capilla San Sebastián Martir. Muebles La Colonia. Iglesia Cristiana Cristo es Paz. Garage Manuel. Based on the businesses I saw, people living in Ciudad Juárez did nothing but eat, fuck, and pray.

Juanca drove in silence. In the back seat, Brian was holding himself again, his forehead against the window, his eyes lost in the world outside. I focused on the road. Many of the places I was seeing were new to me. However, there were brief flashes of the world I knew, a world I was surprised to see on the other side of the border. A McDonald's. An Applebee's. A BBVA bank. It was an odd mix, a mix that spoke of a place where cultures meet, where languages morph into a hybrid, where people come and go all the time between a space where they have limited opportunity and another that is obsessed with pushing them out, with denying them the very dream the damn place was built on.

We kept driving in silence for a while, the broken, buzzing music filling the car. A word or two would occasionally break through the static, giving us a version too fragmented to understand, a story too broken to follow. In a way, it made sense that this was our soundtrack.

"Who's this Reina dude the priest was talking about?" asked Brian.

"La Reina is not a fellow; she's a woman," said Juanca. "She's Don Vázquez's . . . let's just say you don't get to him without going through her first."

"So she's like a . . . secretary?"

"Nah, B, secretaries type on computers and pick up the phone and shit; La Reina shoots motherfuckers in the face and feeds people to the crocs. She doesn't fuck around. She's a gabacha, but she has one of the biggest pairs of cojones in Mexico. Don't mess with her. Ever. And don't say shit about the way she looks. I'm not kidding about her shooting people in the face and feeding them to the crocs."

Juanca turned left on a smaller street and slowed down. There were houses on one side and a few small businesses on the other. Cars were parked on both sides of the street, the bigger SUVs and pickups halfway up the sidewalks. We stopped in front of a long single-story building with white walls streaked with dirt and water stains. On top of it was a large sign with blue letters that read EL IMPERIO. A loud, repetitive bass made it sound like the place had a heartbeat. My guess was no one complained because no one wanted to mess with Don Vázquez. Better to live with a headache than to die without a head.

Juanca looked around, craning his neck as if to see beyond the door, and then drove on. About two blocks down he found a spot he liked and pulled up to the sidewalk.

"We're here."

A shorter drive meant there was no need for uncoiling and stretching. We exited the car and Juanca led the way.

As we walked down the street, I took in the houses. Their size was more or less the same as those in the neighborhood where Juanca lived. However, they looked different. Many of them had exposed cement blocks for walls, and those that had second floors had the type of construction that makes it obvious the second floor was added after the house was built and had been done with a small budget. There was graffiti on some of the houses and the bits of grass I could see were yellow, dead clumps that hadn't been cut in ages. As I was looking at the top of a house that had a halfway-built second floor, a strange shadow appeared, a blackness deeper than the surrounding night. My heart jumped. Then the figure barked at us. The dog's white teeth flashed in the darkness, an eloquent threat.

The man standing at the door of El Imperio was massive. His black shirt barely contained his muscles. He was my height, so about five-nine, but he must have outweighed me by a hundred pounds, and every pound of that was muscle. The sides of his face had slabs of beef attaching his lower jaw to his skull. The added face meat made him look like a Cro-Magnon who shaved regularly. The veins in his biceps were small snakes that moved under his skin as he shook Juanca's hand and waved us in with a smile.

The inside of El Imperio was dark. Neon blue lights hung over the dance floor. The place was a large square with a bar up against the wall opposite the door, bathrooms and a few pool tables in the back, and a DJ booth tucked into a corner next to the dance floor. Sweaty bodies moved to the beat of house music. The rhythm was repetitive and heavy, the same steady, frantic heartbeat we'd heard as we drove by.

At the bar, a few men sat on round stools, most of them resting elbows on the bar, their bodies turned away from the dance floor. They reminded me of the Mexican I'd met at the bar while I waited for Brian. Then I remembered the man in the bathroom and what went down in the parking lot.

Be careful, ore.

The men didn't look at us as we approached. They were all nursing drinks in red plastic cups or cans of beer. The bartender was a young woman with a face full of metal and the left side of her head shaved. The hair on the right side was dyed green and fell over half of her face all the way down to her shoulder on her left side. She wore a black sleeveless shirt. A green dragon was wrapped around her right arm, its head taking up most of her shoulder and disappearing briefly under the shirt's straps before emerging once again on her chest, its head vomiting red and orange fire that reached the woman's opposite shoulder.

Juanca crossed the length of the establishment without stopping or looking at anyone. He went up to the side of the bar, lifted a chunk of it, got behind it, and signaled for us to follow. The bartender looked at us, anger flaring in her dark eyes, her right hand reaching for something under the bar, but then she recognized Juanca. Her eyes softened. She nodded at him with a smile before returning her attention to the men sitting at the bar.

There was a black curtain covering the wall. I hadn't noticed it in the scant light. Juanca pushed it aside to reveal a door. He opened it and walked through while holding the door and the curtain with his arm. We followed.

Instead of a street, we found ourselves in some sort of backyard. It was a few hundred feet across, just dry dirt and clumps of dead grass between fences we could barely make out in the dark. Across from where we stood, there was a second building. Unlike the building that housed El Imperio, this one had walls covered in rusted corrugated zinc sheets and looked a lot like a warehouse. It had a double door in the middle of it and no windows. Two men stood by the door, both holding AK-47s.

"¿Qué onda, Manuel?" Juanca yelled.

The man on the left squinted. His face broke into a smile.

"Hijo de la chingada, llegó el elegido," said the man.

We walked across the backyard and approached the men. They were clearly happy to see Juanca. Juanca introduced us and we shook hands. They smelled like beer and gun oil. The man who had called Juanca the chosen one was named Gerardo. He said the other man, Antonio, was glad to meet us, but couldn't say shit about it because he had no tongue. My mind jumped to San Antonio and the two cut tongues I'd seen in that awful house . . .

"¿Vienes a ver a Don Vázquez, no, culero?"

"Pues a ver tu cara de pendejo no vengo, güey."

The men laughed and opened the doors for us.

We entered a place that was somewhere between a club, a bar, a boxing arena, and a warehouse. The noise inside was a different beast, a constant drone of voices instead of thumping house music. Smoke from cigarettes, cigars, and, judging by the bittersweet smell, weed hung in the air like a physical presence you could cut through with a knife.

Toward the middle of the place, about fifty people stood around in a circle, screaming like crazy. Juanca moved us closer to the action and we squeezed into the circle.

In front of us was a round bare cement pit with the floor painted lime green. Two roosters were exploding into the air and crashing against each other. One was almost entirely white, the other so brown it was almost black. With every move the birds made, the people around us went into a frenzy as if an electric shock had passed through the room.

Cockfighting is not a sport; it's a spectacle, bloody and fast-paced. It's also illegal. I'd been to a few fights with my abuela at a club gallístico behind the one restaurant in town she liked. When my mom was busy or had vanished on one of her benders, my abuela would take me with her. It was no place for a kid. It was no place for an old woman either, but she loved it. She used to tell me the trick to picking a winning rooster was to look at their head movement. If they were jerky and nervous, they wouldn't focus. Funny how that also applies to people.

In front of us, the roosters jumped again, the flapping of their wings inaudible over the ruckus. The birds collided in midair before falling away from each other. Tiny feathers floated to the ground.

The roosters circled each other, their heads bobbing, and then took to the air again. The white one stuck a spur into the side of the brown one. They fell together, a frenzied jumble of feathers. As they pulled away, blood shot from somewhere on the wounded bird. The blood traced an arc in the air and landed across the left side of the white rooster, immediately turning into a silent, crimson line of poetry on the shiny white feathers. The onlookers roared. Most of them were men with clenched fists and sweaty faces. Their skin glistened under the harsh halogen lights that hung over the pit. They yelled with their mouths open, the fight between the birds a ritual of blood to appease some old god, the outcome the difference between going home broke and going home drunk and with a roll of pesos in their pocket.

The smell of warm bodies smoking, sweating, screaming, and drinking was all around us. The birds were approaching each other again, the brown one moving like something was broken inside it, when Juanca tapped me on the arm. He signaled with his head to follow him. I extricated myself from the mass of excited, shouting people and followed him.

"What the fuck is that all about?" asked Brian.

"Pelea de gallos," said Juanca. "Cockfights. You never seen one?"

Brian shook his head. Juanca smiled.

"It's an easy way to make money if you know what you're doing. People love it. Champion roosters are big fucking business in a lot of places. Don Vázquez also has dogfights at his other place. Those are ugly, man. The dogs usually end up with their faces all fucked-up. All the roosters have are espolones and their beaks, but dogs have mouths full of jagged teeth and powerful jaws, you know what I'm saying? And they can go on for a while. I had a cousin who trained them. He used to tie them to a stick in the middle of a pond and keep them there until they almost drowned. He turned those dogs into killing machines. When dogs fight, if the fight is bad enough, you have to take the loser out back and shoot them. Sometimes the owners or trainers get shot along with the dogs. It's nasty. Same thing happens here, but less often. I prefer this place."

We crossed the large room and reached another door. This one had only one man in front of it. He nodded at Juanca and opened the door for us.

The room inside was dark and had a large bar in the back with an entire wall of liquor bottles behind it. Instead of a cockfighting ring, it had pool, blackjack, poker, and roulette tables. Men and women sat at most tables, large piles of cash in front of them. Long lamps hung from the ceiling, throwing weak white light over everything. AC units decorated the walls here and there. They managed to make the air only slightly colder than it was outside.

At the bar, a tall, blond woman with sinewy arms was talking to a short man with a beige ten-gallon hat. She turned to us as we approached. Her eyes lit up and her mouth curled into a huge smile that revealed teeth too perfect to be real. I felt like I'd seen her before.

"I hope my eyes are not deceiving me and it's really the one and only Juan Carlos walking into my arms this very second!" Her English was perfect. Combined with her skin, height, and blond hair, I guessed she was a white girl from somewhere north of the border.

The end of the bar was open. She reached it in three steps and turned to us. She wore a thin pink dress that ended right above her knees and revealed a curvy figure.

Juanca and the woman embraced. There are different types of hugs, and this one spoke of a long friendship full of good times and a dash of the kind of bad shit that pushes people together.

When their bodies separated, the woman held Juanca at arm's length and smiled again. Now that she was closer to one of the lights that hung over the tables, I could see her better. Her makeup made her look paler than she was and some of it had piled together and cracked a bit around her brown eyes.

"You look good, you sexy motherfucker!" Then she turned to us. "And who are these fine gentlemen accompanying you this evening?"

"Reina, these are Mario and Brian," said Juanca. "Mario, Brian, this is La Reina."

She stepped forward, her hand outstretched. I took it first. She had a nice grip, and in the lean muscles of her arm I could see her measuring my own grip as well.

"The name is Jessica Kayden King. Everyone calls me La Reina. You can call me Reina or you can call me Jessica if you can't roll your *R*s. Never JK. Call me anything else and I'll shoot you in the face and feed your ass to the crocs in the back even if I fuck up a nail in the process."

The perfect smile remained in place while she talked. I'd heard the term *bubbly* being used when describing someone, but this was the first time in my life I'd met a person who made me think of it. La Reina shook Brian's hand and then returned to the bar.

She reached under the bar and pulled out the biggest gun I'd ever seen. She kissed it and looked at us. "You gentlemen see this fine piece of stainless steel?"

La Reina stretched her arm out and pointed the gun between Brian and me. Even in the darkness I could see the letters etched on the side of it: SMITH & WESSON.

"You know what this is, white boy?" La Reina asked, looking at Brian.

"Yeah, it's a ridiculously large gun used to bring down elephants."

"Ah, a white boy who's not a gun nut! Well, bless your heart. This right here, gentlemen, is a miracle of gun engineering. This is four pounds of power and death. I call it the Goddess stick because if God was real, she'd be a woman and this would be her dick. This is a S&W500 Magnum. Do you know why its barrel only holds five bullets? I'm sure you don't, so I'll tell you: it only holds five bullets because you don't even need six. I could line up the three of you and pop your heads like melons dropped from the top of a building with a single pull of this beautiful, shiny trigger."

"So . . . that's what you're gonna shoot us with if we call you something else?" asked Brian.

La Reina smiled. "You're not as dumb as you look."

La Reina pulled her arm back and brought the massive weapon close to her face. She looked at the barrel of the gun, stuck her tongue out, and licked it lasciviously. Somehow the gesture wasn't out of place.

"Enough of that," she said as she placed the cannon back under the bar. "I'm sure Juanca is aching to talk to Don Vázquez and get the show on the road. Follow me, gentlemen."

As we walked, the shouting from the other room increased violently.

"Shit," said La Reina, turning around.

She trotted to the door we'd used to get here and opened it. On the other side, frantic screaming came from the people who had been around the pit. We approached. La Reina pushed her way through the bodies. At the center of the action, a short man wearing jeans and a blue T-shirt was waving the corpse of the brown rooster around.

"What the fuck is going on here?" yelled La Reina.

"The bird, it has no . . . no scar!" replied the man with the rooster.

"No scar?"

A woman stepped forward. She had dark eyes and a head full of dark curls framing her face.

"He saying the bird no have no wounds, you know? It never be in a fight before. The man said it was champion, but it never fight."

Her English skills were much better.

"Ah," said La Reina. "Someone tried to be too smart for their own good." She grabbed the dead rooster and held it up. "Who's the owner of this bird?"

A man was pushed toward La Reina. He was shaking. His white button-down shirt was soaked through with sweat.

"¿Es tuyo?" La Reina asked. The man nodded. La Reina turned to the irate man in the blue shirt.

"You need to take care of this. Now," said La Reina.

The woman with the curls translated. Blue shirt smiled, reached back, and pulled out a switchblade. The blade popped out hungrily, its tip slicing the air.

"Well, lack of honesty has a price," said La Reina. She looked around and spotted a short man with a beard that made him look like a caveman. "Bring the man some plastic."

The short man left. La Reina walked up to the man who'd tried to cheat and grabbed him by the neck. She turned him around and made him look at everyone else. The man had his hands against his chest, as if protecting himself from cold weather.

"¿Ven ustedes a este cabrón?" La Reina asked loudly in accented Spanish. "In Don Vázquez's house, sometimes you win and sometimes you lose. But you never cheat."

The crowd had been relatively quiet, but a few of them screamed their assent when she said this.

La Reina lifted her left hand and signaled for the man with the switchblade to come closer. The man stepped toward her, the blade in his hand catching the light from the overhead lamps. The man La Reina was holding started mumbling apologies and looking around, probably looking for a friend, a savior, anyone willing to say a word in his defense. He found sweaty faces looking back at him with darkness moving behind their eyes.

The guy who'd left to get the plastic came back holding a white tarp like the ones painters use to cover furniture while working. He shook it and allowed it to gently fall to the floor.

"Clávale el cuchillo," said La Reina. Two men appeared and held the cheater's arms. The man in the blue shirt lifted his hand and quickly stabbed the other man in the gut. The man howled. La Reina let go of his neck. The men who were holding up the cheater let go and he dropped to the plastic.

The men wrapped the plastic around his legs and started dragging him toward the back of the place.

Part of the crowd had dispersed, back to their games and drinks. The ones who'd stayed were laughing or screaming.

"Se lo chingó por tramposo," said a woman with a black shirt and tight jeans.

La Reina looked at the man. He was still holding the knife. The cheater was squealing like a pig as the men pulled him outside through a door next to the bar.

La Reina looked at the floor. "They better not make a mess. And if they do, they better clean up after themselves."

"See?" said Juanca. "Told you it gets bad in here from time to time." He smiled.

"Sorry about that, gentlemen," said La Reina. The man who had brought the plastic appeared next to her.

"All done, boss," he said.

"Where did you take him?"

"Back alley."

"Good. Did you two finish the job?"

Instead of answering, the man looked at his shoes.

"Oh, for fuck's sakes."

La Reina sashayed away and walked back the way we came.

She opened the door at the back of the room and looked at us. Juanca jogged to her.

"Let me check on this real quick. I don't want trouble tomorrow and that poor bastard . . ."

She turned right, walked all the way to a gate by the fence, and opened it. Then she turned slightly left into an alley between the two houses. We could see down the alley from where we stood.

The man was curled on top of the plastic. He was moaning and holding his gut.

"See? Gonna take this poor sucker hours to die. He might try to get up and make it home while bleeding internally. Not a nice way to go. Cheating at the fights is bad, but not this fucking awful." She looked at Juanca. "Got a knife?"

Juanca dug in his back pocket and pulled out a small pocket-knife with a wooden handle and gave it to La Reina. She pulled the blade out with a click, walked up to the man, yanked his head up by the hair, and slit his throat. Blood spurted out onto the plastic. La Reina let him drop back down. The man gurgled a few times and his legs kicked out. Then he was still. La Reina bent forward and cleaned the blade against the side of the man's jeans before closing it and returning it to Juanca.

"That's better." She looked into Juanca's eyes. "He's not suffering now."

Without another word, La Reina retraced her steps and returned to the bar. Once inside, she kept walking and took us to another door on the left wall. It opened into a new room with no one inside it. She entered the room and began walking parallel to the wall. Near the back wall was a white door. She opened it for us and stood on the other side holding it, a smile on her face.

The space we entered looked somewhat like an office. The walls were covered in framed photos and posters of bullfighters.

A large AC unit whined on a wall. Near the back wall, two men with AK-47s stood by, cradling their weapons with such ease I was sure they slept with them. One of them was muscular and resembled Juanca in many ways, including the ink that covered most of his arms, hands, neck, and face. Behind them was one of the biggest aquariums I'd seen in my life. Large dark shapes swam in there, but the water was so brown and murky that I couldn't see them clearly.

In the middle of the room was a chubby brown man with a gray mustache sitting behind the desk. He wore a white guayabera with intricate embroidered designs that started on top of the shirt's pockets and ran down his torso on both sides. A thick gold chain with a massive cross with Jesus hung from his neck. Don Vázquez.

He leaned back in his chair and crossed his hands over his belly. Golden rings decorated a few of his short, stubby fingers.

"Juanca," he said, standing up. "Ven aquí y dame un abrazo."

Juanca went to the man and they hugged. Don Vázquez closed his eyes as they embraced and then planted a kiss on Juanca's cheek before letting go with a pat on the cheek. He turned to us.

"Are these the Americans that are going to help you?" His English was heavily accented but he seemed comfortable with the switch. A true businessman.

"Yes, Don Vázquez. These are Mario and Brian."

"Mario," said Don Vázquez slowly, his bushy gray eyebrows twitching closer to each other. Something pushed most of the air out of my lungs. If you lined up all the people who'd died because of this man, the bodies would probably reach Austin. My name in his mouth was all too much.

"Un placer conocerlo, Don Vázquez." What the fuck was I supposed to say?

Don Vázquez laughed as he approached me, hand outstretched.

176

"Conocerme nunca es un placer, Mario. Conocerme a mí es una oblicagión, el resultado de una mala decisión o una pesadilla. ¿Tu amigo habla español, Mario?"

"No, señor, Brian entiende un poco, pero no habla español."

"Ah, then we will speak in English. I want everyone to feel welcome and I want everyone to understand exactly what they have to do."

Brian knew we were talking about him. He also knew the man had switched languages for his benefit. He stepped forward and offered his hand.

"Pleased to meet y—"

"Thank you, Brian, but I was just telling your friend Mario that meeting me is never a pleasure; meeting me is something that happens to people because they have made a bad decision."

Don Vázquez's voice was deep and calm. He was slightly shorter than me. Rotund. His skin reminded me of my grandmother's—a shade that brought to mind old pennies and reminded me of the Taíno Indian in her blood. I had no problem imagining Vázquez's bloodline lifting still-beating hearts up to the sun before the Spaniards came.

"I'm sure you are all tired, yes? I say we get down to business so you gentlemen can get some rest tonight." Don Vázquez turned to Juanca. "Did you bring me what I asked for?"

"Claro que sí, jefe."

Juanca put his hand in his pocket while moving toward Don Vázquez like a kid eager to please. He pulled out the handkerchief with the toe wrapped inside it. The walls in El Milagrito's room came back to me, the rattle of the crosses like the sound of a thousand angry insects.

"Here you go, Don Vázquez."

Don Vázquez took the toe carefully and began to unwrap it. Behind him, something thumped against the aquarium's glass. A dark thing that looked just like the starfish-shaped creature I'd seen in the tunnel was quickly moving left along the inside of the glass. Its long, black tentacles sent a shiver down my spine.

"There are things in this world that have no explanation," Don Vázquez said, pulling my eyes from the creature. "When you come across these things, you have two options. Option one is to try to make things make sense. This is what most people do. They experience something and they try to mold the event to their experiences, to understand what happened using the filter of what they already know. This never works. It only leads to confusion and frustration, yes? The second option is to accept that strange things happen, that the impossible sometimes is real. When you accept it, you can move on with your life. Our ancestors invented gods for this reason and they were happier because of it."

Don Vázquez stopped talking, his eyes on us. The skin under his left eye bulged out like there was something underneath trying to break out.

"I only tell you this to prepare you for what you are about to see," he continued. "There is no point in trying to understand it. You just need to know that what's going to happen outside is a good thing that will make your job easier. It will keep you safe."

Of all the things we'd encountered since crossing the border, Don Vázquez's quiet eloquence was the most surprising one. Facing your own prejudices and learning that they are wrong is a powerful thing. I had no problem thinking of myself as an intelligent person despite my shitty position in life, despite my junkie mother, my accent, and my brownness. I had read and studied hard because I had believed education was the surefire path to upward social mobility. I had devoured books because I didn't want to end up like my mother or any of the men we lived next to in Houston. I had learned to speak English and Spanish as well as I could because I was convinced speaking intelligently would open doors for me, that it would keep some of the racism my father feared so much away from me. I was sure that shit made me special. Then I had kept on bettering myself because I never wanted to feel like Melisa, a brilliant woman, had to look down on me, that she would have me say something incredibly stupid in front of her friends from work or the other moms in her book club, some of whom had Ivy League educations. However, I never expected to find the same intelligence in others. Don Vázquez, in my head, was no more than a drug lord, a killer whose goal was to take over the trafficking world and make all the money in the world flooding the US with drugs and Juárez with violence. I was sure he was all that, but the words that came out of his mouth made me think of a patient theology teacher talking to students who needed to understand the possibility of an interventionist god, the possibility of miracles happening in the everyday world.

Don Vázquez finished unwrapping the toe. He held it up so we could see it.

"This is a piece of God." He turned to the men in the back. "Este es un pedazo de Dios hecho carne. Con esto en mis manos soy invencible."

The toe now looked slightly gray, and blood had dried on the nail, making it look black and dirty. Don Vázquez brought it to his mouth and kissed it before carefully rewrapping it and placing it in the front left pocket of his guayabera.

"Follow me."

It was a command, not an invitation.

CHAPTER 21

Don Vázquez led us out of his office, through the bar where we'd met La Reina, and back out into the courtyard. There, he turned right. The men who'd been in his office began walking with us. I noticed they were both missing fingers.

We walked along the side of the building and turned right again where the wall ended. Once we'd circled the building, we came upon a concrete pool at least three times the size of the pit they had inside for the roosters. It was round and about four feet off the ground. Two lampposts had been installed at its sides. Despite it being raised off the ground, it was low enough that I could see inside it. The light from the lampposts fell on the quivering brackish water inside. A short concrete slab hung over the water with a metallic staircase attached to it. In the center of the pool was a round island of dirty concrete.

"Raulito, Manuel, traigan a la bruja y a Rodolfo."

Something moved in the water, made a splash. The sound made me peel my eyes away from Don Vázquez and look. I immediately recognized the shape. It was a crocodile. The top of its head was above the water, its eyes and nostrils gliding along. It was huge.

"Holy shit, the croc thing was real!" said Brian.

Don Vázquez smiled. "They are real indeed, and usually quite hungry too."

"Why the fuck do you have crocs out here in the back of your club, man? You know . . . if you don't mind me asking . . . sir."

Don Vázquez smiled. Brian was obviously nervous. I wanted him to shut the hell up and follow instructions. The less he talked, the smoother things would run.

"Many years ago I read in a newspaper that Pablo Escobar had hippos on his property," he said. "Hippos are dumb and too big, but I liked the idea of having exotic animals. I was thinking about getting a tiger or a lion, something strong with a powerful mouth that could eat whoever fucked with me, but then I watched a documentary with my daughter and changed my mind. The documentary talked about how crocodiles have a . . . serum in their blood that helps them fight off infection. They get hurt, but they never get sick. You can cut one with a machete, drop him back into that nasty water full of shit, and he won't develop an infection. I loved that about them. Do you know why, Brian? Because I am like these crocodiles; I'm always swimming. I swim in the darkness, surrounded by shit, but I never get sick. Anyway, I sent some of my men across the border. I found a guy I do business with who could get me what I needed. The animals in there all came from Louisiana. You ever been there, Brian? They have a lot of crocodiles out there. Anyway, these are my American employees."

Don Vázquez's smile looked different under the light outside.

"So if the crocs are real, that means all the stories are real?" asked Brian, his eyes glued to the surface of the dark water.

"And what stories would those be?" Don Vázquez's features seemed to rearrange themselves. Something within him too.

"Well . . . we've been hearing a lot of talk about, you know, feeding people to the crocs and whatnot. The lady inside . . . with the big gun . . ."

"La Reina," I helped him. I really wanted him to keep his mouth shut now.

"Yeah, La Reina said something about throwing us in there after shooting us in the face if we called her anything other than La Reina."

Don Vázquez laughed. The sound didn't fit our surroundings.

"La Reina will definitely shoot you in the face and throw you in there herself."

"That's . . . impressive. I like a woman who can handle herself."

"The strongest flowers are those that grow between the cracks, my friend," said Don Vázquez.

"How'd she end up here? You know, if you don't mind me asking. It's just . . . she's not a local, is she? She looks like she should be in the movies or something."

The motherfucker wanted to bang her.

"La Reina came to Mexico looking for work. She moved here because healthcare in the US is garbage. She had some stuff she needed to take care of and wanted some plastic surgery for her face. Faces are important. I've helped a lot of people change theirs forever, sometimes for better versions and sometimes for faces they'll want to hide. It depends on what they deserve. Anyway, La Reina was good with a gun, so as soon as she started working here, she made a lot of noise. You know, a blond gringa who killed men like it was a joke. She was fearless and they said she never ruined her makeup. Soon I was hearing stories about her daily, so I decided to reach out and send her on a suicide mission. If she lived, I'd hire her. If she died . . . well, she died. Someone was cutting into my product between here and the tunnels, so I asked her to find out who it was. I gave her no info. A week later she came back with a video on her phone of two rats cutting my meth with milk powder. I asked her if she could take care of it. Two days later she showed up wearing a blue sundress with yellow flowers on it and pulling a little red cart behind her with a foam cooler on it. The heads of the two rats were in there. She opened the cooler and pulled them out to make sure I got a good look at them. I liked her style. Death in a pretty dress. She started working for me that day. I got her the medical care she needed. Now she runs things when I'm not here. When someone misbehaves, she feeds them to the crocs. I tell her to keep teaching the men respect because respect matters. That's why I'm letting Juanca do this, so he can get respect for his family, for Omar. She really loved Omar, so I know she's happy you're here. Make sure you keep it that way."

I glanced over at Juanca, to see if his face would betray any emotion, but his expression was flat, eyes glued to Vázquez. I didn't like that Juanca's brother had something to do with this job. Revenge is as normal to humans as hunger or thirst. We need it. We crave it whenever we feel someone has done us wrong. But it also makes you do dumb shit.

Brian opened his mouth to say something, but the men who'd accompanied us came back around the corner of the building. The one called Manuel was holding a guy by the arm. A few tattoos covered his arms and bare chest. Manuel was pulling him like he was cattle. The man had duct tape covering his mouth and his hands were tied behind his back. Above the duct tape, the fear in his eyes said everything his mouth couldn't.

Raulito was behind them, walking slowly. Next to him was a bent figure covered in a long white camisole sporting a variety of dark stains. As they stepped into the perimeter of light around the pool, I saw the woman more clearly. She was old and looked weak. It was as if the man wasn't so much holding her up as he was dragging her. When they got closer, the woman lifted her head. Her eyes were empty, the pink flesh inside her eye sockets glinting under the light, and her arms ended in stumps instead of hands.

"What the fuck...?" Brian's voice cut through everything

and pulled me from whatever place I'd been in before and dropped me into the creepy reality in front of us. This was real. The woman was real. The toe in Don Vázquez's pocket was real. I wished I was back home, holding Anita while she slept peacefully, looking at Melisa's beautiful, peaceful face smiling at me. I wished it with everything I had and then reached into an impossible space between memory and impossibility and found even more with which to wish for it, for them.

Manuel walked past us. The man he was holding looked at us, the panic in his eyes growing, pleading. The same profound sense of unease I'd had in El Milagrito's room rushed back. A bad thing was going to happen.

I looked away, toward the faraway fence. Beyond it was an empty street with dilapidated cars parked in front of a few houses. A single lamppost poured soft light onto the pavement and side-walk. Underneath it was a short figure. I couldn't see its face or clothing. It was a black smudge under the light, a silhouette without details. It looked like the thing I'd seen in my kitchen.

"¿Tienes lo que necesitas, Manuel?"

"Sí, Don Vázquez, tengo todo," replied Manuel as he made his way to the stairs.

The man Manuel was holding started fighting, planting his feet on the ground and refusing to move. Muffled words and screams came from behind the duct tape covering his mouth. He probably knew about the animals in the water.

Don Vázquez dug in his left front pocket and brought out a phone. He tapped it a few times and held it up to his ear.

"Reina, dile a Marta que traiga la troca. Vamos a empezar en un minuto y no quiero tener que esperar por la caja."

Manuel was struggling with the man now. He was holding the AK-47 to the side and looked like he was thinking about putting it down so he could handle the man better.

"Mario, would you please give Manuel a hand?"

My feet were moving before the words *of course* left my mouth. Power's a strange thing. Some have it and some don't. Those who do have a certain way of speaking that renders options nonexistent. Don Vázquez had been warm, even friendly, so far, but this was his kingdom and his demeanor made one thing clear: cross me and you'll quickly become croc shit.

"And you, Brian, give Raulito a hand. We want to make sure everything is under control and we can do things right."

There it was again. A hand. My eyes flew to the stumps at the old woman's wrists. Why would they mutilate her like that?

I didn't turn to look, but I heard Brian move. I had no idea why the other guy would need help handling a woman who looked like she had one foot in the grave, but I wasn't about to start asking questions.

"Juanca, Marta va a estar aquí en cualquier momento. Cuando llegue, ayúdala a bajar la caja de la troca."

I grabbed the man's left arm. He was fighting with all he had. Whatever he was saying behind the tape was getting louder. Adrenaline was making him stronger than he should have been.

"Hay que subir a este pinche cabrón a esa plataforma."

We moved together. The man tensed his legs, so we lifted him up and carried him forward. His body was slick with sweat, but we managed.

Approaching the crocodiles was surreal. Every instinct was screaming at me to move away from that water, but my body was obeying Don Vázquez's orders, almost as if it were an independent entity.

Manuel and I had to pull even harder when we reached the stairs.

The concrete platform jutted out into the brackish water. It was about four feet long by six feet across, so we managed to fit in there somewhat comfortably, but it didn't have any sides, nothing to hold on to. Fear gripped my heart and squeezed. I leaned into the man, fearing he would decide to take one of us with him.

"Brian, I need you to listen to me, okay?" said Don Vázquez. "You need to help Raulito bring la bruja over here. Don't be gentle with her. Whatever you think she's capable of, multiply that by the biggest number you can think of. That's why we had to cut off her hands. Pull her hard and get her away from here fast and everything will be okay. Are you ready?"

Brian looked like he was about to pass out. He wasn't ready. The bags under his eyes had darkened at least two shades since we'd been out here. The overhead light from the lampposts wasn't helping his cause. He nodded.

The bruja looked limp between them. The stumps on her arms reminded me of El Milagrito. The hand around my heart squeezed harder.

"Cuando estés listo, Manuel..."

"Agárralo fuerte," said Manuel. I grabbed the man's arm tighter, using my forearms to hold his bent arm against my body while keeping my leaning stance in case he tried to push me away. His elbow dug into the bottom of my sternum.

Manuel did a strange sideways squat and finally put the weapon down. Then he reached back and pulled out a large black folding knife and flicked the blade out with his thumb. When it clicked into place, the man we were holding started bucking like an angry horse. The elbow dug deeper into me and a foot smashed against my shin, but I held on. I lowered my body, widened my stance, and dug my shoulder into his jerking torso. Instead of trying to get him under control, Manuel gripped the blade in his fist and threw his arm back. His fist flew over to my side and jammed the knife into the man's stomach right above his jeans. He stabbed him so hard I heard the skin pop.

Manuel dug the blade deeper into his belly so that only the handle was visible. The man howled behind the tape, his legs kicking around. We were almost holding him in the air. Manuel dragged the knife back toward him like a fisherman yanking his line back to set the hook. The man's skin ripped a few inches and then the blade stopped. Manuel pulled again. A gash opened in the man's lower stomach, revealing flesh, muscle, and the yellow fat that lined his insides. I turned away. The muffled screams rang from his skull. I was sure the tape was going to fly out at any moment.

Blood from the wound spilled down. His jeans sucked up most of it, quickly changing color in the process. The rest spilled onto the concrete in front of him, the grayness greedily soaking it up. Manuel let go of the man's arm. We stumbled a bit and I had to struggle to keep him up by myself. For a second I feared he was going to leave me alone with him, but Manuel got behind the man and wrapped his left arm around his neck. He brought his right arm around, the knife leading the way. He buried the blade almost in the same spot he had the first time and then pulled it across his lower belly.

Manuel sliced one more time and then pressed his body into the man and pulled back by the neck while thrusting his hips forward. It looked like he was fucking him from behind. With the air cut off, the screaming stopped. I let go as his body jerked back. Manuel's arms held him up and bent him backward. The place where Manuel had cut was now a deep, red chasm of flesh. Something pink was pushing out of the wound. A hundred impossible things flashed in my brain simultaneously. When the first pink snake popped out, my heart stopped. Then I realized it wasn't an alien or a demon—the pink stuff was the man's intestines.

The man bowed forward. Then Manuel pushed and pulled again, yanking with his arm and thrusting his hips into the man's lower back. Shiny rosy coils speckled with blood burst out of the man's body, uncurled while tumbling down his legs, and plopped into the filthy water.

An explosion of teeth and green scales erupted out of the water. The crocs clamped down on the pink cords and spun around, splashing water and pulling more guts out of the man.

"¡Ayúdame a detenerlo, güey!" yelled Manuel. Of course. He couldn't hold the man, not while the crocs were pulling at his innards, trying to yank him into the water. I held the man's arm. His body was shaking but there was no way he was still alive.

Every time the crocs' jaws snapped shut, it sounded like someone hitting hollow wood with a hammer. Their teeth were incredibly white under the lights, the inside of their mouths a soft pink that was almost white and seemed not to belong anywhere near such a deadly, dirty place.

Snot ran down the tape covering the man's mouth and his eyes were rolled back. The splashing beneath us continued. Something was clutching my lungs and pushing the air out of me. Inhaling was hard. The smell of blood, stagnant water, and shit crawled up my nose. My throat tightened. I forced myself to look away and not gag.

"Ya, güey, jálalo."

Manuel and I pulled the man back toward the stairs. His feet dragged. His entrails stretched. A croc was pulling at a long, pink rope that poked out of the wound all the way to the water. The thing stretched and refused to break. We pulled harder. The croc shook its massive head like an ancient, green, scornful god. The intestine broke. We felt it give with a snap. My heart traveled to my throat and pounded the sides of my neck like a trapped animal hurtling itself against a cage.

We navigated the metal stairs and placed the dead man on the floor. I stepped back, feeling wobbly. Behind me, the splashing continued. The crocs were fighting for scraps.

The man's lower abdomen had caved in. Chunks of... something were poking through the stretched slit. Blood was spilling slowly from the wound. The front of his pants was entirely black.

Brian and Raulito showed up. They lowered the woman next to the man. Manuel reached down and ripped the tape off his mouth. Blood had pooled in there, some from his wounds and some probably from his stifled screams, the panic and hopelessness that had scratched at his throat.

The woman looked like she was about to collapse on top of the man. Her bent body swayed. Her limp arms hung at her sides. Then she jerked her head up. Her back was to the lights, which obscured her face and made her empty eye sockets look like black holes. Her nostrils flared. Don Vázquez appeared next to her. He bent down and got close to her face.

"Es hora de comer, Gloria. Chúpale el alma."

Don Vázquez placed his left hand on the back of the bruja's head and pushed her down. She fell forward, swinging her arms. At her touch, the dead man's chest rose. She lowered her head even more and started sniffing the man's neck like a dog as the man vibrated like he was running a high fever. She sniffed her way to his lips. Then she opened her toothless maw and placed it on the man's bloody mouth.

I was sure the man was dead, he had to be, but his legs started bucking as soon as the woman pressed her mouth to his. The slash in his belly flapped like thin lips. The woman stayed where she was.

A voice whispered something next to my left ear. I turned. No one was there. Then I heard the voice again. It sounded like a word was flying around me, the voice that uttered it an invisible insect floating around us.

The man stopped moving. The woman removed her mouth from his. She stood up with an unnatural movement, like a limp doll shot up by coiled springs hidden underneath it. A long, powerful hiss erupted from her bloodstained lips. The voice in the air multiplied into unintelligible hisses. Then a soft voice joined them, whispering words in a language I'd never heard. The voices intensified while the old woman's hiss continued. Brian looked around, confusion fighting panic on his face. That meant it wasn't just me who could hear the voices.

"Agárrenla bien," Don Vázquez said, his voice unperturbed.

Raulito stepped forward and clamped his hands around the woman's left bicep. A second later, Brian did the same on the other side. Together, they pulled the woman back.

Her body twisted; her legs kicked out. Her face had contorted into a mask of anger. When the black holes where her eyes should have been landed on me, something cold pressed against the back of my neck.

Don Vázquez stepped forward and gripped the woman's shaking head.

"Gloria," he said. The woman carried on. Don Vázquez squeezed her head, the muscles in his forearms tensing under his ochre skin, veins snaking under the thin skin covering the back of his hands.

"Gloria, escúchame."

Don Vázquez's words weren't getting through to her. She opened her mouth again, the lower jaw distending like a snake's. At the back of her throat, the thick purplish stub of her severed tongue vibrated in a silent scream. I turned my head. On the street across the fence, the black figure under the streetlight was solidifying a bit. Judging by the nearby cars, it stood about four feet tall. Its inky blackness seemed to soak up light.

A sound like the wet, phlegmy grunt of a wounded creature erupted from Gloria's mouth. It snapped me back into the situation in front of me. The guttural sound lingered, the shape of it in my ears not matching the shape of her mouth. The disagreement reminded me of dubbed movies.

Don Vázquez had pulled out a gun at some point, a blocky thing with a short muzzle. He had it pressed against Gloria's forehead. "Ya córtale, pendeja. Te necesito aquí, Gloria. Un favorcito más y te mando de vuelta a tu recámara."

Gloria hissed again, but this time it was the sound of something deflating, the expulsion of air of someone who's letting go. The other sounds I'd heard had quieted.

A vein in Brian's neck pulsed under the strain of holding Gloria. Both men were struggling. Seeing her like that, her body a mass of wiry muscles and rage, the lack of teeth and severed hands made sense. Gloria wasn't human. If Don Vázquez needed two men to control her without hands or teeth, I could only imagine what she'd be able to do with ten fingers and nails—or talons—at the end of each digit.

Without moving the gun, Don Vázquez reached into the front pocket of his guayabera and pulled out the wrapped toe.

"Así me gusta, tranquilita. Ahora escúchame bien. Estos muchachos"—he moved the gun and pointed at Brian, me, and then Juanca—"necesitan protección. Aquí tengo un pedazo de El Milagrito. Te lo voy a dar para que hagas lo que tienes que hacer."

At some point I had stopped having expectations or trying to guess what was going to happen next, but watching Don Vázquez unwrap the toe and carefully place it in Gloria's mouth caught me by surprise.

The moment Gloria closed her mouth, the inside of her eye sockets became strangely luminescent, emitting a faint pinkish light that reminded me of the bizarre fish that live at the bottom of the ocean and produce their own light. Her body began convulsing.

"Dude, what the fuck?"

Brian let go of Gloria and took a step back. His voice was a few octaves higher than normal.

"Agárrala, pendejo," said Raulito.

"Her feet, man," said Brian, ignoring the order. "Look at her fucking feet!"

Gloria wasn't levitating, but the balls of her feet, which were whiter than I expected and covered in thin blue veins, weren't touching the ground. Her toes caressed the dirt without effort as if her body was being held by someone. My mind went back to the parking lot at the bar, my dead neighbor floating next to my car, his face gone . . .

"Hold her. Now. We have to keep her under control."

Don Vázquez's voice, the undeniable authority it carried, broke through to Brian. He latched on to her arm again, his lips mouthing something I couldn't make out.

While Gloria twitched, I heard the rumble of a motor behind us. Headlights came our way and then turned. A black F-150 circled the pool, stopped, and then backed up toward us.

Violent gagging made me turn back.

More than vomit, what came from Gloria's mouth when she opened it resembled solidified smoke. It was thick and somewhere between white and gray. Instead of dropping like a liquid, it floated in front of her face the way liquid floats in zero gravity. It poured from her mouth and made a roundish form in the air.

When the last of the floating goo left Gloria's mouth, her body crumpled. It seemed to take Brian and Raulito by surprise because they jerked their arms to keep her standing. A second later, the gray blob that had been floating in front of her face dropped to the dirt, as if it had somehow morphed into a liquid. It splashed Gloria's feet and made a small gelatinous puddle.

There was no sign of the toe.

CHAPTER 22

Manuel knelt next to the dead man. He hooked his thumb on the open flesh and pulled the wound open. He stuck his hand in the man's stomach and dug around a bit before dipping his knife into the wound. His hand came down twice.

"He's fucking dead already, man," said Brian. "What else are you gonna do to him? What the fuck is this all about?"

Manuel moved his hands a bit more and then cut again. His hands emerged from the gaping flesh. The right one held the knife. The left one held something round and pink with something lighter attached to it. He held it up to show Don Vázquez. It had a tube at one end. It was the man's stomach.

"Now the—"

Brian ran four or five feet, bent forward, and vomited. He placed his hands on his knees and dry heaved.

Don Vázquez stared at him for a moment before carrying on. "He's ready."

Manuel turned and flung the stomach into the croc pit. It landed with a splash. A commotion ensued and water exploded into the air. The dinosaurs from Louisiana were enjoying one last snack, their clacking jaws a symphony of death.

"Pónganlo en la caja," Don Vázquez said.

* * *

A door slammed behind us.

"Aquí le traje la jaulita pa'l amigo, jefe."

A woman was standing next to the back of the truck. She was about five feet tall, but almost as stocky as the man we'd seen at the door. Her head was shaved on the right side of her head and all her long black hair fell over the left side, covering her shoulder, just like the first bartender we'd seen. She wore tight jeans and a sleeveless black T-shirt that showed her muscular arms. The ink on them wasn't clear in the scant light, but her collection reminded me of Juanca's.

In the bed of the pickup there was a metallic crate, the kind used for large tools.

"Juanca, help Manuel with Rodolfo," Don Vázquez said.

Juanca grabbed the man's arms. Manuel grabbed his legs. They lifted him up. His stomach collapsed, the flaccid meat dropping into the empty hole of his lower torso. They brought the body over doing that odd walk people do when carrying something heavy and unwieldy. They heaved the body onto the bed of the truck and then climbed onto the bed and grabbed it again. When they reached the box, the woman in black opened the door and the man dropped into the box with a loud thud.

She let the metallic door clang shut, slid the bolt into place, slipped the padlock through the holes in the two pieces of metal, and locked it tight.

The woman told Juanca the key was in the ignition.

While the men talked, Brian came over. He looked sick and kept trying to spit the taste of vomit out of his mouth. The knot between his eyebrows was shiny with sweat. His skin was paler than usual. Darkness had crept into the bags under his eyes, which were teary and bloodshot from vomiting.

"You okay, B?"

"No, man, I'm not okay. This is . . . whatever comes after absolutely fucked-up. We need to get the fuck out of here. Like, now. Please."

As if on cue, Juanca walked to the car, turned it on, and turned on the AC, all without getting in.

Don Vázquez came up to us. Juanca joined him.

"Your brother would be proud of you. Make sure they see Rodolfo."

Juanca lowered his head. Don Vázquez turned to us, his large, grandfatherly mustache curled up in a smile.

"Let's do you first."

Don Vázquez moved a couple steps back and stood next to the puddle of whatever had come from Gloria's mouth. Juanca stepped forward. Don Vázquez bent down, stuck his thumb in the puddle, and stood up again. He brought his hand up and ran his finger across Juanca's forehead. Juanca closed his eyes. Don Vázquez bent down again.

"Your turn, Mario."

I didn't know what that liquid was, but I knew I had seen it coming from Gloria's mouth, and that I didn't want it anywhere near my face. Despite my own wishes, I stepped forward.

Don Vázquez's slimy finger touched my forehead. The gray gunk was colder than I expected. Then I was falling backward. My arms shot up. My eyes closed by themselves. Something cold expanded in the center of my chest, simultaneously emptying everything inside me and filling me up.

I felt weightless. A light exploded in front of me. It was so bright that it burned away my eyelids and entered my head, wrapping around my brain until cold whiteness was everything.

When my eyes flew open again, the light was gone.

In front of me, Don Vázquez ran his finger across Brian's

forehead. Brian's eyes closed for a second. His arms jerked like he had bumped against something. His eyes opened quickly. He drew a breath and looked around. I knew he'd experienced something.

"Gentlemen, you are now under the watchful eye of... I guess you can call him the Holy Spirit, yes? If all goes well, you'll just open the door, watch the action, and then collect the money. Easy, right? If you do something stupid and it fucks everything up, I will come looking for you, and I always find the people I look for, is that clear?"

We nodded. His smile hadn't wavered, even when he was threatening to kill us if we fucked up. The thing under his skin moved again, this time only on the right side of his face. Juanca said he'd make sure they saw Rodolfo's face. They hugged again. Don Vázquez shook our hands briefly and then walked away. As his men were lifting Gloria up, he turned back to us.

"You'll be safe for a while, but I suggest you move quickly. I'm sure even angels get tired of waiting around."

CHAPTER 23

J uanca jumped in the driver's side and I rode shotgun. Brian, again, got in the back and immediately curled into himself.

The truck's lights illuminated the empty space in front of us, but we could see a gate at the back of the property. The woman had left it open. As we started moving forward, I looked out at the pool one last time. Then I remembered the shadowy figure and glanced toward the street outside. The figure was still there, more solid than before and closer to the fence. It was definitely humanoid in shape. It seemed to be watching us.

We drove by a cement building and I lost sight of the figure. A part of my brain wanted to dig deeper, to go where the figure was and get some answers, to get...something. But like Vázquez said, it probably wasn't something I'd ever understand. We'd had enough with the long night behind us and the disemboweled body in the back of the truck.

The darkness in the streets seemed deeper now, like the absence of light was trying to hide something other than the day. We drove down a few streets lined with houses and accentuated by an occasional bar or club. Juanca turned on the radio. The car's speakers were new. Strident accordion wails filled the car for a while.

"What did he do?" asked Brian after a few minutes.

"What are you talking about?"

"The dead guy in the back. What did he do to deserve that? Why not just...I don't know, shoot the bastard in the head or something. I'm never gonna be able to get his eyes outta my head. I thought they were going to pop out of his skull. And his...fucking...pink innards, man. Why? Why do that to him?"

I wanted to be somewhere else, so I looked at the dark buildings and occasional neon signs and thought about mi angelito.

Anita had a huge plastic boat she loved to play with. It opened down the middle and had little cabins and a cockpit with a tiny brown steering wheel. When money was tighter than usual, I'd take her to Savers and let her pick whatever she wanted. Most times she went for a bag of random toys, but the boat was love at first sight. It took on water and never floated straight, but she played with it for hours. What she didn't know was that it broke my heart to see her so happy with a chunk of plastic I'd paid four bucks for. I wanted to buy her the world. I wanted to buy her all the toys and then a bigger house to keep them in. I never did any of that, and that shit still hurt. It was a failure that would haunt me forever. But maybe I could make up for it. Maybe Melisa and I could have another kid, fill a new house with laughter and kisses and toys. I would buy that kid whatever he or she wanted. I would get Anita's face tattooed over my heart. Promises aren't worth shit, but I still promised myself I'd do everything in my power to make all of that happen.

My thoughts had made me lose track of time, but when Juanca spoke it startled me, so I knew he'd been quiet for a while. Brian's questions had probably hung in the air for that time, making things awkward again.

"You gringos just don't understand."

"We just watched a man getting disemboweled and then

having his guts pulled out and eaten by crocs, man! What the fuck am I missing here? You want a motherfucker dead, you grab a fucking gun and shoot him. Done deal. Not personal enough for you? Stab him. Grab a big knife and stab him in the liver or something and he'll bleed out in a couple minutes. Or you can stab him a hundred times while looking him in the eye if you really want to show him how much you hate him. Easy. What we saw today? That was something else. And whatever the fuck that old lady was doing isn't right. I'm not even sure I want to know about all that."

"You know what, Brian? I really think you need to shut the fuck up," Juanca said. "You signed up for this because you want the lana, right? I get that, you know what I'm saying? Estamos todos chingados. We're all in the same boat. But you have to understand that this isn't your world. We have to send a message when we kill someone here. That backstabbing asshole in the back? He's one of the men who killed my brother, okay? We got him, we got the information we needed from him, we gave him the death he deserved, and now he'll never rest in peace. Fuck him. You think there's a lot of violence around here? You don't even want to imagine what it would be like if we didn't send messages."

"Never rest in peace? What if we get pulled over and they search the back? What the fuck are we even supposed to do with the body?" asked Brian.

"I'll tell you soon enough," replied Juanca.

There it was. *Sending a message.* Vengeance. Not knowing had made me uncomfortable because it meant that the big question mark ahead of us tomorrow had a bunch of little question marks attached to it like pulsating tumors.

"Killing is killing, man," said Brian. He sounded defeated, out of his element, sad. Whatever his relationship to Juanca had been before this, it had morphed into something ugly. "I think you send a pretty strong message when you send someone to meet their maker. The rest is just, I don't know, theatrics. Anyway, can we get something to eat? I'm starving."

"Must be all that vomiting you did back there," said Juanca. I knew it stung. The lack of a reply was a good measure of just how much. Men often complain about women because they know how to hurt us with words. We do the same. I think the only reason we complain about women is because they do it better.

After a minute, Brian spoke again.

"I'm feeling like this whole fucking thing is hopeless and I don't know why," he said.

"When was the last time you smoked ice?"

"Before we left my house."

"Your brain is telling you things, man. It might show you some things too. Weird shit. Monsters and all that. Stay cool. We'll get you something to eat soon and then I'll get you something to help with the quitting once we get home."

"Yeah, that must be it. Must also be why I want to eat a fucking bullet right now more than I've ever wanted to in my life."

He was looking out the window. There was no trace of a smile in his face. He was being honest. Venting. He wanted to kill himself. This wasn't the face of a man about to blow his friend's brains out. I never should have let Juanca get in my head.

"Stay cool, B," I said. "We'll be done in a day, back home in two. You're gonna be a rich man soon. And the withdrawal won't last forever. Just think about how damn happy Steph is going to be when you tell her you're clean."

Brian made a sound that was somewhere between a cough and a grunt. I let him be. The battle in his head had nothing to do with us.

We kept our mouths shut after that. The silence in the cabin was masked by the music coming from the radio, but there was nothing to cover the tension. When you throw people together, their personalities crash. The carnage coming from that crash depends on many variables, and added stress is a huge factor. So is fear. We were a ticking time bomb. If we stopped by the side of the road to take a leak and Juanca shot Brian, or vice versa, I wouldn't be surprised. I thought about what Juanca had told me at the barbecue joint when Brian was in the bathroom. The tiny voice in my head kept repeating the same thing over and over again: *Never trust a junkie, pendejo. Never trust a junkie, pendejo. Never trust a junkie, pendejo.*

CHAPTER 24

I lost track of where we were. At some point, instead of turning right and heading back to the church, or where I was pretty sure the church was, Juanca took a different exit and started driving down a smaller road. The space between houses became bigger and businesses disappeared. The area was sparsely populated.

Once you leave the center of the city, Juárez withers away and then comes to an abrupt end before you hit an area that, according to some signs, is near Mount Cristo Rey. If you're there, you're basically a stone's throw away from El Paso.

Enveloped in darkness, we hung a tight left onto an unlit dirt road. Juanca flicked on the long lights and drove on. There was nothing out there. A couple miles later, a trio of garages surrounded by stacks of old tires and mounds of scrap metal came into view in front of our headlights. A hand-painted white sign at the top of it said GARAGE CARLOS in blocky blue letters.

Juanca slowed down but didn't stop. We approached the building in the middle. It had double garage doors in front of it. Juanca flipped the visor down. There was a black garage door remote there. He pressed it and the door on the right started to rise. No light came on.

Light from our headlights crept into the cavernous blackness that appeared behind the door, illuminating rusty jacks and jack stands, a gigantic red compressor, a few benches, two lifts, and a bunch of tools and tall toolboxes pressed against the walls. As we pulled in, Juanca kept looking around, circling between every window and the rearview mirrors.

The interior of the garage looked as greasy, oily, and cramped as every other garage I'd ever seen. Two yellow lifts took up most of the space in the center of the garage. However, there was a huge space behind the lifts that was entirely empty. Juanca slowly drove around the lifts and parked there. He pressed the remote again. An overhead motor hummed and the door rolled back down.

"What are we doing here, man?" asked Brian. He shifted around in the back seat. His head popped up between the front seats.

"First thing we're gonna do is wait. We wanna make sure we're completely alone."

When the garage door closed, Juanca rolled down the windows and switched off the engine.

Darkness swallowed everything; our eyes adjusted. Other items in the garage became visible, slowly emerging from the gloom like apparitions. I thought about the shadowy figure I'd seen while we were in the back of El Imperio and wished my pupils would dilate faster.

Juanca opened his door and stepped out of the truck. I did the same. Juanca was looking around and stretching.

I looked down. The floor of the garage looked like the gray, dirty floor of a garage. Then I looked around. There was a thin black line about six feet from me. It was too straight to be a crack.

"So the truck is already where it needs to be, and now we . . . take a ride down?"

"You're pretty proud of yourself for figuring that out." Juanca almost smiled.

We walked back to the truck.

As I approached my door, Juanca told me to stop.

"The switch is on your side. On top of the toolbox there."

He got in the truck. It roared to life. I went over to the toolbox and pressed the large button on the wall. Something large clanked under the floor and the hiss of a hydraulic system followed. The ground beneath the truck shook and began to descend. I walked back to the truck and climbed in.

Our descent was smoother than I expected. It also felt longer than I thought it would.

We were going into the earth with a dead man in a metallic box. Who knew what other shit this tunnel would throw at us. That would be weird enough, but there was more at stake, and we all knew we were far from done.

The bottom of the lights suddenly vanished into the dark. The wall of dirt in front of us finally gave way to the entrance of a tunnel. It was big enough for the truck, which made the previous tunnel we'd used look ridiculously small in comparison. This one was impressive. They had dug into the soil and rock and then installed lifts to take cars up and down, all to traffic drugs. I wondered how long it had taken and what the cost had been. Brian was apparently thinking the same thing.

"How the hell did they build this?" he asked.

"Money, B," said Juanca. "Money is why you're here, right? With enough money you can do whatever you want. Hielo paid for all of this. Don Vázquez even brought in some lady from the University of Texas to help him make sure the whole thing wouldn't collapse on our heads. It took a while, but they got it done. There are some bigger ones here and there. I know of one in California that can fit two cars at once, but this one is one of the best in Texas."

The platform shuddered to a stop. Juanca switched to drive and released the brake. The truck crept forward. We bounced as the front wheels abandoned the platform and landed on the ground. We bounced again when the back wheels did the same.

We were in the tunnel. It felt like we'd accomplished something. Ahead of us, the headlights bathed the dirt walls and reached into the darkness before dissolving into nothing. Beyond them, the tunnel was a stolen chunk of starless night.

Juanca told me to get out and find the switch attached to a cable near the left side of the lift. I squeezed out of the truck and used my phone's flashlight to find it and press it before going back to the truck, the lift humming back up behind me.

We drove slowly into the darkness. Occasionally the lights would show us strange, ragged holes dug into the sides of the tunnel. I tried to push the screech from the previous tunnel down into a shadowy corner of my brain. It was a useless exercise.

Juanca leaned forward on top of the steering wheel, his eyes glued to the illuminated dirt ahead. He was squinting a bit, trying to see into the darkness beyond the lights.

"Fuck!" he yelled as he stomped on the brakes.

My hands flew up and slapped the dash. Brian thumped against the back of my seat.

In front of us, lit by the top half of the headlights, two skinny gray legs coated in something slick and shiny quickly retreated into the darkness.

A second *fuck* erupted from the back seat.

A jarring screech followed, reaching us through the closed windows and the hum of the AC.

"Did you see that? Did you fucking see that thing? What the fuck was that?" Brian's breathing bordered on hyperventilation. Mine didn't, but the hand that had wrapped itself around the nape of my neck as I watched a man be disemboweled came back so quickly, I heard a slap.

"Pinche hijueputa criatura . . . I'm gonna kill that sumbitch!"

"Was that . . . was that one of those things you were telling us about back at your place?"

"Yeah, B, it was."

"Should we . . . go back? Should we get the fuck outta here?"

"Nah, we'll just give it a minute, give it time to find a hole and get lost."

"Find a hole? You mean it will go away by itself?"

"Yeah, they usually do. Hopefully it was alone."

"Hopefully? What if it wasn't?"

Juanca didn't answer.

"Juanca, what if that thing wasn't alone?"

"Well," he said under his breath, giving the truck some gas and rolling us forward.

CHAPTER 25

W

e crawled forward. The light ahead of us unveiled a few inches at a time. If the drive from San Antonio to El Paso often turns into the same mile again and again, the drive in this tunnel was the same infernal chunk of earth again and again. The only difference was that, instead of trees or dilapidated barns, the tunnel had holes that made me shiver with the possibility of what they contained, and occasional spots on the dirt walls where strange, somewhat luminescent mold grew. We scoured the space they exposed like our lives depended on it. Under any other circumstances, I would have explored the stuff on the walls or at least taken a picture with my phone, but these weren't normal circumstances.

Juanca slammed on the brakes.

A thing was hunkered down in front of us; its gray head was down as if it had been sniffing the earth. It jerked its head up when the light hit it. Huge white eyes with no pupils looked at us. The mouth was a nightmare of protruding teeth. They looked like yellow fangs and glistened under our light. The creature stood, its head vanishing again, its legs two ropy wet things that made me think of a malnourished dog. The screech made us jump.

"Fuuuck!" cried Brian.

The thing moved forward. The rest of its body was slowly revealed as it walked toward the car and more light fell on it. It had no discernible sex. A gray paunch sat under an emaciated set of ribs that were much longer than human ribs. Its muscular arms hung forward as if it was used to walking using its arms as well as its legs.

"Put this fucking thing in rev—"

CLANK.

The truck rocked a bit. Juanca smashed his hand on the horn and the sound erupted from under the hood. The creature recoiled, screeched again, and then jumped on the hood.

"Shit, that didn't work!"

Juanca started lowering his window.

"What the fuck are you doing, man?!"

Instead of answering, Juanca switched the gun to his left hand and stuck it out the window. He angled the gun and squeezed off a shot. It missed the creature. The angle was wrong. I lowered my window.

"What the fuck," Brian yelled from the back. "Roll the window back up. It's going to crawl in here!"

I pushed my head and shoulder out and aimed. I pulled the trigger. The shot hit the creature in the shoulder. It screeched again.

A liquid the color and consistency of used oil poured from the hole in the thing's shoulder. Its muscular arm trembled. It slid forward on one arm, its face closer to us, the hole full of jagged teeth about two feet from my face. Juanca shot at it again. His angle was better this time. It was also better than mine. The left side of the creature's head exploded in a mixture of gray and pink. The creature fell to the side and then jerked sideways, falling off the hood and plunging into the dark.

CLANK. CLANK. CLANK. The sound came from behind, though.

"Mario, get in," Brian yelled. I slid down into the car as fast as I could and closed the window. If there were more of them, the glass panes probably wouldn't hold, but I didn't want to serve myself up on a platter either.

I looked back toward Brian with a nod.

"It's the fucking box. It's moving. I think that thing is trying to grab it!" yelled Brian.

The truck surged forward. We heard what I'm sure were claws digging into the plastic of the truck's bed, but the box was still there. A few seconds later, another screech came from behind us. Juanca accelerated a bit more till we were cruising, but for the rest of the ride, all I could think of was getting the hell out of that tunnel and away from the strange creatures and their damn yellow teeth.

"How much longer, man? I hate being down here with those things."

"Yeah, I love it down here, man," said Juanca. "Just shut the fuck up. We should be at the platform soon."

The soil beneath our wheels crunched from time to time. Pebbles occasionally made a different sound. Nothing else showed up. No more creatures or bloodcurdling shrieks. However, those gray legs, white eyes, and sharp teeth were never far from our thoughts.

The ramp we finally came to looked just like the one we'd used to descend into the tunnel. Juanca brought the truck onto it and told Brian to activate the lift and get back in the car.

"Fuck that! I'm not leaving this car. Those things are out there," said Brian.

He had a point. I opened my mouth to argue but then thought each wasted second could bring those things closer. Gun in hand, I threw the door open and ran to activate the lift and get my ass back in the truck.

As we left the darkness below, our headlights again came

to an abrupt stop on the exposed soil a few inches in front of the grill.

The darkness around us morphed into something different, less solid. It went from impenetrable to something akin to pre-dawn, when the density of darkness magically attenuates as if fearing the coming light. As we got closer to the end of our ride, it became obvious that someone had left a light on for us.

Finally, earth gave way to a garage similar to the one we'd left, and for a second I feared we had somehow driven in a circle and were still on the outskirts of Juárez with a disemboweled corpse stuffed in a metallic box and nowhere to go except back into the rabid ground. I wished the corpse part wasn't accurate.

The platform rattled to a stop. The hydraulic system hissed like an angry dragon. Around us, grimy garage equipment covered every inch of the place except for the area surrounding the platform. It was a smaller space than the one we'd used on the other side. This one had a single lift and a few drums of used oil pushed against a corner. Photos of women in skimpy bikinis covered the walls. Some had tattoos and tiny neon triangles of cloth that spoke of our times, but others wore larger pieces and had hairdos that were at least a couple decades old. The mix was jarring.

"Now we get some tacos, or what?"

Juanca sighed. "Yeah," he said. The anger had left Juanca's voice. The tone reminded me of the tone I'd used with Anita here and there whenever she wanted to play the same game over and over again or when she wanted me to play with her while I was answering emails, trying to watch a movie, reading something on my phone, or wasting time on social media. Every second I hadn't spent with her was now a tiny, angry ghost pummeling at my heart.

"Yeah, B," Juanca said again. "Now we get out of here and get those tacos."

CHAPTER 26

Brian was still pushing trash into the taco bag when we turned onto Juanca's street.

Instead of parking outside, Juanca told me to open the gate for him and he pulled up in reverse. That way the bed of the pickup would be hidden from passersby.

Once we were inside the house, Juanca vanished into the hallway and came back with towels.

"There's only one bathroom. Don't make a fucking mess in there or my amá will get mad. No se orinen en el pinche piso. Take turns and shower. I'll bring some shit so you can set up the sofa for you two. I suggest you get some rest."

"You expect me to get some sleep after the shit we've seen, man?"

Brian had always been somewhat of a jokester. He was a junkie, sure, but a junkie with wit. Plus, the ice always gave him this uncontrollable energy. That was all gone now, replaced by fear and a strange attitude. He wanted the money, but he didn't know what level of fucked-up shit he had signed up for, and it was affecting him. His eyes were sunken and he looked even paler than he had that morning. The sheen covering his forehead was, much like his hunger and tiredness, a perpetual reminder of the chemical war raging in his system.

"Perfect, then. Take a shower. That sweat from going clean stinks. I have some Adderall if you want it. It can help you with that shit. Like I told you, we need you sharp. We can even cop some ice if you need some. Whatever it takes, just don't fuck this up."

"I just feel so damn tired all the time. Last time I smoked meth was . . . fuck, before we hit the road. Started feeling tired a couple hours after that. Now it's worse. It's like there's a fucking black cloud inside me and it's full of voices that keep reminding me about every single bad decision I've made in my life and then they tell me to kill myself. And I'm hungrier than ever."

"It's all good, man. Luego te va a doler la panza, güey. Te van a dar como calambres."

Brian looked at me. He seemed lost. Panza. Calambres. He needed a translation.

"Cramps," I said.

"Yeah, cramps," repeated Juanca. "The Adderall might help with all that, and your head will be clear for tomorrow. I'll get them to you later. Now take a fucking shower. You smell like a dog that slept in the rain."

Brian nodded, threw the towel over his shoulder, grabbed his backpack, and headed to the bathroom.

Juanca went into the kitchen. I sat on the sofa and pulled out my phone to scroll through Melisa's profile pics again. There was another text there, reminding me that my pain had a price tag on it and I still owed most of it. I ignored it and tapped my photo album.

Scrolling through the photos on my phone was too painful, but seeing Melisa's face brought me a strange mixture of hope and guilt.

The shower started running.

Nothing had changed. Melisa hadn't posted anything. I realized I wasn't really expecting her to post but kept checking because it was an excuse to see her face. I missed her. A lot. My guilt had become a rock that sat atop my chest at all times and became even heavier whenever I thought about her. What I'd done made me unworthy of forgiveness, unworthy of the love of the most important person in my life. Thinking about it made it hard to breathe. It also made me want to hurt myself for being such a fucking idiot.

Juanca returned and sat down next to me. I wanted to think about something else. The sounds at the back of the truck while we were in the tunnel came back to me.

"I wanna know why there's a body missing its guts sitting in the back of the truck as we speak. What are we supposed to do with it?"

"Podemos hablar de eso luego, Mario, pero ahora necesito hablarte de otra cosa," said Juanca. "Yo sé que estás solo y te sientes como la mierda, pero todo hombre debe tener el derecho a decidir si vive o muere si no ha hecho nada que amerite la muerte."

I know you're alone and you feel like shit, but every man should have the right to decide if he lives or dies if they haven't done anything that merits death.

He spoke quickly, his eyes digging into my pupils. I had no idea what he was talking about. He took a deep breath, his eyes still anchored to mine.

"Brian me dijo que te va a meter una bala en la cabeza mañana por la noche después de que terminemos el trabajo."

Brian told me he's going to put a bullet in your head tomorrow night after we're done with the job.

His voice bounced in my head, bloated with the promise of death, the stench of a gutted friendship, the sting of betrayal.

"You really think Brian is going to kill me? Because he seems more likely to turn the gun on himself right now. Cut the mind-game shit, man, so we can focus on tomorrow." Under normal circumstances my wording would have been stronger, but I couldn't get the images of all that I'd seen during the day out of my mind. Juanca was a sick fuck. I had no time for his games.

Juanca looked at the bathroom door, then back at me and laughed.

"El hijo de la chingada might even try to kill me. People go fucking crazy when there's money on the table, you know what I'm saying?"

He ran his hands down his thighs and sighed. "Así es todo en la vida."

He got up and started rummaging around inside a closet. I sat in silence, my thoughts moving around at the speed of light. I wanted to blend into the sofa and disappear, to travel back in time and go back to sitting in front of that crumbling sofa in Houston and throw rocks at the rats that scurried in and out from beneath it. I leaned back. The gun pressed against me. Its blocky shape was a comfort, a message, a premonition—it was the tiny hand of my angel telling me to stay alive just a little longer.

Juanca came back with some sheets and two pillows. He threw them on the sofa next to me.

"You two can take care of that later. Es un sofá cama. Si lo abren caben los dos." Juanca pulled his phone from his pocket and walked outside.

The water was still running. I looked at my phone and unlocked it. Without thinking, I tapped the photo gallery icon. I scrolled down fast three or four times, the pictures blurring into moving colors. Then I stopped.

There was a lot of blue. There was a gorgeous tree screaming in silent green against a cloudless sky. Next to that image was one of a large body of water and a tiny head poking up from it. I tapped on that one. Anita's face filled the screen. She was playing in a lake we'd taken her to a few months before she got sick. We spent hours collecting clamshells from the shore. Whenever she found an open one that still had the two halves attached, she moved it around in the air and called it a lake butterfly.

I zoomed in, using my fingers to make the photo bigger. Her smile was there, a genuine, beautiful thing untouched by the ugliness of the world. It broke me all over again. My eyes filled up. My vision got blurry. I blinked. Tears rolled down my face. My chest bounced once, twice—an animal caught in a trap. I put the phone down and grabbed my face. The tears kept coming. My lungs refused to work properly. I looked for the anger. It was a refuge. I couldn't find it. I wanted to hold my baby. I wanted to kiss my wife. I wanted to laugh at something, at anything. I wanted everything I'd had and lost.

Juanca came back in. I brought my head down and tried to control my breathing. A moment later I felt his hand on my shoulder. "Mira."

I couldn't make myself look up. His hand moved away, but some of its warmth remained, the soft breath of a lazy ghost.

I wiped my face with my hands.

"Bathroom's free." Juanca nodded toward Brian, who was drying his head with a towel.

"That shower gave me life, man. I'm feeling a bit better. You got cereal or something, Juanca?"

"Kitchen. Cereal is on top of the fridge. There's milk in there if you want some. Door next to the fridge is the pantry. Get whatever you want, just don't be noisy about it."

"Cool."

"You wanna jump in the shower or do you want me to go first?"

I wanted to wash my face, blow my nose. I wanted to do something, to move, to be away from Juanca and Brian. I wanted to be alone for a while.

"Nah, I'll jump in there. Then I can help Brian set the sofa up and we can try to get some rest."

I picked up my towel and then my backpack. The walk to the bathroom was short, but it felt like moving away from an entire world.

I got the water running and took off my jeans. They were dirty from the tunnels. The smell of earth came from them, reminding me where we'd been and what we'd seen, reminding me we would be going back down there soon. I rolled up the pants and sat on the toilet. A thousand showers with Melisa came back. Some were great. Sexy encounters with a dash of humor because she loved how making love in the shower always looked great in movies and it was nothing like that in real life. Some other showers were emotionally charged and contained tears. When Anita took a rare nap, we would often put her on our bed and shower together with the door open so we could talk while getting the shower out of the way. Every memory looked like a better place than where I was, including the arguments and accusations, the talk of money and critiques about my inability to find a better job despite being bilingual and smart. A shower with Melisa was a place I would do anything to get back to. No, it was a place I was doing everything to return to, and two hundred thousand dollars would give us enough of a running start. With that kind of money, we could stay in our new home for a bit and work on loving each other, on reconnecting, instead of having to worry about work and rent and utilities and the rest of the shit that becomes the dark, rotting core of your life when you don't have enough money to cover everything every damn month.

Possibility is a dangerous thing. It's almost as dangerous as hope. You start asking yourself what needs to be done so that the thing in your head, the thing invading you, becomes real. I knew Anita wouldn't come back. The days of wishing for the impossible were over. There is no time machine to undo death and bring someone back from the dead. But Melisa was alive. Maybe she was thinking about me in that very moment, remembering my hands on her back, her fingers washing my head after a rough day at work. Maybe there were enough pieces left of what I'd broken to start again. Money, an apology, and a promise to change could be the start of it, but I knew there needed to be something else, something huge, to make it happen, and I had no idea what that could be. A new place would be nice, but not enough. A new dream for us sounded great, but that could only come after. We were young and could try again, but that alone wouldn't cut it. We could make another miracle.

I wanted to make another miracle.

CHAPTER 27

B rian had pulled out the sofa and put the sheets on it by the time I came out of the bathroom. He sat on a corner of the sofa facing the TV, hunched over his phone.

A voice was coming from his phone. He said something that sounded like "Yep, I'll pick up the three ricks," but I couldn't really hear. A woman responded. He hung up. Probably Stephanie. Maybe he was trying to say "I love you" but couldn't because masculinity is weak like that and showing we love someone somehow makes us less manly. Or he could've been telling her the time was almost here; he would shoot me in the head and take my money so they could buy themselves and their baby a new life. In a way, I understood them.

"Think we'll be able to catch some shut-eye?" Brian asked.

"I'm sure as hell gonna try, man."

"I am too but . . . I don't know. Saw some shit today."

"We did."

"Buddy of mine told me a story once. He said he grew up in Hill Country. His grandparents were farm folk. They had a bunch of acres somewhere near Blanco. Anyway, he said there was a thing living in their barn, a strange creature with a big head and large black eyes that hid in the woods during the day and came into the barn to sleep or something at night. Now, my buddy, Jake, he didn't hit the bottle or nothing. He was a regular dude. I had no reason not to believe him. He always told the same story too. You know, liars usually tell a bunch of lies, but when someone always tells the same story, it's probably true..."

Brian took a deep breath. I had no idea where the story was going, but I was listening.

"Jake told me more than once how he refused to go out to the barn at night. One time his grandpa sent him out there to get some shit and he says he walked in and saw the thing in a corner, a long, humanoid creature. Spooked the shit outta him. He told his grandpa and the next day told his mom. They said he'd probably just seen a barn owl. Those things get pretty big out there. Plus, you know, he was a kid, it was dark, all that.

"Thing is Jake kept an eye out and saw the creature a few more times—you know, caught glimpses through the window at odd hours when waking up or going to the bathroom. When he saw it, the thing was always either leaving the barn or walking along the edge of the tree line behind it. It was always just a flash, a hint, you know? Like, enough to know it was there but not clear enough to actually know what the fuck it was. Jake's bedroom had a window and he could see the barn from it, so he became obsessed, staying up at all hours of the night trying to get a better look at the damn thing that was living in the barn. He never got a good look at it. Instead he and his grandpa started finding mutilated animals out on their property and in the nearby woods. Cats, dogs, possums, raccoons, a few deer, you name it. Weird thing was no animal would scavenge the bodies, like they were poisoned or something. Jake tried to get his grandfather to listen but the old man just told him barn owls don't kill large dogs and that he should stop watching movies that were rotting his brain. I guess things stayed the same for a while, but then, on a night like any other, Jake was in bed and heard a sound like someone screaming far away. The sound woke him up and when he turned to look out the window, Jake saw the thing right outside his window. He said the head had no feathers and its toothless, round mouth was open. The thing saw Jake move and instead of vanishing, it slapped a hand on the glass. Not a paw or a talon, man, like, a fucking hand. Jake ran to his grandparents' bedroom and dragged them both to his room, but the thing was gone by the time they came in. Jake was so freaked-out about the thing somehow hovering right outside, peeking into his window, that he convinced his grandpa to grab his rifle and try to hunt the creature down. After a lot of bitching and moaning, his grandfather finally agreed. The next night, they waited by the window. They didn't see the damn creature. Jake said they should try again and his grandpa said no, but then they went out the next morning and found three dead chickens outside the chicken coop, their bodies torn to pieces by something that drank all their blood and, like, ate away at the soft bits. The dead chickens made Jake's grandpa angry, so he said all right, they'd spend one more night dozing off in front of the damn window. Well, around one in the morning they saw movement to the left of the barn. Something was exiting the woods and making its way to the barn. Jake's grandpa told Jake to wait inside the house and went out there with his rifle and a flashlight. According to Jake, he opened fire as soon as he walked into the damn barn. Then Jake heard the screeching sound from far away and then a second shot.

"Jake and his grandma ran out almost at the same time. They walked into the barn. There was blood on the floor and the rifle was there, slightly bent as if some giant had tried to break it, but they couldn't find Jake's grandpa at first. Finally, they called the cops and two guys came out to help them look. About half an hour later, one of the pigs had the brilliant idea of shining a light upward. That's when they found Jake's grandpa. The man had been attacked by something or someone and then that something or someone had pulled him all the way to an exposed beam near the roof of the barn. They had to get firefighters with big ladders to get the body down.

"Way Jake told the story, his grandpa's body had been viciously attacked. Someone had punched a hole through the left side of his body. He said you could see his ribs and lungs. There was also a large cut between his neck and shoulder that made the cops think some crazy killer with a machete was out there in the woods. Here's the kicker: they never found a weapon or anyone to pin the murder on. Jake kept the article that came out about it in the local newspaper in his wallet. It was short and vague as fuck, but it said the man had been 'viciously attacked by an unknown assailant.' That's fancy talk for seriously fucked-up, you know? I know it said that because Jake would show it to me all the time, or at least whenever we drank together."

Brian had started talking out of the blue and dropped that story on me. Then, just as abruptly, he went quiet. I had no idea what he was trying to say.

"Why are you telling me this story, B?"

"I . . . don't know, Mario. I guess I'm trying to say that I get it, that I accept sometimes weird shit happens, okay? But today was . . . it was a lot of it. Maybe too much. I believe Jake. I think there was something strange out there in the woods and it killed his grandpa. Maybe it was a deformed maniac or an alien. My guess would be an alien based on the descriptions. Anyway, the point is I accept that we live in a weird-ass world. Still, what we saw today . . . it makes me worry about what's gonna happen tomorrow. Something weird happened to me when Vázquez put that sludge on my forehead. I saw things. It felt like I was falling backward for a few minutes, but it all went down in, like, a second. And what the hell are we supposed to do with that damn body stuffed in that box in the back? I don't know, man. This is getting too creepy for me, but I know it's too late to back out and I need that money. I just want to do what we have to do tomorrow night and then get as far away from El Paso as possible."

Brian had been staring at a spot on the floor near the kitchen. He snapped out of it and looked at me. He was afraid. So was I.

However, I didn't want to let him know. Fear is often seen as weakness. This was not the time to be weak. I thought about what Juanca had said.

If Brian was planning to kill me, I didn't want him thinking it would be easy.

I sat on the opposite side of the bed and grabbed my phone. I wanted to do something so we could keep the conversation to a minimum. For all I knew the man sitting next to me, the man who would share that pullout sofa with me for the night, could be plotting to put a bullet in my head like I was trash, and yet he was telling me a story about a creature killing an old man in a barn because he was looking for . . . comfort? I had no idea.

I unlocked my phone. No texts reminding me of my debt. No new emails. No new notifications on Facebook. Melisa hadn't posted anything.

Juanca stepped out of his room carrying some clothes and went into the bathroom. I opened Google and thumbed a new tab open. I had about twenty of them already open. Some were news sites. Others were random things I'd clicked on or searched out of curiosity in the past few months. I started closing them. It was something to do. One would come into view as soon as I killed the previous one. I had apparently looked up the street value of meth at some point. I had no recollection of it. I closed that one and then the next one, which was an article about *irregardless* being recognized as a word. The moment I closed that one, another page appeared. It had a lot of text. At the top was a title from the past, words from a time in which I desperately wanted to understand what no one did: "Rising Rates of Acute Lymphoblastic Leukemia in Hispanic Children: Trends in Incidence from 1992 to 2011." Apparently I hadn't read the whole article. It was another unfinished thing from that time, another loose end. I didn't want to read it now, but the stuff I'd read about while desperately looking for answers, for a solution, came rushing back. I remembered not understanding most of what I'd read and being frustrated that no one had a clear answer for me when all I was asking for was a bit of hope.

I stared at the words on the screen. So much knowledge, so much research, and no one could save mi angelito. She was "a fascinating case." Death made her special. I didn't want her to be special. I wanted her to be like all the kids who went into remission. I wanted her to be boring and not a puzzle that defied the doctors and had them standing in front of us, looking lost and fishing for words that meant nothing and did nothing for Anita.

I remembered that all the articles I'd read had made me feel stupid. I didn't know what some of the words meant. As I stared at the screen, some of them popped up at me. What the fuck is *histologic*? What are *atopic conditions*? Ignorance is dangerous, but knowing takes time and effort, and that's something many of us don't have. Every hour I spent performing some menial task for minimum wage was wasted time I could've spent becoming a doctor. If I had been an oncologist or a researcher, maybe I could've saved Anita. Or maybe not. Maybe Melisa had gone out with that friend of hers, the one who teaches yoga and is always talking about veganism but smokes two packs a day. Maybe she had been too skinny. I remember she didn't want to gain too much weight during the pregnancy.

No. Blaming Melisa was stupid. It always had been. But I couldn't fight it because if it was her fault, then it wasn't mine. Guilt is a painful thing, and humans have a talent for finding ways of blaming things on others to steer clear of it.

I thought about texting Melisa. Not one of those long texts where you try to have an entire discussion, just one word: *Sorry*. Or, better yet, *Perdón*. We go back to our native tongue for important things. We return to our native tongue to speak of our mothers, the food of our childhood. We return to our native tongue to ask for forgiveness and to pray. I know Melisa would read a *Sorry* and understand it, maybe even accept it, but she would feel a *Perdón* in her heart.

I put my phone away. There would be time for texting her later. There would be time for rebuilding once I was home and not sitting a few feet away from a junkie desperate for money and a psychopath with a disemboweled corpse in his mother's house.

Outside, the night was pregnant with the possibility of the wretched earth, with secret agendas and promises of death, but they were all quiet, the way all things are before they actually arrive. I paid attention to what the silence was whispering to me.

CHAPTER 28

My body needed sleep, but my mind couldn't let go. The body in the back of the truck had me worried. Sending a message to avenge Juanca's brother's death was all well and good, but not if it got us killed. And I didn't like these mind games Juanca kept playing.

Brian tossed and turned for a few minutes and then his breathing changed. He had his right forearm over his eyes and his mouth open. His entire body relaxed into the lumpy foam of the pullout sofa. I thought about killing him.

He'd been one of the only people to come visit me after Anita's death. When all you do is work, friends drift away. Brian had been there. He'd offered me drugs and then jobs. In a way, he'd helped me.

But now maybe I was the only thing between him and a lot of money.

There were knives in the kitchen. It wouldn't have to be too big or even sharp. A serrated one would do the trick. I could slice his throat; he would gargle and thrash around, but it'd be over quickly, especially if I sliced hard enough to cut the jugular and carotid on both sides of his neck. How hard would that have to be? What would be the best angle? How much pressure would I have to apply? I had once read about how long it takes for someone to bleed to death and remembered the many things that affected that equation. I knew Brian would panic, which would work in my favor. I would also be severing important veins, which would make everything faster. I also remembered the word for bleeding to death: *exsanguination*. I had never used it, but I had learned it because being a brown guy with an accent is hard and knowing fancy words helps. Plus, *exsanguination* is a better word than *histologic*. Exsanguination sounds like a dark ritual or a death-metal band. Histologic sounds like the history of logic, and there is no logic in this world.

The idea of killing Brian slowly drifted away, pushed by thoughts of how much blood there would be to clean up after all was said and done. I didn't want Margarita to find a dead gringo in her living room.

I looked at the windows and wondered what it'd be like if I suddenly spotted a round face with big eyes looking at me. I wondered if the messages I'd been trying to ignore were also hidden in my own nightmares, waiting for me to see them and do something...or run in the opposite direction. I went through the recent visions that had stuck with me, the ones I'd had after Anita's death:

The ghost of my neighbor accosting me in a parking lot, his face covered in skin, his feet a few inches off the ground.

Anita, my sweet angel, hanging from a lamppost as some giant creature bellowed in the darkened sky behind her.

I stopped there. None of those gruesome images had anything to do with what I'd seen today.

I closed my eyes and pushed that darkness away, filling my head instead with the endless blue of the Caribbean. I thought about the ocean. I thought about my mother's smile, its fleeting presence disrupting everything around it with an explosion of energy and beauty. I thought about her two tattoos, two small fish, both on her left ankle, one next to the other. "Your brothers . . . or sisters," she told me once. "One got lost on the way here because my body was polluted. The other one was a tired little soul that wasn't ready to deal with the ugliness of the world, so its tiny heart never started beating." There, after words about death, after words about lost babies, a warm, sad smile. Then the words that kept me going in awful times: "But it was all worth it, mijo, porque después viniste tú."

My mother was a ghost that haunted me in life. In death, she was sometimes a memory so sweet it drowned out everything else, but other times she was a reminder of how addiction can turn angels into rotting demons.

I thought about the impossible green of El Yunque, where my abuela took me a few times. There were small worms that came out of the soil one time after it rained. They blew my mind. Knowing there was an entire universe under my feet was too much for my young brain. I spent weeks thinking about worms underneath the house and the street, worms under the tiny church in town and under the grocery store, their slick bodies burrowing, always burrowing.

Another time we found huge snails, their shells dark brown and as big as dessert plates. That day we had driven down to Loíza to see a carnival after a few hours of walking through the slippery paths of the rain forest. I must have been about ten years old then. We stood on a crowded sidewalk in Loíza and watched schoolkids my age play bomba and plena as they marched down the street, flags waving. Then came the adults, the powerful reverberation of drums a frenetic wall of sound that pushed their bodies forward. Finally, there were demons. Some were eight or ten feet tall, dressed in colorful garb. Their faces were multicolored and had horns sprouting from them in all directions, their beaks huge and menacing. Vejigantes. Fear gripped me. Demons danced and walked down the streets and people danced with them, celebrated their arrival. I asked my mother about them, hiding half of my body behind her with the pretext of my question. She yelled something about a celebration and someone killing Moors hundreds of years before. Then my abuela jumped in and said the vejigantes attacked people with a dry cow bladder full of seeds. Images of the horned demons slaughtering cattle in the middle of the night to remove their bladders filled my brain. Before me, the towering demons danced, their flowing robes the opposite of their rigid horns. They scared me. The smiling faces around me made no sense, as if they were possessed. The drums were too loud, incessant, their sound a small, invisible hammer pounding my chest and ears.

A vejigante stopped in front of us. It was huge. Half of its face was red with white dots and the other half was blue with red dots. Three horns sprouted from each side of its head, the top ones curling toward the front like those of some mutated bull. Its elongated body moved from side to side. I was sure it was going to fall on top of me.

I heard a scream over the music, a harrowing sound that froze me in place. The vejigante leaned over. Something flashed in the sunlight. The vejigante's long arm came at me fast.

Even all these years later, my breathing became a ragged, wet thing as I thought about the vejigante swaying above me, its horns rippling like epileptic snakes.

The past is the present trapped in a perpetual echo.

The present is just an amalgamation of everything that preceded it, molded together with memory.

The future is the floating unknown that shifts between nothing and possibility, between death and new beginnings, between uncertainty and hope.

We are the knowing, insignificant fragments of flesh trapped in the space between all three, aware that every sentence we start is made up of a silent half waiting in the future and whatever we just said already an irretrievable chunk of the past.

I inhaled as deeply as I could and then exhaled, my breath shaky.

The darkness around was full of the tiny sounds of the night. An old AC rattled somewhere nearby. The fridge hummed. Once in a while, it birthed some ice cubes. Brian breathed. I stayed put, unmoving, my eyes closed.

Too much inside me was focused on the past. I was always in the past. I needed to see the future. I needed to vanish, to somehow shoot across miles of arid land and darkness and open my eyes in my own bed, away from the border and Brian and Juanca and the body in the back of the truck and Anita's screaming ghost and the fucking guilt about what I'd done to Melisa and whatever was waiting for us the following night. I wanted to sleep and to not dream and to wake up feeling like carrying on was the right decision. That's all.

Outside, an occasional car drove by, their sound like a large insect. Other than that, I was alone with my thoughts. None of them resembled anything I wanted to approach at that time and in that situation.

At some point, the hum of the fridge stopped and I lost the battle to sleep. Tomorrow would be full of death. I only had to make sure the death wasn't my own.

CHAPTER 29

The sound of Margarita coming out of her room woke me with a start. I reached for my phone. Almost noon.

"Buenos días," she said. "Nomás los molesto porque tengo hambre. Ustedes duermen como Juanito, igual que los osos." She said it without a smile.

I said good morning to her and she entered the kitchen. Something about that threw me off. I was expecting a bit more warmth from her. I needed it.

Few sounds in life are as comforting as an old woman preparing something in the kitchen. It always reminds me of my abuela. My mother never cooked, but our time in Puerto Rico was full of delicious home-cooked meals. That's when I learned sofrito is a miracle and that arroz con habichuelas is something your DNA makes you crave. My abuela would cook arroz con gandules, pollo asado, tostones, and other delicacies and then feed me until I couldn't breathe.

Margarita came out of the kitchen and pointed at Brian, who was still sleeping. "¿El señor come chilaquiles?"

"Si usted va a hacer chilaquiles, a mí no me importa lo que este coma, señora."

She smiled.

"Bueno, si no le gustan los chilaquiles puede comer cereal de ese que hay encima del refrigerador."

She turned and reentered the kitchen. A second later she came back out.

"Disculpe que le pregunte, señor . . . ¿usted perdió una hija?"

Did you lose a daughter?

My life had been reduced to a loss.

Margarita came over, her old feet barely leaving the ground. She wore the same robe from the night before. Her hair was now in a bun with no loose hairs poking out of it. Her face was wrinkled, but she looked fresh, rested.

"Quiero que sepa que Diosito tiene un lugar especial en el cielo para los padres de los angelitos que él se lleva antes de tiempo."

I want you to know God has a special place in heaven for the parents of the little angels he takes away before their time.

What do you say to that? How do you tell a sweet old woman that God is dead? Do you shake her and ask her if losing two sons to the streets isn't proof enough that we're nothing but godless animals slaughtering each other on our way to nothingness? I stayed silent. She took one more step and placed her hand on my head. She smelled like lavender and mothballs. The skin under her arm hung and shook like the short, thick wing of a peaceful bat. In front of my face, her other hand shook a bit, the spotted skin thin over big green veins and tendons.

Just like the previous night, something tightened in my chest. I was sure the time of tears had come and gone, but now random acts of kindness opened my wounds almost immediately and my heart pushed salt water into my eyes.

Margarita's hand lifted; its almost weightless presence stirred memories of my abuela touching my head, holding my hand. My mother tucking me in. Melisa's embrace. Anita's soft hand. An entire life shaped by women. Then my own hands, first picking up Anita, then shoving Melisa. I was oblivion. I shouldn't exist.

I looked up at Margarita's face and it blurred behind my tears. She gave me a nod and a sad smile. She understood how fresh my pain was, how deep. Her silence was comforting.

"Usted va a volver a ver a su hija. No esté triste."

You will see your daughter again. Don't be sad.

Margarita returned to the kitchen and then stopped. She turned around and spoke again, her voice much lower.

"Anoche tuve una visión mientras rezaba por ustedes."

Last night I had a vision while praying for all of you.

She stopped and looked at Brian. I did the same. His breathing was deep. His mouth hung open a bit. He was still knocked out.

"Ese hombre es avaricioso. Si usted se despista, él lo va a matar."

That man is greedy. If you don't pay attention, he will kill you.

Margarita shook a bit as a shiver visibly ran through her. Had she really had a vision of Brian killing me or had Juanca put her up to this? Too many coincidences often mean there is no coincidence at all.

"Cuídese," said Margarita. She turned and went back to the kitchen. I sat there in silence, wondering what the day would bring, worrying about my death and what I had to do to keep it from happening.

A few minutes later, Juanca stepped into the kitchen, dressed in a blue T-shirt and clean jeans. He had on cowboy boots and a big belt buckle shaped like Texas.

"Look at that lazy motherfucker." He chuckled, his thumb poking back toward the living room. "Yo, B, wake your ass up!" Brian just moaned in response.

"You get some rest, Mario?" Juanca asked.

"Not really."

"No worries; you're gonna sleep like a baby as soon as this is all over. Money makes for a hell of a pillow."

"What's the plan for today?"

"Plan is simple: First, we eat. Then we're gonna go see the dudes who are gonna keep an eye on things from afar tonight. They have some guns for Don Vázquez. We have to check them out before they put everything in the truck we're gonna use. Tonight's the night. We want to be there early and prepare everything, you know what I'm saying?"

I took a quick shower. Given how all of our pit stops so far had ended in blood, I wasn't particularly keen on adding another detour, especially when it involved guns. I threw on a black T-shirt and a clean pair of jeans.

By the time I came out of the bathroom, everyone was sitting down at the small table in the dining room. The chilaquiles had filled the house with a wonderful smell. I joined them and we ate in silence. Margarita could have opened her own restaurant. I told her so. She thanked me with a smile that reminded me we came from different worlds but inhabited the same loss.

Juanca wolfed down his food and then stood up and went to his bedroom. I had a feeling he didn't want to stick around and have us asking questions in front of his mom. I had no idea what was going on in his head, but whatever it was, he wanted to ponder it alone. Brian kept shoveling food into his mouth like a man eating his last meal. As far as I was concerned, it could very well be just that.

We talked while we finished, but my mind kept straying back to what Margarita had said. She was doing the dishes but would occasionally look over her shoulder at us.

"I'm going to feel much better when I'm back home with Steph and my nice green bricks." Brian stared off into space and sighed.

He patted his belly, letting out a belch before standing. "Muy delicioso," he called out to Margarita. She nodded at Brian but before she turned back she made eye contact with me. Her words from earlier came back to me.

Brian had said something to Stephanie about "three ricks," but I hadn't been able to hear anything else. Three ricks didn't mean shit to me. Then something clicked. Three bricks. Three hundred thousand dollars. Brian wasn't supposed to be taking home three bricks. Each of our cuts was two hundred K.

Fuck.

Si usted se despista, él lo va a matar.

A promise? A threat? An idea?

Si usted se despista, él lo va a matar.

A message from La Huesuda, telling me I had a chance to go with her now or to postpone our dance in the streets of the barrio that's on the dark side of the moon.

Si usted se despista, él lo va a matar.

An invitation to strike first, to make sure that fucking bullet stayed in the clip instead of blasting its way through my skull, ripping through memories of Anita and Melisa, of my mother and the beach, of miles on the road and hugs from good friends.

CHAPTER 30

We were on I-10 again almost immediately, heading northwest. Juanca said the men with the guns had a safe place where Texas met the New Mexico border.

"They set up a place that also operates as a granite supplier. Texas Stone Works. It's legit. Well, you know, sort of. It makes it easy for them to get as many trucks as they need and they also use it as an excuse to buy guns. You know, because they have to protect their business and land and all that. We're gonna get some guns from them and switch the box from this truck to the one they're gonna give us. It'll be a clean one with Texas plates. It'll be all prepped to carry the guns and will have some space for us to stash the money, probably under the back seat or something. They'll let us know."

"Are these dudes the sharpshooters you talked about back at my place?" asked Brian.

"They're dicks but it makes things easier, you know what I'm saying? They've found ways to not get too dirty and make a lot of money with minimal work and almost no risk. They have the New Mexico and El Paso cops in their pockets, so if one of their trucks that's involved in something shady gets caught, they can fake a report saying it'd been stolen. These cabrones have been doing this for a while. They're leeches, man. Pinches remoras. Between little gigs like this where they prep a car or shoot someone from afar and the gun stuff, they make a ton of lana."

We drove some more in silence, each of us thinking about the night ahead. I knew two things: I was going to keep my eyes open and I was going to kill Brian. Three bricks? Fuck him. He was a desperate junkie with a baby on the way. An extra hundred thousand dollars was too much temptation.

The funny thing was killing Brian didn't feel like killing a friend; it felt like making a move to stay alive. Our survival instinct doesn't care about the past; it only cares about keeping our blood inside our bodies. An extra hundred thousand for staying alive was a hell of a sweet bonus.

We stayed on the road for about half an hour and finally pulled up in front of a six-foot, solid wood fence that had nothing but brown hills on the other side of it. There was a huge white tarp with the name TEXAS STONE WORKS written on it hanging from a portion of the fence a bit farther down. Juanca pulled out his phone and sent a text. A few seconds later, the chunk of fence in front of us started sliding to the left and we drove in.

The dirt road dipped after about a quarter mile. A cropping of small white buildings came into view. One of them was clearly the front for the business. It was larger and whiter than the others and the top half of most of its front was made of glass. Slabs of granite of various colors could be seen inside. There were no cars parked outside. We drove past it and kept going to a few other buildings farther back. As we approached the last building, which looked like a dilapidated hangar with gigantic doors for digging equipment or something else that size, its door started going up. Juanca stopped the truck and waited. Then he rolled the truck into the building, parked, and killed the engine.

Two tall men were waiting for us on the other side of the door. They stood next to a desk covered with papers, a computer, and at least a dozen disposable coffee cups. Both were big and had beards. They reminded me of the men at the barbecue joint. The shorter of the two wore faded jeans, brown cowboy boots, and a black T-shirt with something on it. The other, who must have been at least six-three, wore blue jeans that looked new, black hiking boots, and a white T-shirt with nothing on it. He had bright blue eyes but they didn't look friendly.

We stepped out of the truck and walked to them. Juanca introduced us.

"Mario, Brian, these are Steve and Kevin."

The shorter man offered his hand. His shirt had a baldheaded humanoid figure with the side of its face all messed up. Underneath it, it read GEORGE A. ROMERO in small letters and then DAWN OF THE DEAD in big letters.

"I'm Steve," he said. "Y'all can call me Stewie."

The bigger man reached his hand out as well, with the same serious face he'd had since we arrived.

"Kevin, but you can call me Kevin."

If it was supposed to be a joke, no one laughed. The tall man held on to Brian's hand for a second after Brian introduced himself.

"I'm gonna go ahead and guess you're not Mexican, Brian."

"You'd be guessing right, Kevin. Born and raised in Austin. Lived in Portland for a bit. Hated it. Came back south and found my town full of hipsters and college kids."

"When you're done rolling with these motherfuckers . . . well, we can always use white dudes who don't mind getting their hands a little dirty to help us with buying guns. Just let me know and we'll talk. It's good, easy money and it's better than running around with drugs and meeting sick fucks who'd like nothing more than to put a bullet in you."

Juanca cleared his throat. "We should get down to business. I want to make sure everything's in order."

"Relax, man," said Stewie. "We have everything under control, as always. This isn't Mexico."

Juanca glared at him.

"Yeah, we have some beauties to show you," said Kevin.

Kevin moved to the wall on the right and pressed a button. The door started going down. Then the big man led the way and walked us farther into the depths of the spacious hangar.

There were eight or nine cars in there, most of them pulled apart, and some heavy machinery that had seen better days. More than a granite business, it looked like a garage. There were car doors on the floor and stacks of tires and rims everywhere. Back seats were sitting on the floor, some sliced open and drained of their soft contents. One car looked like the cars in cartoons when they have an accident and all that's left is the chassis, motor, seats, and wheels. Kevin and Stewie moved to a dark red Ford pickup. We stood next to it, close to the bed on the left side of the truck.

"This right here, gentlemen, is a 2016 F-150," said Stewie. "The inside is in pretty good shape. Nice AC. Seats look good. Pretty comfortable. The MPG sucks, but that's a Ford for ya, right? Anyhoo, the beautiful thing about this baby is not in the front. No, the beautiful thing about this baby is like Jennifer Lopez's most endearing quality: all in the back. Let me show you. Can you hand me that crowbar, Kev?"

The big man reached down and picked up a crowbar that was on the floor. Stewie grabbed it and placed it under his arm.

"We wanted to make sure that you could still use the space in the cabin to stash the money." While he spoke, Stewie rummaged in his back pocket and pulled out a socket wrench.

"The lights are still fully functional, so make sure you mention that when you hand it over to whoever is gonna take

the guns out. Tell those idiots we'd like to keep using this one
for a couple more months. Every time we send something that
way, those fucking savages scratch it, dent it, or fuck something
up. I'm sure they've fucked up their whole country and that's
why wetbacks can't wait to get over here!"

Stewie pulled the tailgate down and used the socket wrench
on the screws that held the taillight on the left side in place.
With the screws in his hands, he wiggled his fingers around
the taillight and pulled it back. The taillight came out with two
loud pops. The back of the taillight had the cables that led to
the bulbs, one brown and one blue. Stewie twisted both and
carefully pulled the bulbs out of the taillight. He placed the
socket wrench back in his pocket and inserted the crowbar into
the hole where the taillight had been.

"Kevin, give me a hand and make sure we don't fuck up
the paint."

Kevin walked around Stewie and pressed his hands against
the side of the pickup. Stewie leaned back while holding the
crowbar in place and yanked on it. The metal screeched and the
side panel of the pickup's bed popped out. Kevin caught it and
lowered it until it rested against the side of the pickup.

Inside the panel were a few cables and some gray material
that looked like foam. Taped to that with strips of duct tape
were half a dozen AK-47s in two rows of three, all slightly
angled, their barrels crisscrossing in the middle. Nearer to the
cabin and close to where the taillight had been, there were
more guns, also taped to the gray material.

"Holy shit," said Brian.

"Pretty sight, ain't it?" asked Stewie. "Six AK-47s and six
Glock 19s. The total is forty-seven thousand six hundred
dollars. That's with the good neighbor discount, of course."

"How the hell do you fill up a truck with brand-new AK-47s?
Do you guys build them?" asked Brian.

"Nah, man, we buy them all from legit gun shops," said Kevin. "Remember I told you I had a gig for you when this was done? This is what I'm talking about."

"You buy all this at regular gun shops?"

"It's easy and risk-free, man," said Stewie. "Easiest money you ever made. Plus, we get to keep some and do a bit of patrolling around the border. You know, keep the riffraff out and whatnot."

"How the fuck?"

"You need to forget everything you think you know about gunrunners," said Kevin. "There's good money in drug trafficking, but it's dangerous as fuck. That's why we stick to guns as much as we can. The cartels need guns, a lot of guns, and we supply them with whatever they need."

It almost made me laugh. These two patriots were part of the problem. The cartel situation was bad, and the guns that made it so bad came from guys like Stewie and Kevin. It made me curious.

"How come Brian here gets a job offer and I don't? This gun money sounds pretty good to me," I said.

"Oh, no disrespect... Miguel, was it?" asked Kevin.

"Mario."

"Mario, right. Don't take this the wrong way, but this is a gig for folks with papers. White folks, *comprende?*"

Papers. He was implying I wasn't a citizen of the United States of America. He was calling me an undocumented immigrant because of the color of my skin. I thought about shooting him in the face.

"I'm an American citizen."

"Oh, that's awesome, man," said Stewie. "However, you're still... you know, Hispanic... or Latino. I don't know what you people are calling yourselves these days. Don't care, either. Point is, the sellers we work with would think you're buying stuff for the cartels."

"And they don't think that about white folks like you and me?" asked Brian. The fact that he opened his mouth meant what had happened in the car after we left the barbecue place had affected him. Juanca's words about staying silent had sliced him to the bone. This was his white guilt talking.

"Hell no," said Kevin. "Listen, this isn't about racism or anything like that; this is about the system and how it works. White folks hunt. We protect our property from . . . undesirables. We head to the shooting range once in a while. It's all good. Brown folks are different. Tango Blast. MS-13. The Mexican Mafia. Sureños. A brown man with a gun is just bad news and gun sellers know it. Can't blame them."

"Okay, it's the system, got ya. I wanna know how it works," said Brian.

"Bro, you're a white man, and that means you can walk into any gun shop in this town and get a gun, no license required. This is the way we do things in the great state of Texas. It's also how they do things in a bunch of other states. Listen, all you gotta do is fill out this little form called a 4473 that's issued by the United States Bureau of Alcohol, Tobacco, Firearms and Explosives. You're gonna lie a bit on it, okay? Few small lies, no biggie. The thing is no one knows or fucking cares. After you fill that thing out and return it to whoever is working with you at the shop, it's gonna be stored in the back with thousands of others just like it. That form doesn't have to be digitized or anything, so the moment it enters the mountains of others like it in the back of the store, everyone forgets about it and the gun becomes a ghost. Then you're free to sell it to the Mexicans. Easy peasy. Guy like you could make a pretty penny buying stuff for us. All you gotta do is say the word, man."

We were there to get a vehicle full of guns and somehow Brian ended up getting a job offer and I was called an undocumented immigrant. That's how systemic racism works.

It was so dumb it was almost funny. It was the story of my life: my education and my résumé never looked as good or as trustworthy as a white man in a suit. This time around, I was losing a job opportunity to a sweaty junkie with bloodshot eyes who'd been eating Adderall like candy.

"I don't give a shit what Brian does after we get back here, but I do care about what's going to happen tonight. Did you talk to the people I told you about? I'm sure those fuckers are on their way right now. That's the last I heard."

Juanca's voice was strained. He was worried and apparently as angry as I was. He didn't like not being in control. He also probably hated these assholes as much as I did.

"It's all good, man!" said Stewie. "Listen, the Sinaloa Cartel doesn't mess too much with routes that cut straight down through El Paso, and they steer clear of Juárez. Keep in mind that we're sort of in the middle, and Sinaloa is on the west coast. We have a guy keeping an eye on this truck. They already made their delivery in Houston and are heading this way."

Stewie went to the desk and rummaged around for a bit. He held up a map.

"Come here and I'll show you where we're gonna hit 'em."

It was a topographical map. It looked old and used. There was a coffee stain between Albuquerque and Santa Fe. Kevin placed his index finger on a chunk of elevation lines.

"This is the place you were talking about, the Florida Mountains. As you've probably noticed, things here are pretty fucking flat. Not so here. You say they have to come through here, right?"

"Yeah," said Juanca. "They won't enter Mexico through Nuevo León, Coahuila, or Chihuahua because it's dangerous. They'll use the stuff they built right here, close to Sinaloa. This place is where they have one of their biggest tunnels. They usually skirt along this ridge right here to stay out of view. The entrance is somewhere near Whirlwind Road and Pol Ranch Road. They have it covered and only drivers know where it is. I drove this route myself a bunch of times. Anyway, we don't want to risk these cabrones getting too close, so we're going to hit them as they start skirting this area."

"Copy that," said Kevin. "Juanca, you said you needed to be close, so we're gonna have you guys here. Stewie and I are gonna take their tires out from the top of this ridge. That'll get them to stop pretty damn fast. The terrain out there is no joke. Then y'all do whatever you need to do. Once the deed is done, we collect the money and burn the car. You three will have to get on NM-9 and haul ass back to El Paso or Juárez or wherever the fuck you're going. As you know, this is a bit of a ways out, about an hour and a half from El Paso proper, so plan accordingly."

"We got our shit together. I'm here checking on you two, not the other way around," said Juanca.

"Listen, Juanca," said Stewie. "I know this is your gig and whatnot, but we're putting our asses on the line here and . . . well, I'd like to know what it is that you have planned for when we stop them. These dudes are gonna be on edge, man. They'll surely be carrying a serious chunk of change and my guess is they'll have some boom sticks to make sure the dough stays with them. Plus, you're bringing four men with you, which tells me you know you need to take care of them fast. Can you at least tell us what we should expect in case things go south out there?"

Juanca stepped toward the big man, who was at least half a foot taller than him, and looked him in the eye.

"You want to know what's gonna go down out there? Okay, I'll tell you, *Steve:* What's gonna happen out there is I'm gonna open up a box of pure hell on those cabrones. You can stay back and watch while you wait for your money or you can fuck off and get your money later from Don Vázquez. It's all the same to me."

"That . . . doesn't tell us much, Juanca," said Kevin.

Juanca turned to the taller man. "I know it doesn't. If I told you what I have planned you two would chicken the fuck out. Just have your rifles ready and make sure you hit those wheels when you have to. I don't want you to miss because it's dark or because you're nervous or some shit. You have one fucking job, so make sure you do it right. There's a lot riding on this."

"We're not fucking amateurs, man," said Stewie. "We have equipment to shoot at night as comfortably as we do during the day."

"That's fucking fantastic, Steve. Then I suggest you two worry about those shots and let me take care of the rest."

Stewie raised his hands and took a step back.

"Whatever you say, Juanca."

"Good. I'm gonna move some stuff from our truck to that one. You know, unless there's anything el—"

"Yeah," said Kevin. "Is the chick with the dick still working for Vázquez? We haven't heard the wild stories in a while."

"True," said Stewie before Juanca got a chance to answer. "Is your brother still banging him . . . her?"

Juanca's hand moved back. Then it stopped. He took a step toward Stewie. They looked like they were about to kiss. Juanca's hands became fists. They hung at his sides like a couple of grenades ready to go off.

"You mention my brother again and I'll fucking cut your balls off and shove them in your mouth before emptying my clip in your face, is that clear?"

I heard Stewie swallow. Kevin cleared his throat.

"We're good," said Kevin.

Stewie stepped back. Juanca stayed where he was. Then he snapped out of it and turned to us.

"Let's go," he said.

I turned and took another look at the burgundy pickup. The

taped AKs looked like some kind of art piece, a critique of gun culture or some shit. Instead they were just death machines on their way to do what they did. I'd had no idea that it was dudes like Kevin and Stewie doing all the buying for the cartels, but the more I thought about it the more it made sense. Mexico gets all the shit, but most of what they produce is shot, swallowed, smoked, and snorted on this side of the border. And the guns come from here, from assholes like Kevin and Stewie, fucking leeches that make a killing working the border while also patrolling it for kicks, probably while dressed in their best tactical gear from Walmart. Why would I have expected it to be different?

"What was that all about?" I asked Juanca when we reached our truck. "Are you sure we can really trust those guys?"

Without taking his eyes off the box sitting in the truck's bed, Juanca replied, "I don't trust them. I don't trust anyone."

Besides the big metallic box, there were two other boxes in the truck. Brian helped us move the big one to the burgundy pickup and then Juanca and I grabbed the smaller ones because Brian wasn't looking too hot. His forehead was covered in sweat and the bags under his eyes made him look like he hadn't slept in a week. His eyebrows were pushed together as he looked from the back of the truck to me and then to Juanca.

"All moved, boss," said Brian. "Are you gonna tell us what the fucking deal is with the dead guy in the damn box?"

"I need him for something," said Juanca. "You'll see what I mean soon. Don't wo——"

"Nah, man, I'm tired of that shit. I don't wanna see later. I'm asking you now. What's the——"

Juanca took only one step toward him. The look on Juanca's face cut Brian's question in half and made him cross his right arm in front of him and hold his left elbow. He looked like a kid expecting a punch from a bully.

"These motherfuckers got on my nerves and I have no patience left for your bullshit, B," said Juanca. "You're getting paid. A lot. This is a fucking job. You took it. Now do your part and I'll do mine. In the meantime, shut the fuck up and stop bothering me about shit that has nothing to do with you. It's too late to find anyone else, so let me know if you're gonna keep being a pain in the ass, yeah?"

Brian suddenly found his shoes very interesting. He mumbled something.

"What?" asked Juanca.

"I said we're good. Just nervous is all."

"Stick those nerves up your ass and keep them there until we're done, B. Seriously."

"Yeah, I will, Juanca."

Juanca looked at the boxes and then told us to hit the bathroom at the back of the place. We had a long drive ahead of us. I went first. When I came back, things had calmed down a bit and Juanca was telling Brian to take it easy with the pills. Apparently he had pulled out the little bottle and popped a few more. I didn't know if an Adderall overdose was a thing, but if it was, Brian was on his way to one.

Brian went next. The moment he walked into the tiny bathroom and closed the door, Juanca spoke without turning to face me.

"Me tienes que decir qué vas a hacer para estar preparado."

Killing a man is one thing, but killing a man you know is another. Shooting some asshole who diddles kids in the back of the head is making a contribution to the world, a good deed. Killing a man who's about to become a father and who reached out to you in your time of need is an entirely different thing. However, when the options are kill or die, the answer is always the same. If Brian was planning on killing me after we got the money, that meant I had to get him before that happened but after the job was done. That meant shooting him as soon as we took care of business but also making sure I didn't eat a bullet first. Suddenly I wanted Juanca to help out, to play a role, to keep an eye on the bastard. The weight of that murder was too heavy to carry it alone.

"Cuando se acabe el asunto, necesito que nos pidas que te ayudemos con las cajas, que nos mandes a buscarlas o algo," I said. If Juanca sent us to fetch the boxes for him, we'd have an excuse to head together to the back of the truck and his hands would be busy. Then I could shoot Brian.

"¿Y qué pedo con la lana?"

There it was, the question I'd been dreading. *And what about the money?* It was a short question that contained worlds.

"No me importa. Si te parece la dividimos."

"Hecho. Ahora escucha: yo te ayudo y digo la mierda de las pinches cajas si después me ayudas a decorar a esos cabrones."

I had no idea what he meant by "decorating those fuckers," but I agreed. Whatever it was, it paled in comparison to how much I needed his help.

"Hecho."

"Si crees en Dios, estáte tranquilo, Mario. Dios sabe que solo lo vas a matar porque él tiene planeado matarte ti. La gente se va al infierno porque le hacen mal a alguien que no se lo merece, no por defenderse."

People go to hell for doing bad things to those who don't deserve it, not for defending themselves.

Those words, then and there, meant everything to me. Padre Salvador's words came to me: *Men who do bad things for the right reasons are always forgiven in the eyes of the Lord . . .*

I closed my eyes and thought about the bullet that would kill Brian. It would exit the gun and tear through the brain that housed his memories. To blow a man's head open is to violently push chunks of his past out into the world. It was a small price to pay for keeping my memories of Anita intact, a small price to pay to live another day and have a chance to start my life from scratch, to hold Melisa again until her warmth made me forget what I'd done to her forever. Yeah, I know the word *rationalization*. Melisa taught it to me. She'd like to bring it up whenever she felt I was making excuses for doing dumb things. In this case, I didn't mind it.

"Guys, why don't you head to the shop with the new truck?" asked Kevin. "It'll be weird for all of us to leave at once. Hang around a bit and then follow us when you see us leave."

"Okay," said Juanca. "Tell Brian to meet us there."

We jumped in the truck and drove it out to the front of the store, but we didn't go in.

In front of us, a heavy woman came out of the store. She was carrying a baby and dragging a toddler by the hand. The baby was crying. The toddler, a girl with a head full of messy brown curls and a pink outfit covered with smiling cartoons, was resisting, screaming. She was fighting the way we all fight. We come into the world fighting, covered in blood and crying, and we go out fighting disease, calamity, age, or exsanguination. The point is we need to fight. Always. Giving up is never an option.

Brian came back and Juanca left to use the bathroom. We sat in the truck in silence, watching the heavy woman drag her child across the parking lot to a dilapidated Honda Accord at the end of the building. Suddenly a man with a crew cut exited the store holding a few pamphlets. He was short and wore blue athletic shorts with flip-flops and a white wifebeater. He walked over to the toddler, took the arm the woman was holding, and yanked the girl up. Her tiny feet left the ground. The first time he hit her, Brian sucked in air through his teeth, said "Damn!" The second time he hit her, I opened my door. The man aborted the third hit because I yelled at him. He looked up. Confusion and anger fought a battle on his face, neither winning. I was on him before knowing exactly what was going to happen. My fist flew sideways. It caught him in the jaw. *Clack.* My knuckles screamed. He dropped the girl, but she landed on her feet. He staggered back. The second shot was a straight right. It landed between his nose and mouth. His teeth dug into my flesh. Pain shot all the way to my elbow. The cartilage in his nose crunched like a drumstick being pulled from a chicken. His eyes rolled to white and he fell back with enough force to make his head bounce against the concrete as he hit the ground. The woman was screaming up a storm, holding her children. Both were crying.

"When he wakes up, tell him I'll be watching him the rest of his sad life. If he puts a hand on his kids again, I'll be waiting, and if I have to hit him again, I won't stop until he's not breathing, you got that?"

She didn't get it. She didn't get it because she was screaming. I felt hands on me.

"Bro, you're bleeding!"

It was Brian. I turned and pushed him. Was this motherfucker coming to rescue the asshole who'd just hit a kid?

"Your fucking hand, man! You're gonna need it tonight."

My hand. Pain that had been hiding behind a hill of adrenaline ran out and kicked me in the brain.

"Damn." Brian whistled. "It takes a real monster to put his hands on a kid like that." My chest tightened.

"I leave you motherfuckers alone for one minute and you deck some asshole in the parking lot?" Juanca's voice registered above the chaos. "Man, get your stupid ass in the car and let's get the fuck outta here. We don't need this shit right now."

He wasn't wrong, but what I'd done felt more right than whatever amount of right Juanca was, so I didn't care.

CHAPTER 31

I n the Caribbean, night falls on you like someone flipped a switch. The sun doesn't crawl down the sky to hide behind the ocean—it drops like a piece of radioactive fruit an angry kid hit with a stick. In Texas and New Mexico, that's not the case. In the American Southwest, the sun comes down politely, like it's letting you know it's about to get dark. It plants bruised kisses in the sky and often spills orange, pink, red, and purple watercolors on the clouds.

The New Mexican grasslands are as expansive and gorgeous as they are repetitive and mundane. Yeah, that sounds contradictory, but you have to be there to understand. On one hand, the desolate terrain reaching out endlessly in all directions makes you realize how amazing the world can be when there are no buildings around, no malls fucking things up, no people making noise around you. Open land accented by low mountains and endless sky is a reminder of a better time, a time before humans.

I was aware of Steve and Kevin following us as we exited I-10 and went off road, but I couldn't see them now. I was sure those motherfuckers had bailed.

The pickup moved well and the big wheels and good shock

absorbers did their job, but the uneven terrain made the box bump around and slam against the sides of the bed. Knowing there was a body banging around in there was unsettling.

Ahead of us to the right, the earth gradually turned darker and rose up. Up close, the Florida Mountains were like dry brown scars on the land.

Juanca drove into a dry riverbed and then stopped behind a hill and killed the engine. Darkness swallowed everything.

We stayed put for a minute, getting used to the dark.

"This is the place," said Juanca. "Hopefully those mother-fuckers are setting up shop somewhere around here. The top of any of these hills should give them a clear shot of the car without being exposed. After they blow out a tire, we'll do our thing."

"Is there any way for us to get close without being seen?" asked Brian.

"Not really, but it'll be dark and they'll be confused, so we have that going for us," said Juanca.

Brian nodded a few times and looked around.

"You wanna run this by us again, Juanca?" he asked. "I was picturing the desert, and this whole . . . mountain thing is freaking me out a little."

"Those fucking Proud Boys are gonna climb a hill somewhere around here and lay low at the top. Kevin said they have a ton of fancy equipment that will help them see the truck way before it gets here. They're gonna blow out at least one of its tires. I also asked them to shoot out the window so their screams and shit can be heard."

"For what?" asked Brian.

"For that," said Juanca, pointing at the back of the pickup. "I'm gonna move our car forward a bit when shit starts happening and leave the tailgate down and the box open. One of you has to be on the lookout. The other has to help me unload Rodolfo in the back. Once they're all dead, we'll get the money. Easy work, easy money, cabrones."

Easy wasn't what I was thinking.

"Nah, hold on a goddamn minute," said Brian. "Exactly what are you suggesting we do with that empty sack of meat in the box?" Juanca was caught up in sending some message that was probably going to get us all killed.

"You'll see." Juanca's mouth stretched into something resembling a smile.

"Fuck, I knew you were gonna say something like that. You've been cagey as fuck about it. Same as that whole thing about you not wanting to kill more because you'll go over your quota or whatever. You're not gonna stay in the car and make us do all the work, are you?"

Juanca turned around to look at Brian.

"No. These men I get to kill. They're the last. After this, I'm done. I told you. You can't imagine what that visionaria told me is coming my way if I kill one more person after that. These last bad guys and I'm out."

I still had questions, and one of them was pressing against my lungs.

"And what if those two racist fucks don't show up?" I asked. "We lost them a while ago."

"They'll show up."

"How do you know? Looked to me like you didn't trust them back at their place."

"I don't trust them one fucking bit, but they'll show up because they want their money and probably are eager to watch some Mexicans die. Those cabrones put on their Cabela's shit and patrol the border when they have nothing better to do. Wouldn't be surprised to hear they slice the gallons of water that folks leave out here for people who are crossing on foot. They've probably pulled the trigger on a few people coming through . . ."

"Fuck," said Brian.

"No, fuck them," said Juanca. Then he looked at me. "Don't worry, they'll do what they're getting paid to do. Just be careful and keep your eyes open in case they try to kill all of us and take all the money."

That last comment hung somewhere between a joke and a possibility.

Juanca clicked on the radio. The lights from the dashboard illuminated his face as he turned to me.

"Solo unos cuantos muertos más."

Just a few more dead guys.

Brian took a deep breath.

"Guys, I... I don't fucking wanna die out here."

No one said anything. Silence had grown to be our pet, and Juanca's line had invited it to come into the car and settle down between the three of us. Juanca pulled out his phone. I did the same. There was no text asking me for money, which was rare. Instead of unlocking the phone, I looked at Juanca for a bit while he scrolled. It was hard to see in the darkness. I felt like he was hiding something. We all were. I was worried about those things, especially the ones Brian was hiding.

I unlocked my phone and went to Facebook. Melisa's last post was the same one she'd had up for months, asking for prayers for Anita. I went to her profile pictures again. There was a photo of her with a hat sitting against a redbrick wall. I'd taken it on a trip somewhere and she'd loved it, which was weird when it came to photos of herself. Her love of that photo was understandable. She looked amazing. Her eyes were light brown suns radiating caring into the world and her smile was so genuine it was contagious. I stared at that photo for a long time. Memories came and went. Laughter. Fights. Love. Anita. More fights. Most of the fights had to do with money. Not enough money to pay the rent. Not enough money to pay the internet bill. Not enough money to pay the car insurance. Not enough money to pay water and gas and electricity. Not enough money to pay our student loans. Not enough money to pay for a vacation. Not enough money to get better health insurance. Not enough money to pay for nice dinners. Not enough money to get all the groceries we needed. Not enough money to get a new car. Not enough money to help her mom. Not enough money to get a new computer. Not enough money to fix the damn shower. Not enough money to move. Not enough money to get Anita everything we wanted. Not enough money to leave behind our shitty life. Not enough money to move up in class, which is the only palliative for being brown there is in this fucking country. Not enough money. Never enough money. Fucking money, always.

Now I was going to get the money. Three hundred thousand dollars. My face felt strange. I realized I was looking at Melisa's picture and thinking about the money . . . and smiling for the first time in a long time. Smiling right before killing some men.

CHAPTER 32

We waited and then waited some more, but it didn't bother us. The music filled the space around us and our thoughts and phones kept us entertained, each inhabiting a private world while sitting in the truck.

In the back of my head, the sound of static in the shape of Brian's face kept me from being able to concentrate on an idea or a pleasant memory for long. Juanca was shady as hell, but he probably gave zero fucks about who he had to split the money with if one of us killed the other, so why warn me about Brian?

Killing a man who's done you wrong, a man who should no longer be in this world, is one thing, but killing someone because they may or may not do something in the future is different.

The buzz in my head became real. A text. Juanca read it.

"It's showtime, cabrones."

Juanca lowered the windows and turned off the AC. The sounds of the desert immediately entered the cabin. Insects and emptiness. Then, a gunshot. A crack that broke the night in half. Another gunshot followed. And another. Juanca turned the ignition and drove forward.

"What the fuck are you doing, man?"

"Tenemos que acercarnos."

He drove around the hill in front of us. We heard a motor roaring and then the distinct slam of metal against unyielding earth followed by screams and two more gunshots.

Steve and Kevin had done their job.

As we rounded the hill, we saw lights coming our way. We waited. Another shot rang out, this time coming from the car. The car's lights moved wildly and then slowed down, stopped. About three hundred feet in front of us was the car we'd been waiting for, a huge dark blue Suburban. Juanca killed the engine and jumped out.

"¡Ayúdenme!"

I jumped out and joined him at the tailgate. We heard more shots coming from the car. Juanca pulled down the tailgate and reached for the metallic box. I grabbed the other side. More shots came, this time with a few screams. Someone was barking orders, getting the men organized. We couldn't see what was happening near the car. We dragged the box to the edge. Juanca shoved his hand into his pocket and brought out the key to the padlock. He opened it and stopped.

More shots rang out and a scream of pain echoed throughout the mountains. Juanca asked me for help lifting the heavy door. There was no time for questions. I did as he said. We both pulled it up. Once we had it open, the stench of death and shit crawled up my nose and made me gag.

"Get in the car! ¡Rápido, cabrón!"

His voice had gone up a few notches. We ran back and jumped in our truck. Juanca turned the ignition and rolled up the windows. Two more shots rang out, their sound muffled by the glass.

I could see there was a man in the passenger seat of the cartel's Suburban, head down, with dark blood oozing out of a hole in his neck. The rest of the men were flanking the sides of the car.

"Where the fuck is Rodolfo?" Juanca asked.

"Who the fuck cares?" I readied my gun as three men darted to the right near the vehicle. Another figure moved toward the back. Three shots rang out. They were aiming away from us. They had made out Steve and Kevin.

There had to be at least ten men out there in the dark, the flashes of their weapons lighting the night like firecrackers at a party.

"Fuck it, it's on us. Let's go."

Juanca opened his door, jumped out, drew his gun, and trotted forward while crouching. Brian and I followed.

The sound of guns going off came from everywhere at once as it bounced off the hills around us. I aimed at the car and waited for someone to move.

Behind the big car, a man with a black cowboy hat ran out of the darkness and ducked as if to grab something from the car. I pulled the trigger. The sound of my bullet smacking against the metal of the car rang out. I fired again. The man jumped back. My third shot caught somewhere that dropped him. The night turned darker. I wanted more.

In front of me, Juanca was kneeling and aiming. I couldn't be sure, but it sounded like he was laughing. He was shooting at someone to the left I couldn't see. Somewhere behind me, Brian was shooting as well. I didn't like having him behind me with a gun, so I ran behind Juanca and got next to him.

A lanky guy wearing jeans and a yellow shirt stepped out from behind the Suburban. His eyes were on us. Surely our shots had given away our position. He had something long in his hands. He squeezed the trigger. The land in front of us flew into the air. It was a fucking machine gun. I scrambled back, covering my head. I couldn't swallow I was so scared. The volley stopped. The ground behind us dipped a bit, so I was sure they couldn't see us.

I saw movement to my left. There was another round of bullets, this time aimed to my side. Brian screamed. I heard his body hit the ground. The air oofed out of his lungs.

"B, you okay?"

"I'm hit! I'm fucking hit!"

Shit.

I poked my head up and looked toward the man in the yellow shirt just in time to see the left side of his head go up in a red mist. My ears didn't even register the shot.

"Ha!" said Juanca. "Keep shooting, pendejos!"

A figure moved toward the man Juanca had just dropped. I saw dark shorts and a dark shirt and aimed for the center of it. My first shot did nothing. The second bent the figure in half. It felt great, and that made me feel bad.

Another automatic weapon went off. To my left, where I thought Brian was, the ground erupted into the night sky, sand falling on us a second later.

"Fuck!" Hearing Brian scream meant he was still alive.

Juanca ran back at a crouch. I followed. Behind us, someone was barking orders again. I caught "alrededor" and my heart sank. *Around.* They were going to circle us. We were fucked.

Whatever gun Kevin and Stewie had brought had sounded different from every other gun out there. More than firecrackers, every shot that came from them was a blast that reminded me of a demolition. I wished for it now, but they must have been hit. Or the chickenshits decided to bail. Either way, we were alone, outgunned, and outnumbered. It was only a matter of minutes.

Juanca jumped behind a small bush. We both looked back at the car. A figure in jeans and a white T-shirt ran in front of the car with a rifle held up to its face. I aimed. A shot rang out before I pulled the trigger. The running man's head jerked back, a small cloud of mist puffing into the air behind him. His arms flailed. The rifle went flying. Momentum carried him forward a few more feet before he slammed into the dirt.

The shot had come from the side. I looked away. Brian was limping toward us, gritting his teeth.

When he got close enough and dropped down next to me, I saw he had his belt tied under his left knee.

"You hit bad?" asked Juanca.

"What the fuck is a good hit, man? Hurts like a motherfucker. Let's get these assholes so we can get the fuck outta here. I need a doctor."

Juanca scoffed. I had darker thoughts.

We looked back at the car. Men were moving too fast to get a clear shot. Many had vanished. I was worried about the ones I couldn't see.

"I think they're coming around this hill," I said. We all looked back, our eyes straining to pull the darkness aside as a round body appeared, a silhouette in the truck's lights. I lifted my gun and squeezed off a shot. The bullet clipped his left shoulder. Juanca and Brian squeezed off shots almost simultaneously. Both bullets found their mark. The man made a noise like a cat drowning in syrup. He dropped to his knees and brought his weapon up with shaky hands. Juanca shot him again. The man's head shot back. He dropped with a thud.

The choreography of violence we see on screen and the fast, messy nature of violence in real life have nothing in common. The former is the ballet of martial arts movies and the precise, quick deaths delivered by heroes to the bad guys that get in their way. The latter is a shotgun blast that punches a ragged hole in someone's chest, a croc pulling at a man's intestines, or whatever was happening in front of us.

A loud growl came from behind us. Then, almost immediately, it came again.

"What the fuck is that?" Brian sounded panicked. I turned, gun up and ready. They had circled around. We had to kill as many as possible before they killed us.

"Rodolfo!" said Juanca.

A scream caught in my throat. For the first time in my life, I understood why people say "frozen in fear." Rodolfo stumbled toward us, his eyes cloaked in shadow. The skin of his face appeared to be sliding off.

"Relax, cabrón. Tenemos protección," said Juanca before squeezing off another shot.

A man screamed something near the truck. It was strange, but I heard Rodolfo whimper; then his head jerked in the direction of the scream. Then he was off, his gait somewhere between a jog and the way people move when they're falling forward.

The man spotted Rodolfo and shot at him before ducking behind the cartel's Suburban. If any of the bullets reached Rodolfo, it didn't seem to faze him. He made an awful cry and leapt like a cougar. I thought he was going to land on the hood of the car, but he sailed across it and slammed against the man. The rifle flew up and disappeared into the night.

We heard a scream that morphed into a wet gargle. More shots popped off. A skinny man with a crew cut approached the area where Rodolfo was and stood still as if unable to process what he was seeing. Juanca shot him in the chest. Fear's grip on the back of my head became a vise.

Another shot rang out. A man with a baseball hat, jeans, and a white shirt had caught Rodolfo in the arm with a bullet, pushing the limb back a bit, but it did nothing to stop him. Both figures crashed together. The momentum made them drop and roll. Rodolfo bounced back to his feet like a marionette that's been yanked by its strings. With one hand, Rodolfo grabbed the man he'd tackled and lifted him back to his feet. Then he pulled the man toward his face and bit him on the cheek. The man screamed. Rodolfo pulled back with a chunk of flesh between his teeth.

The man pushed at Rodolfo and then punched him. His fist connected with his face and shoved it to the opposite side, but that was it. Rodolfo pulled at the man again, this time turning his head and biting him in the neck. When he pulled away, blood spewed from the hole. In the sideways light of the headlights, the blood looked black.

"What . . . what the fuck is that?"

"Eso es un espíritu hambriento."

A hungry spirit, except it was the corpse of a man I'd watch die a day earlier. It didn't make sense, but things that don't make sense happen all the time.

The man he'd bitten was screaming. Shots kept going off behind him and from the dark behind the car. They reminded me someone could approach us from behind at any moment, but the spectacle was too hard to look away from. Rodolfo kept pulling the man he had grabbed in for a bite and then pushing him back. The man was losing strength. His knees buckled. Rodolfo—the thing that had been Rodolfo—held him for a second and then dropped him on his face. The man didn't move.

Rodolfo turned to us. His body caught the light coming from the headlights at an angle. The hole in his stomach looked like a gaping black mouth. The lower part of his face was covered in blood. He was chewing the man's flesh. His eyes landed on us. There was enough light for me to see them. Tears were streaming down his bloodied face. He looked at me and stopped for a second. The awful cry erupted from his mouth again. It wasn't anger; it was agony. In the monster was the man, and he was looking out at the world from behind those eyes. I remembered the look on El Milagrito's face and understood both were normal people trapped in bodies that had betrayed them. Underneath the sloughing flesh of the beast, Rodolfo was still human. He was, like me, a haunted man that had become something else.

The thing that had been Rodolfo snapped its head sideways, dropped to all fours again, and took off into the night. The gunfire was dying down a bit.

"He's probably trying to catch the last motherfucker. One dead inside, one on the other side of the car, couple we got moving this way... and that fat one right there... dude in the yellow shirt, the motherfucker with the rifle who just got his face chewed... makes seven, so we're missing one or two more, at least by my last count. I think we're gonna get them all."

"What the fuck, man?! What the fuck? What the fuck?" Brian looked like he was going to faint in the dark. His skin was shiny with sweat.

"That was a lot of dudes. How the fuck did they all fit in that damn Suburban? And what the fuck was that thing? He had no guts. He had a fucking huge hole where his guts used to be. I saw... I saw that man die, Juanca! What the fuck did you get me into here?"

"Relax, B. It's over. You did good. I saw you put down a few."

Brian smiled. "Yeah, I did." He breathed deeply and put the gun in the back of his pants. He looked at his leg. His jeans were covered in blood, but he seemed relatively okay.

"Let's get back in the car."

We walked back slowly, Juanca and I with our guns held high, and got into the truck. We were all breathing heavy. Juanca turned the ignition and flicked on the lights.

"What are you doing?"

"No puede quedar vivo ni un pinche cabrón."

Juanca grabbed his cell and made a call as the truck acceler-ated. The phone rang and rang. No one picked up.

He hung up.

Juanca turned the pickup around and drove toward the Suburban. We stopped about fifteen feet away. He left the lights on and the motor running.

CHAPTER 33

The ground around us was littered with corpses. Fear was riding my blood. One of those men could still be alive, holding on so he could put a bullet in one of us before drawing his last breath. I didn't want to do whatever came next.

Juanca cleared his throat and turned to me. The way he looked into my eyes contained a world of meaning, and I couldn't begin to decipher it.

"Would you guys mind getting those two boxes from the back in here while I send a text? I gotta check on something real quick."

"Sure, man," said Brian. "Whatever gets us the fuck outta here." I heard his door open and instinctively opened mine.

This was it. No more thinking. Death was about to show up again. La Huesuda. Fuck.

I swung my body and stepped into the dry soil of the desert.

Brian was almost at the back of the pickup. He was limping a bit, taking his time. I felt panic creep into my veins, threatening to seize my muscles and stop me in my tracks. I focused.

Pull the gun out.

Aim.

Shoot.

Survive.

Brian had been the one who showed me how to use a gun. His words and actions came back to me whenever I held one.

In my head, Brian plucked the gun he'd given me in my apartment ages ago out of my hands. He turned the gun to the side and pointed at the safety he'd been talking about to show me how to use my thumb to click it off.

Two hands.

Don't turn it sideways like the idiots in the movies.

Again, remember the fucking safety. And get rid of it.

Kill or be killed.

Kill or be killed. The easiest decision ever.

Kill or be killed. A mantra. A plea.

Without thinking about it, a whispered prayer escaped from my mouth, asking for forgiveness, asking for protection, asking for a strong hand to hold death with it, for a strong finger to change the world forever in a fraction of a second.

Padre nuestro que estás en el cielo...

"Hey, Mario, you gonna give me a hand with these?"

...santificado sea...

"Yeah, just a sec."

...tu nombre; venga a nosotros tu reino...

I reached back and pulled the gun out.

...hágase tu voluntad así en la tierra como en el cielo...

My right thumb found the safety and clicked it off. My index finger slipped around the trigger.

...danos hoy nuestro pan de cada día y perdona nuestras ofensas...

I rounded the truck. Brian was reaching down into the waistband of his boxers. He kept his gun there because he said he didn't like the feel of a holster or the metal pressed against his lower back.

. . . así como también . . .

I lifted the gun. Brian kept fumbling with his waistband.

. . . nosotros perdonamos . . .

Brian looked at me.

CHAPTER 34

The aftermath of a gunshot is a god cracking his mouth open and letting out a mournful note, a sustained cry that announces the end of a life.

One second Brian was there, his skull intact, his future an unknown thing that included Stephanie, a baby, maybe getting clean, and a lot of money. A second later he was on the ground, the back of his skull an open mess spilling vital fluids into the dirt, bleeding his memories into the earth.

I looked at his body in the dark.

I'd killed him, but I was still alive.

I don't know what makes us want to keep on living, what makes us desperately hold on to anything that will allow us to remain on this earth just a little longer despite the pain that comes with it, but I do know that, whatever it is, selfishness resides at its core; selfishness is its black, dangerous heart.

I blinked and realized I was still holding the gun up, the barrel a silent threat aimed at the dark immensity of the New Mexican desert. I lowered my hand, took a step toward Brian.

Brian's eyes were open, staring at nothing. Moonlight reflected on their wetness. But he wasn't Brian anymore, not really. The thing that made him who he was had been removed by the bullet that traveled across the inside of his skull. The thing at my feet was a sad, sick sack of bones, lingering chemicals, muscles, and organs.

Guilt. Pain. Relief. Anger. The feelings came and went. They grew in my chest, crashing against each other like wild waves in a hurricane.

"You okay?"

Juanca's voice came from under a wet blanket, barely registering under the sustained note of that mournful god.

"I'm good."

"Want me to get his shit?"

I shook my head. When you put a bullet in a man's head, the least you can do is get his wallet from his back pocket.

"You did what you had to do, you know what I'm saying? Don't think about it too much."

I placed the gun back in my pants and exhaled.

The body wasn't as heavy as I'd expected. When I grabbed Brian's shoulder to turn him over, the bones pressed against my hand. He felt like a child.

I turned Brian around and lifted his T-shirt. The wallet was in his right back pocket. I plucked it out and shoved it into my left back pocket. Then I looked at the back of his head. Between the darkness and his blood-soaked blond hair, the damage was an amorphous, wet, dark mess. The lack of details was a good thing.

Back inside the truck, Juanca was texting someone.

"What are we gonna do with him?" I asked.

"If you're worried about it, we can set him on fire. If not, we'll just let the creatures out here eat him. Between the heat and the animals, he'll be gone in no time. Whatever you want, man."

He didn't seem concerned. I envied him.

Before us, night filled the desert.

THE DEVIL TAKES YOU HOME

"What now?"

"Ahora tú me ayudas a mí."

Juanca exited the truck.

"Help me check them. Make sure they're dead."

The guy in front of the car was a mess. Rodolfo had removed the entire left side of his face. His eye was hanging from a thread of gore and rested on the red muscle and blood that covered his cheekbone. The guy in the car was almost as bad. The bullet had entered his right temple and made a hole there, but it had blown a much larger hole when it came out the other side. It made me wonder if Steve and Kevin were dead. The inside of the car was splattered with blood, brains, and chunks of bone. Next to the car, the bearded guy had been eviscerated just like Rodolfo. However, instead of having his guts turned into croc food, his were next to him, the long pink loops uncoiled and reaching out into the night around him like a dropped garden hose. Two more men were sprawled a few feet away, both with puddles of blood around them. Farther down, I saw a few more dark lumps on the ground.

Juanca pulled out his phone and walked to the back of the pickup, back toward the body. Suddenly he stopped.

"Where the fuck are you?" Then listened. "Wish I could give a fuck. If you want your money, come and get it."

Juanca killed the call.

"Ya viene Steve. Espéralo ahí nomás. Voy a buscar al último cabrón. Quiero verlo para estar seguro de que esté muerto."

"So they're alive?"

"Nah, just Steve," he said.

"What happened?"

"Steve says they blew out the tire and then the window, but Kevin wanted more. He started coming down from the hilltop and they saw him. He caught one in the neck and bled to death in their truck."

I looked for something like sadness inside me and found contempt.

Juanca nodded and got in the truck. He drove forward slowly, zigzagging a bit, the high beams on. About a third of a mile out, the lights fell on the last guy. His body was an unmoving lump on the ground, a miniature version of the hills we'd hidden in while waiting for them.

The truck drove up a bit more and then stopped. Juanca got down and walked over to the corpse with his gun drawn. Then he got back in the truck and turned around.

As he approached, I saw a second pair of lights in the distance. Steve.

Juanca reached me and parked a few feet away. He stepped out of the truck and came to stand by me. We waited for Steve in silence.

A few minutes later, Steve pulled up next to a body and climbed out. He left his truck running. He walked toward us. His face was red, his eyes bloodshot. He chuckled.

"Enjoyed the show, Manuel?" he asked.

"Mario."

"Right, Mario. Sorry."

"No, I didn't."

"Too bad. I didn't either."

He looked down and choked back a sob. Then he grunted and cleared his throat. It was like the last slice of humanity that was left in him was trying to come out, but he wouldn't let it.

"Where the fuck's my money?" asked Steve.

"Probably somewhere in the back. I'll go check."

Juanca moved to the Suburban, opened the back door, and looked around. Then he walked to the front and touched something before coming back and opening the back hatch, which swung open smoothly. Steve looked at him, shifting his weight from one foot to the other and snorting snot back into his skull every few seconds.

There were several backpacks in the back of the Suburban. Juanca pulled a few, checked them, and dropped them on the ground next to him. Finally he pulled a brown gym bag and let out a laugh. He zipped the bag back up and walked to us.

"You sure it's all there?" asked Steve.

"They ain't making deals with folks who pay in ones, man. Two mil don't look like much when it's hundreds. It's all in here."

"Sweet! Then pay me so we can get the fuck outta here. We made quite a ruckus. I was almost gone by the time you called," said Steve.

"Nah, you bailed early," said Juanca. "I figure you tried to get the fuck out after Kevin got his ass shot. Then he died and you were lost, didn't know if driving away meant you'd never see the money, right? That's why you got far enough away to stay safe but close enough to maybe keep an eye on us with your scope."

Steve looked like a man caught with his pants down. I had no idea why Juanca was talking to him when we had shit to do.

"Just give me my fucking money," said Steve.

"You got it. How much was it again?"

"We said forty-seven thousand six hundred."

Juanca dropped the bag and kneeled. He held on to the corner of the bag with two fingers of his right hand, where he still had his gun, and used his left to unzip the bag. The sides of the bag pulled away a bit, exposing a dark sea of green. I'd never seen so much money in my life, and part of that was mine. My green future.

Steve approached. He sniffed again and rubbed his hands together. He was still wearing the shirt with DAWN OF THE DEAD written on it.

Juanca looked up at him. A few seconds went by. Then Juanca smiled.

Off to my right, I heard someone running. The thud of feet hitting the ground was unmistakable. I pulled my gun.

"Oh, almost forgot, Don Vázquez says thank you for the guns and to keep your mouth shut about other people's business."

"What the fuck are you talk—"

Rodolfo flew into the light and before Steve could turn, Rodolfo crashed into him. They landed on the ground. Steve managed to somehow pull a piece and squeeze off a shot.

Rodolfo made a sound somewhere between a bark and a hiss and came down on Steve. He bit and scratched. It soon became obvious that Rodolfo was much stronger. The second time he lifted himself up and then came down on Steve, I heard a crunch. Rodolfo came up with flesh dangling from his mouth. I turned away. Another tortured wail split the night.

The sounds of Steve struggling soon vanished. All that was left was the wet sound of Rodolfo ripping, chewing, and swallowing meat and gristle. Whenever he stopped, there was a different sound under all that; he was crying. I wanted to get in the car, but Juanca wasn't moving. Then I remembered we were protected.

I watched Rodolfo stand up, his face and torso covered in blood, and smell the night air like a dog. Then he sobbed, dropped down again, and took off into the dark with another howl.

Juanca moved toward Steve. He kept his gun trained on the body, as if he expected Steve to sit up and try to shoot him. Then I thought maybe I was next.

My hand again immediately went to my own piece. I pulled it out and realized I'd never clicked the safety on after shooting Brian. Nerves will ruin you, but throw fear into the mix and you have a recipe for disaster.

Juanca stood next to Steve and pushed down on his head with his boot.

"Está bien muerto."

He stuck his gun back into his pants. I did the same. Apparently I wasn't next.

"Vamos a decorar a esos hijos de puta para largarnos de aquí."

Decorate. There was that word again. It couldn't mean anything good. Nothing about this night was good.

Juanca went to our car. Rodolfo came to mind. The darkness enveloping the little space we were standing in seemed endless, ominous.

"Hey, man, what about Rodolfo?"

"What about him?"

"Isn't he gonna...attack other people? Maybe some folks trying to cross?"

"Nah, forget about him. He'll walk the desert for a while and then collapse. The effects never last too long. He already fed. He'll collapse soon and never get up again...that motherfucker."

"What...what was...it?"

"Rodolfo?"

"Yeah."

"I don't know. Gloria can...do things, you know what I mean? I don't ask questions. You ask too many questions, you end up like Steve over there."

"I have questions, but I guess I won't ask them."

Juanca laughed. The sound was out of place, a grotesque blurt in a quiet church.

"Nah, man, I didn't mean it that way," said Juanca.

"You sure?" I asked.

"Yeah, what's up?"

"Nothing, just...what exactly is Gloria?"

"You don't want to know. A witch. A fucking slave. Once

Don Vázquez got her, shit got weird. Really weird. She killed a few men. They had to pull her teeth out and chop her hands off to be able to control her. I didn't ask about it because things also started working out and we started getting paid. When they killed my brother, Don Vázquez told me we were going to use her to send the Sinaloa motherfuckers a message. And here we are." He pointed at the bed of the truck.

"What now?"

"Ahora los decoramos para que se vayan al infierno como mandaron a mi hermano al cielo."

Juanca leaned over the tailgate and pulled one of the boxes to him. The flaps had been crossed to keep it closed. He pulled them apart and dug in. His fist came up wrapped around a knife.

"Let me get the photos and we'll get to work."

Juanca put the knife back in the box and walked to the front of the car. He opened the passenger's door and grabbed the envelope from the glove box. I didn't need to look at the contents of the envelope; the image of the man with knives jutting out of his sides like he'd visited a sadistic acupuncturist was burned into my mind.

Juanca took out a single photo and walked over to the dead man with the beard.

With the knife in one hand and the photo in the other, Juanca closed his eyes and lowered his head. His lips moved. He was praying, just like I had prayed while killing Brian. For someone who's supposed to be all about good, God finds himself involved in some pretty awful shit.

Juanca bent over, placed the photo in the center of the dead man's chest, and brought the knife down on top of it. The blade dug into the man's torso and stopped. Juanca wrapped his other hand around his fist and leaned forward, pushing his weight on top of the knife. Something gave with a loud crunch and the blade sunk into the man's chest all the way to the hilt.

I thought he was done. He wasn't. Juanca grabbed another knife and another photo and repeated the process close to the gaping hole in the man's belly. This time, the blade went all in on the first try. Then he did it again on his right thigh.

"If you want to get the fuck outta here soon, help me."

The idea of pinning the photo of a dead man to a corpse using a knife was so ridiculous it made me wonder if he was playing, if this was some kind of elaborate joke to lighten the mood. It wasn't. Just like when we were with Don Vázquez, my body moved before my brain thought about it. I grabbed a knife and a photo and walked to the dead man in front of the car. He'd fallen face-first. The side Rodolfo had eaten was facing away from me. I was thankful for that.

I glanced at the photo. The broken body full of knives, the torn-up face with the mustache somehow untouched by the violence. It hit me where I'd seen that mustache before. Juanca's brother.

I thought about his name. It took me a few seconds, but it came to me: Omar. I thought about his name and pictured his mother crying, his brother shattered. Juanca was still a sick fuck, but then again, so was I.

I pressed the tip of the knife against the dead man's back and pushed down. The blade slid in. The skin gave way with a pop and then climbed around the blade, slowly sucking it in like a toothless mouth. There was a crunch and something scraped against the blade. I pushed harder. And harder.

Omar.

Anita.

Vengeance.

I understood.

La Reina. The photo outside the bathroom. Her tears. So

much made sense that I felt like I needed to take a break, to sit down and process everything. But we had a job to do, and the night was far from over.

We go through life trying to inflict pain on those who hurt us. In their absence, anyone will do. It's human nature. To fight against it is to deny ourselves, to turn a blind eye to the ugliness that makes us human, the animal instinct that keeps us going while everything around us burns.

I grabbed another knife and another photo and went back to the man. Behind me, Juanca was sobbing. I placed the photo lower on the man's back and plunged another knife in him. This one had a blue handle that looked like it'd been used for years. I pictured it in someone's hand, slicing into some meat they were cutting for their family. The knife and I were not that different. We'd both come from a better place and ended up in a fucked-up situation. The difference was that the knife was going to stay here and I was going home, and then I was going to find a new home.

I was taking too long. The bearded man looked like Omar in the photo. His entire body was covered in knives. Juanca had put two more photos on him, one in his left leg and one in his face. The rest of the knives had gone in without a photo.

Juanca came back carrying the second box. His face was wet. The tattoos and his dark skin made him look like he was part of the night, a strange creature who lived in the desert and only came out long after the sun had gone down.

"Tengo cuchillos para uno más. Agárra unos cuantos y termina con aquél. Yo me encargo del último."

I grabbed a few knives and went to finish what I'd started. Juanca walked to the last man he wanted to decorate, the one in the car.

Revenge is one of the motors of the world. We want to punish those who hurt us. At least everyone I know does.

Yeah, some say you need to turn the other cheek, but that only comes from those who haven't been smacked hard enough. I understood Juanca. Part of me was angry that he hadn't told us everything, but I knew sending a message to the Sinaloa Cartel and claiming a few bodies in his brother's name was therapeutic. My only worry was how easy it'd be to identify who'd done it. This went against the anonymity he'd talked about in Brian's house. I thought about asking him, but I'd seen how easily he put bullets in people, and I didn't want to survive Brian only to catch a bullet from Juanca's gun soon after. Plus, it wasn't my brother in those photos.

When I went back for another knife, the box was empty. My brain had been pushing the idea that I was only butchering a mass of flesh, like a prize pig. I pulled one of the knives out of one of the dead men's torsos. The knife let out a little squelching noise, but the blade came out surprisingly clean.

I should probably have been a corpse myself by now. What was the difference? I'd pulled my gun a few seconds faster than Brian and now his kid would grow up without a father. My thoughts were too loud, so I stuck the last knife close to the back of the dead man's neck. That one was the hardest, so I left it halfway in.

Once I stood up, my senses reconnected with the world around me, probably in an attempt to escape the knowledge that I'd become a monster.

The first thing I heard was a grunt. When I turned, I saw Juanca straddling the man in the car and stabbing him. He wasn't just pushing the knives into his flesh; he was holding a knife and repeatedly stabbing the man's body. He grunted again.

Somewhere behind him, a screech erupted from the darkness. It made me feel cold despite the clamminess of my skin and the sweat running down my sides. My mouth opened, a question ready to jump out, but the memory of Juanca's words stopped me. Curiosity wasn't going to kill this cat.

Juanca was still stabbing the corpse, but slower. He was getting tired. His grunting had turned into racking sobs. Finally, he stopped. This time, the scream came from him.

After the scream, Juanca punched the man and got off him, pulled out his gun, and shot the man in the head a few times.

Juanca wiped his face and put the gun away.

"You ready to hit the road?" I wanted him back in control.

"Yeah, man. I'm good now. That felt good." He smiled, walked up to the gym bag full of money, and picked it up.

"Somos ricos, Mario."

CHAPTER 35

J uanca had his phone out as we pulled away from the dark, bloody shapes scattered along the hills. The map on its screen didn't show any roads, but Juanca seemed to know where he was going. It was now or never.

"I know you said questions get you killed, but I need to know a few things, especially if we're gonna go back to Austin and never see each other or talk about this ever again."

"You think answers are gonna help you sleep? That knowing something about how Brian was gonna get rid of you will make his fucking ghost haunt you less?"

"I don't need to know anything about Brian. I just want to know how we're gonna make sure no one comes to get us after what we did with those photos . . ."

Juanca placed the phone down and gripped the steering wheel. He didn't look at me but I could feel his anger pulsating behind his clenched jaw.

Finally: "We can't make sure they don't, but we can vanish. If they come for someone, they'll come for me. And I won't be there, you know what I'm saying? I'm heading north, bringing Amá with me. I'm cleaning my face and growing my hair out. I'm fucking done with this bullshit."

I had one more question. I pressed myself against my seat, the gun pushing against my tailbone. It felt reassuring.

"One more question, man?"

I took his silence as an opening.

"What's the deal with Vázquez's partner, La Reina?"

Juanca's jaw muscles tightened under his skin. It almost looked like he was smiling.

"That's not his new partner."

"I thought you said his partner was a chick."

"She is, but it's not La Reina."

"Who the hell is it, then?" I wasn't in the mood for another one of Juanca's mind games. There was too much blood from other people's bodies crusting over on my own flesh to play around right now.

"Gloria."

The image of the bruja sucking on Rodolfo's bloody mouth and then vomiting into the air flashed in front of me. Bile rose in the back of my throat.

"Gloria?" It didn't make any sense.

"That's only one of her names," Juanca said.

"What are the others?"

"Si te digo, no me crees."

"Try me."

"El Chamuco."

"Gloria is the devil?"

"Gloria is a devil. The Devil is everywhere. Sometimes it gets inside people. It's inside Gloria."

"But she's a—"

"A woman. I know. She's an old woman who dealt with the wrong shit as a bruja and got a demon inside her. Are you gonna doubt that after what you've seen?"

I remembered the woman bucking, her feet off the ground. I remembered the thing that came out of her toothless mouth. I remembered Brian struggling to hold her down. Then I looked out at the darkness and thought about Rodolfo. He was half man and half demon. I believed Juanca. It was impossible not to, and I already knew the devil was everywhere. I closed my eyes and wished he would take us home safely.

CHAPTER 36

Despite the late hour, El Imperio was packed. Juanca killed the engine, jumped out, and grabbed the gym bag. By the time we rounded the corner, Marta was heading our way. She frowned and looked behind us. Her massive shoulders were shiny with sweat.

"¿Qué pedo con el gringo?"

"El gringo se hizo comida de coyote."

"¿Neta?"

"Mario le metió plomo en la cabeza."

Marta looked at me.

"¿Por qué te chingaste al gringo?"

"El gringo me quería chingar a mí."

Marta smiled.

"Pues qué bueno que te lo chingaste primero."

Maybe she was flirting. Maybe she wasn't. I didn't care. Her shiny skin and muscles were the best thing I'd looked at in a while. Even her tattoos looked sexy and mysterious. I thought about Melisa, about how months from now maybe I'd tell her about the night a woman who could easily crush my head between her thighs flirted with me.

Marta led the way. We entered through the back of the bar.

The smell of booze and sweat hung heavy in the air, mixing with the smell of cigarettes and the bittersweet stench of weed. I barely noticed any of it.

I did spot La Reina talking to some men at the bar. Her smile seemed to hold them all close. She saw us and came over. Our presence was all the communication she needed. She hugged Juanca for a long time. The music pounded our ears. Heat and humidity had won whatever battle they'd fought with the AC units. La Reina finally let go of Juanca and turned to me. She leaned forward and hugged me. Some people are sweet like that. She was taller than me and smelled like vanilla, strawberries, and tequila. Her hug caught me by surprise, but my arms shot up and I hugged her back. Something brings the fucked citizens of the world together. Suffering makes us family. This woman had probably felt as much discrimination as I had. A trans woman and a brown man, hugging for a brief moment. It was beautiful and strangely comforting.

La Reina pulled away. Her eyes were wet. I pictured her with Omar, both smiling like they were smiling in that photo in Margarita's house. I almost understood her tears. She fixed the front of her long mint green dress and told Marta to take over the bar for her.

Don Vázquez was leaning against his desk when we walked in. He wore a gray guayabera and khakis. The men behind him were not the same as last time. One of them was as big as Osvaldito. A round flap of flesh covered in hair hung from his chin. He looked unmovable. The other one was a large man with a paunch but plenty of muscle. He was tall and had gray hair on the sides of his head. They were both decked out in black. The color went well with the AKs that hung from their shoulders.

"Mi querido Juanca," said Don Vázquez as he gave Juanca a hug. "How did everything go? Where's Mr. Brian?"

"Mario made him dance with La Huesuda."

Don Vázquez turned to me.

"What do they call death where you're from, Mario?"

"They call it La Muerte, but my mother always called her La Huesuda."

"Ah, then your mother was Mexican, yes?"

"No, my father was. He wasn't in my life much, but he left some things with my mother. Words and food, mostly."

For a second I wondered why he was speaking English. Then I remembered La Reina probably didn't speak much Spanish or, if she did, it might've not been enough to follow fast, long conversations with many moving parts.

"Ah, I see. Well, Mario, here in Mexico, death has so many names: La Huesuda, La Dama de la Guadaña, La Veleidosa, Doña Huesos, La Flaca, La Pálida, La Niña Blanca, La Catrina, La Jodida, La Patrona, La Tiesa, María Guadaña, La Seria, La Rasera... the list goes on. What matters is that we know she's everywhere. We know she can come for us at any time and that she can take someone out of the way to make things easier for us. Death isn't a bad thing... well, not always. Sometimes she helps, and sometimes she comes to take us away. I have seen her many, many times in my life. I consider her one of my most important business partners, yes? I have been around her for so long that I can smell her, feel her in the air. I feel her around you. Maybe it's because you've done some things, but maybe it's because she wants to dance with you. I'm going to give you something to keep her away, okay? You will take it with you and everything will be fine."

Don Vázquez slapped me on the shoulder and went to his desk. As he walked, I thought about Gloria. He said La Huesuda was his partner, but apparently so was the devil. Maybe he saw them as one? It made sense. Whatever Gloria had done had made Rodolfo come back from the dead and had protected us against him . . .

Don Vázquez opened the top drawer of his desk and pulled something out. He came back and handed it to me. It was a tiny statue of Santa Muerte. The black figurine had all the details, from the mantle to the scythe.

"Keep her in your pocket. She will protect you. Offer her something when you get home."

Don Vázquez turned back to Juanca and asked him for the money. Juanca gave him the gym bag. Don Vázquez didn't open it. He placed it on his desk and told the men standing by the wall to count out six hundred thousand and put it in a smaller bag.

"I know we said two hundred each, but you get Brian's cut. You can split it however you like. It's a nice little bonus, no?" He smiled and ran his tongue over his teeth. Instead of pink, his tongue was a deep, dark purple.

The men had brought a small machine out of somewhere and were feeding hundred-dollar bills into it. The machine whirred like a beehive. Don Vázquez told La Reina to find us another bag. She left the office and came back almost immediately with a pink rucksack with a mouse on a bicycle on it.

"You know what needs to happen now, yes?"

"We do, Don Vázquez. We're gonna vanish. You don't have to worry about anything."

"Oh, I know that, Juanca. I'm just making sure Mario understands that he needs to become a ghost. You do understand, right, Mario?"

The threat in his voice made it an octave lower. He spoke slower. The smile was gone.

"I do, Don Vázquez. I'm leaving Austin as soon as we get back."

"Good. You know, that's a lot of money. It's more money than most people see in their life. Use it for something good, yes?"

Something good. There were bodies scattered in the desert and an undead man roaming around with chunks of human flesh stuck between his teeth, but now Vázquez was telling me to do something good. Then I thought about Brian, the bits of skull and brain that now served as his last pillow. The bullshit was too much to take.

"Is that what you do with your money, Don Vázquez? Good things?"

It was a stupid thing to say, but something about staring death in the face and walking away decimates the number of fucks you have left to give.

Don Vázquez smiled and took a few steps toward me. The cold fingers grabbed me softly by the back of the head.

"I do what must be done," said Don Vázquez. "I've done this for most of my life. You're here because you have a . . . sad daddy story. Spare me your judgment or I will have to subject you to mine."

There it was. His cold tone and eloquent response floored me, and his threat struck me as the realest thing I'd ever heard. I swallowed.

"I will spend my money on something good, Don Vázquez."

He smiled. "Good."

Don Vázquez made a move with his hand. The older goon came over and grabbed the pink bag from La Reina. He was missing two fingers. At the desk, he placed the money in the bag and brought it to Juanca.

"Thank you, Don Vázquez. Thank you for helping me with this."

"The help was mutual, Juanca. I loved Omar. So did La Reina. He was a good kid. So are you. Anyway, are the guns in the truck?"

"Yes. In the end, they were on the house."

Vázquez raised an eyebrow. Something like confusion mixed with concern rippled across his features.

"Let's just say after meeting Rodolfo, they won't ask anything or tell anyone anything ever again."

"Did you make sure they were dead?"

"I did. Estaban bien muertos."

"Good. See? I told you everything would work out. Rodolfo did his part. I hope no one finds his bones. He deserves to spend eternity cooking under the sun."

Juanca stayed quiet. Don Vázquez nodded. Our meeting was over.

"Go with La Reina. She or Marta will get you a car. Just leave it on your street. One of my men will pick it up soon."

Don Vázquez hugged Juanca again.

"Well, I'm gonna go take care of those guns. Cuida a tu madrecita, chamaco. Ella se merece un poco de paz. Dásela."

Juanca nodded. Don Vázquez shook my hand. His stubby fingers were impossibly strong. He held on for too long.

"Find your wife. Say you're sorry. Make her happy. That's what the girl would want."

I looked at him with alarm. "But how—"

His skin rippled. Something ran over his left eye, eclipsing the white while it was still open. The question died on its way out of my mouth.

El Chamuco.

Sometimes it gets inside people.

The devil was everywhere.

I nodded. I meant it. And vanishing wouldn't be a problem, because I never wanted to lay eyes on Don Vázquez again.

La Reina led the way. She took us across El Imperio. She'd texted or called someone. There was a car waiting for us outside, a brown Chrysler LeBaron that was at least two decades old.

"You know I wanted to go with you, Juanca, but Vázquez needed me here. Things are getting ugly. I'm sorry you had to go through all this. And I'm . . . I'm sorry about Omar. He was an angel. He will forever hold a piece of my heart, and my heart isn't easy to break."

"Thank you for saying that, Reina. Omar loved you. You were there for him when . . . you know, when no one was."

They hugged again. Then La Reina gave me another quick hug and walked back into El Imperio sniffling, the fabric of her dress dancing in the night like a happy ghost.

Juanca jumped into the driver's seat and placed the pink bag beneath his seat.

We started driving to the garage.

The streets were empty. Dilapidated houses rolled by. Shitty cars. Unpainted walls. Yards full of garbage. This place had all I'd known in my life. I'd never lived in a poor part of Mexico, but there is something universal about poverty that allows us to understand the hardships of those who share it with us.

Beneath Juanca's seat, three hundred thousand dollars were whispering a buffet of possibilities.

I'd never lived in a neighborhood where people didn't tie their dogs or put them on their roofs or push shopping carts from the grocery store or the dollar store all the way home and then abandon them on the side of the road. I'd never had the ability to cover all my utility bills in the same month. I'd never gone to the grocery store and not checked my balance on my phone before walking in. I'd never seen a place on television and thought, *I'm going to fly there next month.* I'd never had access to nice things, just like I'd never had access to the same opportunities as those around me. Every job I ever had was always just enough to keep me afloat, to allow me to have a car, a house, and a phone and pretend I was living the fucking American Dream. No, I was poor and brown.

That was about to change.

Juanca turned onto a larger avenue. I clicked on the radio. Guitars and violins came from the speakers. A man was speaking instead of singing. "... edicar como siempre, con el mismo amor, cariño y respeto, a todas las mamás que esta noche me han venido a visitar, sobre todo para aquellas que están un poquito más lejos de mí." People screamed. It was a live recording. The voice sounded familiar. The song started with a line about someone being the sadness of the singer's eyes. Juan Gabriel. I remembered the song. My mother played it nonstop after she got the call saying my abuela had died. My abuela loved Juan Gabriel. My mom played that damn song night and day for a week. I went to sleep listening to it and woke up to it in the morning. The memory was so strong it took me away and I missed a few lines. I tuned back in and heard the singer say he wished that someone's eyes had never closed. Then, two words: eternal love. I remembered what came next, and I wasn't in the mood to think about seeing anyone in the great beyond someday.

Fuck that song. Fuck those words.

I changed the station. An ad for miracle pills came on. Outside, Juárez was a sleeping monster. Inside, fear was slowly being displaced by pain.

CHAPTER 37

Humans can get used to anything if they do it enough times. When we rolled into the garage, my eyes didn't even jump around the place, trying to take everything in. Instead, my heart was beating fast, knowing what was coming.

Just like before, our headlights lit up the slashed dirt in front of the car. The bowels of the earth welcomed us with their silence and endless darkness. At the bottom, the *clang* sounded louder than before. Smaller wheels and old shock absorbers meant everything was closer to us than it'd been in the truck. All the same, I preferred this car without the zombie body in the back.

The tunnel yawned in front of us like a threat. We knew the creatures were out there but pretended that not naming them was equal to them not existing.

Sadness and pain are yours to treat as you wish; forget about them for a while and everything will be fine for the duration of your amnesia. But they always return. Mine came back with a vengeance, the events of the last two days acting like a magnifying glass for the sun of my aching.

An absence can be momentarily covered with anything that can grab your attention and keep it for a while. That something becomes a palliative that allows you to temporarily forget about your pain. You get so used to whatever is masking your grief, however, that you end up just as fucked as you were before that other thing bleeped so hard on your radar that you were able to shift your attention to it.

As we rolled down the tunnel, the radio off and our tires making that weird crunching sound on the dirt beneath us, the cracks in my heart, my sacred wounds, began to throb. I missed Anita. I missed Melisa. Going back home was always going back to my baby and the woman I loved, but now going back home was going back to their absence.

True pleasure is not wanting anything. Sure, some things feel great when we do them, but we often take for granted what we have, and sometimes what we have is enough. The laughter of your child, for example, is something no degree of poverty can touch. Now I had money, a lot of money, but I wouldn't be using it to buy any toys for Anita.

Look at the boat, Daddy!

That fucking boat. Its cheap plastic made her so happy.

"What are you gonna do with your money?" The question was out of my mouth before I realized I'd spoken. Conversation was an escape, a coping mechanism that allowed me to push Anita's beautiful smile and bright brown eyes out of my head.

"I told you, man: I'm heading north. Probably Oregon. They have some beaches up there where the water is cold and there are fucking huge rocks in the ocean. I've seen pics of it. Gonna rent a nice place and then get Amá to come join me. I want her to spend the rest of her days in peace, you know what I'm saying? She's earned it."

"Rent? Why not buy? Now you have the money."

Juanca turned to me for a second. His face was scrunched up. "You serious?"

I didn't know what to say.

291

"Look at me, man. I'm not walking into any fucking bank and getting a house. It's not happening. You shouldn't buy a house. Rent. Maybe get a gig or something. Get you a dirty lawyer that can give you fake papers saying someone died and left you some lana. I don't know where you've been living, man, but your brown skin and your accent are a fucking *problem* for people. I know your mom was a citizen, so you have papers, but you could carry those fuckers stapled to your face and it wouldn't make a difference to racists, you know what I'm saying? A brown man with a hundred thousand dollars in his pocket and rocking a designer suit is still worth only a third of what a white man with a twenty in his wallet and some jeans with holes in them is worth."

The weirdest thing about Juanca's words was that they felt like an attack. My first reaction was to respond, to tell him that I knew exactly what he was talking about. I wanted to tell him that I'd been denied many jobs I was qualified for and had been fired from jobs for bullshit reasons by folks who weren't smarter than me. Or that none of the people who had fired me were bilingual. Instead, I kept my mouth shut because the monster of racism has many heads and some of us get bitten by different ones. I also kept my mouth shut because he was right.

Every time we passed one of those holes on the sides of the tunnel, a small shiver ran down my spine. My brain fed me scenarios I didn't want. Our car broken down and those things pouring out of the holes. A group of them stopping the car with rocks or something and us shooting at them until we ran out of bullets.

The platform was finally in front of us. None of the scenarios in my head had materialized. Maybe God actually managed to throw us a bone once in a while, just like he'd done with Brian out there in the desert. Yeah, I'd killed him with God's help. And now I was the one collecting the three bricks.

Once we were in the garage, Juanca smiled.

"Welcome to the United States of America, cabrón. Got anything to declare?"

"Yeah, we have more than half a million dollars in a little fucking pink backpack."

"Haha. Chinga tu madre, güey. No juegues con mi dinero."

The door went up and we took to the streets of El Paso. They seemed welcoming in their emptiness, like a paved promise of better things to come.

We drove to Juanca's house in silence. He parked and we got out, stretched.

"I'm gonna throw the backpack in my car. Then we can hit the bathroom, get gas and something to eat, and get our asses back to Austin."

"That has always been the best part of your plan, man."

CHAPTER 38

We picked up some snacks at the gas station's convenience store when we stopped for gas. Juanca bought a red bag with some cartoon cars on the front of it. The store had huge statues of La Virgen de Guadalupe under posters of John Wayne. I got a bag of tiny doughnuts and another canned coffee that promised to taste like vanilla. I could hear Melisa telling me those things were going to clog my veins, ruin my pancreas, and destroy my stomach. I looked forward to a long road trip with her. I looked forward to her making a spectacle of grabbing the Waffle House menu with just two fingers while making faces and then using her napkin to clean the silverware once they brought us our food.

The sky was no longer black by the time we hit I-10. Juanca had played around with his phone a bit and we were listening to a strange album where the sound of drones could be heard under beautiful overlapping voices.

"What are we listening to?" I asked.

"Something that relaxes me, but I can find you some Juan Gabriel if that's what you want."

"Nah, I'm good. So, what are we gonna tell Stephanie?"

Juanca looked at me for a long time before answering.

"We tell her the truth—that he died in the desert when we were stopping those motherfuckers. He got shot. She knew this was risky. Vázquez thought Stewie and Kevin's cut might help her move on, make the pill easier to swallow, you know what I'm saying? We'll give her the forty-seven thousand and call it a gift from Vázquez. You know, if you want."

Forty-seven thousand dollars. It was probably more than Stephanie had ever seen.

I finished my coffee, which tasted like cold ass with a hint of vanilla, and ate more than half the bag of tiny doughnuts. I was sure the caffeine and sugar were going to keep me up until we got to Austin, but the voices from the radio were coming into my brain and rocking me gently.

At some point, I must have fallen asleep because the next thing I knew Juanca was shaking me awake as we pulled up to Brian's house.

"Your take is in that bag." Juanca nodded to the back seat. It looked weird without Brian curled up like a rag doll. I got out of the car and reached across the back seat for my bag and the red bag with the cartoon cars on it. My hand connected with something cold and hard. I lifted my bag and saw what it was.

Brian's gun.

My hand instinctively flew to the bulge in my back left pocket. Brian's wallet was still there. My brain played the scene on a loop: I pulled the trigger. Brian fell. The night looked on, unaccusing. I turned him over and got his wallet.

An accusation. Proof of a crime.

Padre nuestro que estás en el cielo...

"Hey, Mario, you gonna give me a hand with these?"

...santificado sea...

"Yeah, just a sec."

...tu nombre; venga a nosotros tu reino...

I reached back and pulled the gun out.

... hágase tu voluntad así en la tierra como en el cielo ...

My right thumb found the safety and clicked it off. My index finger slipped around the trigger like a fleshy snake.

... danos hoy nuestro pan de cada día y perdona nuestras ofensas ...

I rounded the truck. Brian was fumbling with his waistband, reaching for something.

... así como también ...

I lifted the gun.

... nosotros perdonamos ...

Brian looked at me.

... a los ...

"What the—"

I pulled the trigger.

There was no blast like in a real movie, nothing slowed down, no aerial shots. There was just the little *thump* of the gun, a metallic heart pumping death into the world.

The bullet burrowed into Brian's head right above his left eye. A dark dot appeared. A minuscule period to end the sentence of his life. It was no bigger than a quarter, and the universe fit in it.

... que nos ofenden ...

Brian's arms dropped. His jaw relaxed. His mouth hung open, a silent scream I will hear for the rest of my days.

... No nos dejes caer en la tentación ...

He fell sideways.

... y líbranos de todo mal ...

Brian's body collapsed. He was dead.

Amén.

In the movie reel unspooling inside my head, I got the wallet again and again. I got the wallet. Just the wallet.

A tiny explosion that grew: I never got—

Everything stopped. The image in my head froze. Brian. His face down in the dirt. Shirt up. Dirty jeans. Brown belt around his leg.

I got the wallet. I didn't get his gun. I didn't get his gun because there was no fucking gun. He had it in his hand after we shot everyone, but then he'd dropped it in the car, left it in the back seat. He'd been fumbling with his pants because his fucking belt was tied around the wound in his leg instead of his waist.

I shot an unarmed man. My friend.

CHAPTER 39

Guilt had exploded in my chest like the punch of an angry god. I'd blinked, grabbed my stuff, and slid into my car. I made it home and sat on the couch, which means at some point I drove home, but I had no recollection of it. The only thing I could think of was that night. My brain kept reframing it. I'd managed to shift from aggressor to victim. The change was like oxygen—something needed to survive. In my head, the night no longer looked at me unaccusingly.

Excuses. That's what I needed. There were plenty.

Brian was going to kill me. He was hooked on meth. He wanted my money. He got me into this knowing it was going to mean I'd die somewhere in the desert. Brian was trash. Brian didn't give a fuck about those assholes at the barbecue joint. Remember the golden rule: Never trust a junkie, pendejo.

I sat on the sofa and blamed Brian for everything the same way I'd blamed Melisa for everything. I'd lost both of them to violence. My violence. The violence that felt great at first and then made me crash like some weird drug. Neither loss had brought Anita back.

I heard a sound coming from the bathroom. Splashing. A squeal. I stood up. The splashing came again.

Every step between the sofa and the bathroom took a life-time. I feared the sound would vanish if I got any closer, but I had to go there, had to see for myself.

A squeak reached my ears. I recognized it immediately. It was the sound of the tiny rusty hinge that kept the two sides of Anita's beloved plastic boat together.

My feet moved forward as if independent of my body. I simultaneously craved what awaited me in that bathroom and feared its disappearance more than anything else, and that included everything I'd experienced in the last few days.

The bathroom's door showed me a black rectangle. The tub was to the left of that. The splashing was so loud it had to be real. My heart kicked like an angry horse.

My hand flew up, pierced the darkness of the bathroom, and switched on the light. I jumped. The tub was empty.

The gun was in my hand before I thought about pulling it out. The gun I'd killed Brian with. The barrel hit my right front tooth when I put it in my mouth. My finger coiled around the trigger. My thumb flicked the safety off.

One pull. One *boom*. One bullet. That's all it'd take. The pain would vanish. Anita would welcome me. I could do it.

Except I couldn't.

There were three hundred thousand reasons next to the sofa. Reasons to start fresh with Melisa. Reasons to keep going, to know a life I'd never known.

Fuck. Three hundred thousand dollars. After finding Brian's gun, I'd run away. I'd never given Juanca any of my money to give to Stephanie. She would need it. Brian's kid would need it. It was the right thing to do given I'd been the one to kill Brian.

The gun left a weird aftertaste in my mouth. I grabbed the little backpack with the cartoon cars on it and drove back to Stephanie's house.

CHAPTER 40

The sun was high in the sky by the time I pulled up in front of Brian's house, now Stephanie's house. Knowing Stephanie was in there was crushing. I would obviously have to tell her something, to deal with her explosion of grief, with the blame. How the fuck do you stand in front of the woman whose husband you killed?

I grabbed the backpack from the passenger's back seat and stepped out of the car.

I walked up the rickety steps and knocked. A moment later, Stephanie opened the door. She wore a dress similar to the one she'd had on the last time I'd seen her. This one was green and made her eyes pop out at you like crazy.

"Mario!"

She looked surprised. She looked radiant. What the fuck had Juanca told her?

"How are you?" It was a dumb question that popped out of my mouth because I had no idea what to say.

"I'm . . . I'm not okay? I don't know." She stopped talking and looked behind me as if she expected someone else to show up.

"Can I come in for a second? I have something for you."

"I . . . okay," she said.

Stephanie stepped aside and we walked into the house. The smell of ammonia wasn't as strong as the last time I'd been in there.

The door closed behind us. Stephanie squeezed past me and stepped into the kitchen. She had something on the stove. She turned down the heat. On top of the microwave, a new red box had pushed the other bottles back. It said THYREX on the front. I remembered the DHA. I had no idea what this was either.

"What's that?" I pointed.

Stephanie looked at the microwave. She looked confused.

"Thyrex. It's for my thyroid."

Thyrex. The name moved things around in my head. The way she said it, like the name Rick and not the dinosaur. Thyricks. Three ricks. Three bricks. Fuck.

Stephanie cleared her throat and signaled with her hand toward the hallway. I stepped back so she could squeeze by me, and she stepped into the living room. She reached the sofa and turned to me.

I didn't want to spend more time than was necessary in that damn house, so I put the backpack on the sofa and started to say my piece.

"Listen, Steph, I know this didn't—"

"Who was that?"

The voice came from the hallway. I turned around. Juanca walked into the living room.

"Mario."

My name. A single word. He said nothing else. It was enough.

Stephanie walked around the coffee table and moved toward Juanca.

Something was off. Stephanie had closed the door without asking me anything about Brian. She looked at Juanca now. Why

GABINO IGLESIAS

was he still here? Why was the motherfucker barefoot? His eyes landed on Stephanie. They begged her to say something.

"What . . . what are you doing here?" Juanca asked. His voice was smaller than I remembered.

I pointed to the backpack like an asshole.

The truth often sneaks up on you. Things you should have seen suddenly jump at you, covered in insults and screaming, asking how you could have missed them when they were so obvious.

Juanca's familiarity. Stephanie's worried face when she saw me. Brian's gun in the back seat.

Fuck.

Fuck!

I didn't care.

"Listen, man, I just came to give Steph some money," I said. "I'll give it to her and get the hell outta here."

Juanca walked toward me and stood between the TV and the coffee table. "What's wrong, Mario?" asked Juanca.

"Nothing," I said. "Let's just get it over with."

Stephanie moved into the hallway. I turned to look, but Juanca took a step forward and I returned my eyes to him. The gun he'd given me, the gun that had killed Brian, was pressing against my lower back, whispering to me to take it out.

Juanca's eyes jumped to the hallway and back to me. The motherfucker had set me up so I'd kill Brian for him. Now I had a ghost on my back and he had an extra hundred thousand dollars and Stephanie. Fuck him. I reached back, pulled my gun, and aimed it at him.

"¿Qué putas estás haciendo?" He sounded nervous, but his hands stayed put.

I took a step back so I could keep the gun on him while I picked up my money from the sofa.

"Why did you—"

The gunshot and its impact were almost simultaneous.

A bullet punched into the right side of my back, near the shoulder. Air wooshed out of me. The impact turned me a bit. I took a step forward while twisting around. My shin banged against the coffee table.

Stephanie stood in the middle of the hallway, the gun she'd shot me with still in her hands, still aimed at me. She squeezed the trigger again.

The shot hit me in the stomach. Everything inside me broke. I took a few steps forward and the nasty carpet came up to meet my face.

A foot connected with the left side of my head. The world dimmed. The pain in my gut was like hot electricity. Someone pulled my right arm from underneath my body. Juanca. He ripped the gun from my hand. I opened my eyes. Stephanie's bare foot landed a few inches in front of me.

Stephanie and Juanca moved back. The pain exploded again. My scream morphed into a grunt before it escaped my mouth. Darkness came again. The room spun and rose around me. I opened my eyes again. Juanca and Stephanie were standing so close to each other their bodies touched. His left hand was holding the side of Stephanie's belly. The red backpack—my backpack—hung from his wrist.

"You okay, baby?"

Stephanie nodded, a frantic movement that said the opposite was true.

I opened my mouth to curse them, to ask why, to scream Brian's name. Instead, a wet cough took over and a ball of warm, metallic blood climbed up my throat and poured from my mouth. I turned to the side, spat, and tried to push myself up.

"It's gonna be okay. You did exactly what you had to do, baby. You shot him for us, so don't worry. I'm safe. You protected me, okay? You saved me and I love you for it. Now let's finish getting your stuff and get outta here."

The living room was sideways. Juanca was trying to comfort Stephanie. His right hand, still holding my gun, was behind her neck and his left was still holding her belly. He kissed her and then kissed her forehead. She started sobbing harder. Then he led her away, taking my money, my future, with him.

Pressure. I needed to apply pressure to my stomach. I needed to get my phone out and call 911. I started pushing myself up again, gritting my teeth against the pain, allowing anger to flood me with adrenaline to overcome the pain in my stomach.

I wanted to kill Juanca. I wanted to kill Stephanie. I wanted to kill God. I wanted to slice the world's neck against my sorrow's edge.

I sat up just as light burst into the living room from the outside. Then the door slammed.

The wall was nearby, the corner of it before the opening of the hallway. I grunted my way to it. The pain was threatening to pull me under, to allow the darkness to seep in and take over. I thought about Anita. I thought about Melisa. We could start again, even without the money.

I managed to pull myself to a sitting position against the wall. My body was shaking a bit and it was hard to breathe. I needed to get my phone out or I was going to die on that fucking filthy floor, shot by a beautiful monster. I was going to die from exsanguination. It was almost funny.

Shoving my hand into my pocket almost made me pass out. Air wouldn't come into my lungs properly. In my stomach, hot coals were exploding, flashing across my torso.

There was something in my pocket. I pulled it out and looked at it. Santa Muerte. The figurine's grin was there, watching me die. I threw it across the room. I watched it fly and land near a dark, translucent figure. Something. I blinked it away.

The second time I dug into my pocket I managed to pull out my phone. My hands were covered in blood. My pants were soaked with it.

The shadow figure moved closer. I looked at it. My eyes filled with tears. The shadow looked more solid now. It was short and maybe human. I couldn't unlock my phone with bloody fingers. I wiped them on the upper part of my shirt. The screen lit up. I typed in four numbers. The year Anita was born. The phone unlocked.

I needed to call 911, but I went to contacts and pressed on MELISA. I pressed the phone to my ear and heard it ring. I closed my eyes. It rang again. And again. There was a click.

You've reached Melisa. There's a beep coming . . . You know what to do!

I looked forward. The shadow creature had morphed into something blue instead of black. It stood over me, but it was much smaller than I'd expected. Then, from its center a figure coalesced into something gray, solid, and recognizable. An elephant with a tutu, doing a pirouette. I closed my eyes for a second. Then I opened them and looked up, ready to see the face of God.

ACKNOWLEDGMENTS

Writing acknowledgments is weird, but I love it. I could write twenty pages just thanking people and I'd still leave a bunch of them out. I don't want to make the Mulholland folks angry, so I'll do my best to keep it short.

Gracias a Gabi, Ady y Rocco.

Gracias a mis viejos. Siempre.

Thank you to Melissa Danaczko, my wonderful agent and friend. Without her endless patience, encouragement, and knowledge, you wouldn't be reading this. Every writer who sells a book says they have the best agent, but Melissa is truly the best.

Thank you to Josh Kendall. I'm still learning about big publishing, so I don't know if this is the case with every editor out there, but Josh is more than my editor: he's my friend, and that means a lot. Also, he gets what I'm trying to do, and that's priceless.

Thank you to the wonderful authors who kept me inspired, offered me valuable advice and friendship, and then gave me some words about this book: Paul Tremblay, Stephen Graham Jones, Chuck Wendig, Alma Katsu, Josh Malerman, Jennifer Hillier, Brian Evenson, S. A. Cosby, Tananarive Due, David

ACKNOWLEDGMENTS

Heska Wanbli Weiden, David Joy, Chris Offut, John Woods, Steve Cavanaugh, and Daniel Woodrell. Y'all rock.

Thank you to the wonderful team at Mulholland Books/Little, Brown and Company: Alyssa Persons, Massey Barner, Liv Ryan, Craig Young, Ashley Marudas, and Pat Jalbert-Levine. Each of you has a fan club, and I'm the president of all of them.

Thank you to the amazing friends who have been there forever: Jeremy Robert Johnson, Beau Johnson, Cina Pelayo, V. Castro, Becky Spratford, Kimberly Davis Basso, Mark Allan Gunnells, Ted Van Alst Jr., John Edward Lawson, Jon Bassoff, and hundreds of others. Like I said, these lists are never complete.

Thank you to every person out there who read my previous books. You are the reason I kept going for a decade without an advance, a marketing team, a budget, galleys, or anything else. Much love.

Thank you to the ghosts of Juan Andreu Solé and Isaac Kirkman. I know you're watching, and that drives me. Also, a special hug to my friend Petra Mayer, a light in the book world who was lost too soon, for making me the reviewer I am today over at NPR.

Thank you to every bookseller and librarian out there. What you do matters. A lot.

Thank you to Writer's Block Coffee for being my official sponsors. How many writers do you know who have a coffee brand keeping them caffeinated?

Thank you to Puerto Rico and Austin. Thank you to all my friends from back home. The next novel is all about you and the bad stuff we used to do together.

Thank you to you, the person holding this book. You're now part of the dream. Tell your friends about what you just read so we can make this one blow up. And stay tuned; I'm just getting started.

The second time I dug into my pocket I managed to pull out my phone. My hands were covered in blood. My pants were soaked with it.

The shadow figure moved closer. I looked at it. My eyes filled with tears. The shadow looked more solid now. It was short and maybe human. I couldn't unlock my phone with bloody fingers. I wiped them on the upper part of my shirt. The screen lit up. I typed in four numbers. The year Anita was born. The phone unlocked.

I needed to call 911, but I went to contacts and pressed on MELISA. I pressed the phone to my ear and heard it ring. I closed my eyes. It rang again. And again. There was a click.

You've reached Melisa. There's a beep coming . . . You know what to do!

I looked forward. The shadow creature had morphed into something blue instead of black. It stood over me, but it was much smaller than I'd expected. Then, from its center a figure coalesced into something gray, solid, and recognizable. An elephant with a tutu, doing a pirouette. I closed my eyes for a second. Then I opened them and looked up, ready to see the face of God.